"All that, the Spring bore towards me,
And the flower I plucked,
Father's spirit I thought it was,
Dancing and moaning."
Spring, Aasmund Olavsson Vinje

PART ONE

"Governing a large country is like frying a small fish.
You spoil it with too much poking."
Lao Tzu

1

It was morning but his body was telling him midnight. That's why he was trying to siphon the Jack Daniels into the can of Coke. It was only the rattle of the van making his fingers shake. The task complete, Brough held the can up into the flickering sunlight to toast the dawn.

Flashing by to the west were the mountains, same as yesterday: a vertical rock face without snow or vegetation, emitting silence into the landscape. The low sun was making bits of rubble cast long points of shadow across the earth, which was the colour of cigarette ash.

"Helan Shan mountain range famous for excellent *feng-shui*!"

Chun-li's voice startled him. She'd been asleep the moment before, like everybody else except the driver. Brough squinted at her through the makeup mirror: sharp fringe, long hair, face hidden behind a pair of plastic sunglasses.

"*Feng-shui* dictates ideal position for burial is with back to mountains, feet to river," she chirped.

They'd crossed the Yellow River an hour ago: a bleak stretch of churning water. Now they were heading north along a pristine but deserted road, with fields on one side and this rock-strewn desolation on the other.

"Notice small cairns?"

He'd spotted them: little grey piles of rock dotted across the plain.

"Many important Chinese businessmen buried here."

"What," Brough snorted; "they just come here, pick a spot, get buried and pile the stones on top?"

Her voice, trickling like a brook, was starting to charm him, making him think of her, for a nanosecond, without clothes.

"Choose spot, pay bribe to local official, build pile of stones. Otherwise, have to use commercial cemetery. This poster," she pointed to a billboard at the roadside, "advertising commercial cemetery."

The plain was throwing off a white haze that was too dense to be morning mist–this was the dust rising as the sun began to scorch the soil. The leaves of the saplings, regimented along the roadside to infinity, were curled and brittle.

"Other side of mountain range is Gobi Desert," she said, reading his thoughts, "constantly threatening encroachment through passes of Helan Shan."

"How long before encroachment?"

He took a sip of the Coke and waited. There was always that moment of anxiety when you hide alcohol in a fizzy drink: will the Coke just taste like Coke? Will the little kick not happen? But after a second or two he felt that pleasant clunk in his cortex.

"Probably in our lifetime," she replied.

He'd spent eight hours in a plane, three hours at Beijing airport, two more flying to Yinchuan, then six hours in a hotel room with no minibar. In that time he had retained just one colloquial Chinese phrase: the words for "fuck me, fuck me"–hooted mechanically by prostitutes in the adjoining room as they entertained a group of officials. And now it was Friday.

Chun-li had drifted back to sleep; Carstairs was snoring next to her, head back, one hairy fist instinctively wrapped around his camera strap. Georgina, their producer, was draped across the whole back row of seats behind them: hair scraped behind a pair of Donna Karan sunglasses, a man's white shirt, cambric skirt billowing to her ankles, Birkenstocks dangling from her sleeping toes.

Now, through the sun-slant, Brough spotted a flash of colour in the fields: little dots of pink and the silhouettes of human beings moving between the furrows. A few minutes later he spotted some more.

"What's this?" He gestured to the driver, who'd been on autopilot behind a pair of gold-frame aviators.

The driver laughed the kind of laugh you laugh when somebody you don't like has been hit by a truck:

"*Da-gong*," he chuckled: "Har, har! *Da-gong*."

"Chun-li…" Brough whispered.

It was going to be tricky, this. He poked her knee with a biro. She snapped awake.

"Can you tell the driver to stop so we can film *da-gong*?"

"*Da-gong* mean migrant worker," she whispered back, craning her neck to see what he had spotted: "Ah! *Da-gong* also mean day-labourer."

"What's going on?" said Georgina, awake the moment the engine note changed.

"Just pulling over for a quick leg-stretch," Brough said.

"What have we stopped for, David?" She jerked herself upright.

But he had leapt out of the van and was striding into the field, Chun-li tagging behind him, the tail of his linen jacket flapping in the breeze.

There were about twenty of them in the work-gang, stretched in a line; he could see now that most of them were women, bending and swaying, their backs parallel to the earth.

They were wearing headscarves the colour of cherry soup–the Hui minority's version of the *hijab*–and swaddled despite the heat in cardigans, chintzy aprons and marigold gloves. A few blokes up front were scraping at the soil with homemade hoes. On a levee stood two men, Han Chinese, identically clad: white shirts, pressed black trousers, comb-over hairstyles–their faces composed as if for a funeral. Chun-li hurried over and began rabbiting at them in Mandarin.

"David, I mean, we've got stuff like this already," said Georgina, stumbling up behind him. The air was thick with the smell of baking earth and melting tarmac.

"You see," said Brough, ignoring her, "I knew there'd be fucking poverty if we just looked for it. Lying bastards…"

"We don't *know* they're poor, do we? And I'm just not seeing the environmental issue here," she began–but he said, with studied cruelty:

"You ever worked in a fucking field?"

And then:

"Hey Jimmy!"

Carstairs was swaying towards them under the weight of his tripod, camera and kit-bag.

"Jimmy, look at this. This. Is a fuckin' money shot, correct?"

Brough made a finger-frame towards the mountains, which would form a tyre-black colourwash against the pink of the women's headscarves and the dead, white soil.

"It's not the shots, David," said Georgina: "It's…"

"Gimme the stick-mike, Jimmy," said Brough.

Carstairs handed him a microphone with a radio antenna dangling from one end and a mic-flag with the Channel Ninety-Nine logo at the other.

"Hold on a minute, I'm serious here," Georgina folded her arms, "It's a massive drive to Shizuishan and we've already done the peasant thing!"

"Yeah," said Brough: "I-not-poor. I-love-Communist Party. We've done lots of that."

They'd grabbed an hour's worth of filming in the twilight, on arrival: sheep farmers living amid the ruins of the Great Wall. All of them prepared to say–straight to camera–that they preferred pharmaceutical sheep-feed to the traditional grazing methods; that they would have adopted the sheep-feed anyway, even if the grassland had not died, suddenly, beneath their feet.

"Field bosses say no problem," announced Chun-li, picking her way across the soil on two-inch heels. "I just tell them we make tourist documentary about Helan Shan and they are not even requesting facility fee: only to emphasise profound respect of CCP for Hui minority and religion of Islam…"

But Brough was already gone, loping towards the work-gang with the microphone held up like an ice cream and Carstairs struggling up behind him.

"This. Land. Good?" Brough shouted to an old guy at the front.

The old guy stopped, leant on his hoe and smiled–not at Brough but into the space above Brough's head. His skin was Eskimo-brown and his teeth the same.

"Ask him if the land's any good," Brough said. And Chun-li began quizzing the old guy in a tone of voice you might use with a retarded kid.

Carstairs snapped the tripod open and clipped the camera into its mount: he had worked with Brough before, in Chiapas and the Niger Delta, so he was used to snatching what could be snatched without constant sound checks and explanations.

"Why is the land so dry?" Brough's voice became suddenly modulated with concern, now the camera was rolling.

The old guy spoke in short, parched sentences ending with a monotone laugh: "ha, ha, ha". Chun-li summarised:

"Actually this land quite good–that why two rich brothers

decide to buy farms of everyone in area and turn into willow plantation."

"How much a day do you earn?" said Brough.

After a short exchange she reported:

"Old Mister Jin earning 50 kwai for ten-hour day. Actually that quite good. Only problem is Jin family having to pay 700 kwai for irrigating rice field each week. Therefore, including wages of Little Jin," she indicated a fat kid standing gormlessly in the background wearing a cast-off army t-shirt, "combined disposable income equals zero."

Brough turned triumphantly to Georgina.

"Waste of tape," she sang, under her breath.

"How does he survive? I mean," Brough paused to leave an editing space: "Whose fault is it that so many people are poor?"

He felt Chun-li go tense as she translated this, but then relax as she heard the answer:

"Old Mister Jin insist he quite rich," she announced. "Two other sons working in toy factory in Guangdong Province owned by self-made millionaire. Send back wages. Soon Little Jin will also enter toy-making profession."

"Ahh!" said Brough, arching his eyebrows in mock delight.

"Ha, ha, ha," said Old Jin.

"Har, har fucking har indeed," said Brough, to nobody.

"Can we call that a wrap?" said Georgina, not without irony. "Can we get out of this effing field and get on to the next effing city where…"

"But this land is shit!" Brough had grabbed a handful of soil and was crumbling it in front of the old guy's nose. He was suddenly red-faced and shaking:

"Ask him," he took a deep breath, "if it's a Communist country why does he have to pay for irrigation?"

"Da-vid," Georgina was about to try some neuro-linguistic

management bullshit but Brough just tuned it out. He was sweating–sweating whisky-cola it felt like. He could feel the bald patch on his head going the colour of smoked salmon in the sun.

After a long stare at the horizon Old Jin thought of an answer and, with a modest smile, delivered it to Chun-li. She stifled a smirk:

"Old Mister Jin says: Here we eat and drink Communist Party".

"Wrap!" Georgina sang, eyes rolling–a little bit of mania in her voice as she told Chun-li to tell Old Jin thank-you very, very much and to convey our deepest gratitude please to the field bosses. And Carstairs unclipped the camera and was about to move when Brough said:

"But why do you *have* to eat and drink the Communist Party?"

There was a beat of silence.

"Sorry don't really understand question," said Chun-li.

"What I mean is: can he tell me why they have to eat and drink the Communist Party, because if you ask me, though I'm no expert, the *feng-shui* round here might be great for the dead but not for the fuckin' living!"

He could see she thought this insolent.

"Old Mister Jin probably not capable of understanding this kind of question," she muttered.

"Yes but *you* understand it, don't you? You understand why if somebody says they eat and drink a political party it's sensible to ask them why? If I asked *you*, *you* could understand it so why can't he?"

Carstairs, noticing that yelp in Brough's voice that always bubbled up when he was about to lose control, and wondering despite the early hour about the looseness of some of Brough's gestures, said:

"I think we'll need cutaways."

But Georgina said don't waste tape; and Brough threw some

convoluted sentence at her sprinkled with obscenities; and Chun-li flinched at the f-words, which they were spitting at each other now with a violence they just don't warn you about at English lessons. And Old Jin just watched and stared.

While all this happened Carstairs shot a sequence that they could use as setups if they had to.

He framed the master-shot wide, with the work-gang toiling at the bottom, blurred by the heat and dwarfed by the mountain range. Then he shot the women in close-up: the pink of their scarves throbbing neon against the drabness of the mountains; the rough wool of their cardigans, their cracked lips, their tanned and florid faces reminding him of Afghanistan.

One woman stole a smile into the camera and Chun-li told her to stop but Carstairs said no, let her. She looked sixty; others were teenagers. There were no adults of working age here at all.

Then he pulled a sneaky two-shot of the field bosses:

"How did these two miserable buggers make their money, d'you think?" he muttered to Chun-li.

"Maybe win lottery, or discover Rare Earth deposit beneath farm, or exit stock market at top of curve," she began, but Carstairs interrupted:

"For fuck's sake!"

He made throat-cutting gestures at Brough and Georgina on the other side of the field, instructing them to "shut it!" as their shouting was ruining the natural sound.

"There's nowhere for it in the fucking structure," Georgina was yelling at Brough.

"Well fuck the fucking structure!" His knees were flexed with anger, fingers splayed, cowboy boots knocking the tops off furrows as he paced around in the soil.

"It's been signed off! New York have been all over it for a week!"

"Alright I'll phone them!"

He waved his Blackberry into her face as a kind of threat.

"Go ahead. I'm sure New York would love to hear from *you*!"

Brough's mistake had been to use the words "war crime" in a live report from Gaza, after the Israelis had managed to drop white phosphorus onto a school, followed by a series of world-weary generalisations about Hamas, Al Jazeera, Tony Blair and indeed the entire region. The Channel's bosses had pulled him off the story within six hours, citing post-traumatic stress. They'd moved him into "long-form": soft, people-centred reports to fill the half-hour of current affairs they were supposed to air each week, between the freak shows and make-over programs.

"But look at it!"

He made an expansive gesture at the field, the work-gang, the bosses on the levee:

"Look at these two – Gilbert and fucking George! You could tell the whole story here if you wanted to! I bet..."

He checked himself. There was no point. He was feeling shaky, dehydrated.

"So you're the expert on frickin' China now!"

Georgina had sensed his deflation. As he hunched his shoulders and turned away she ventured:

"You know Twyla actually *speaks* Mandarin?"

He muttered an obscenity about Twyla, their boss in London, which Georgina ignored.

"It's all in the structure and the structure's signed off, David."

He forced himself to laugh. At the situation. At himself. He was giggling uncontrollably by the time Chun-li summoned the courage to approach him:

"Why does that old bloke keep staring above my head?"

"Actually quite amusing," Chun-li, relieved, let herself giggle too:

"According to folk religion believed by uneducated people, spirits of ancestors hovering everywhere, just above our heads.

Old Mister Jin tells me he is wondering if Correspondent Brough being advised by mischievous spirit."

Brough's rule was never to drink while working on a serious story, so for the past six months he'd been forced to hike his alcohol intake to lifetime record levels. Now he felt like hiking it some more.

2

There was a condom in the wastebasket. No doubt about it: the smell of burning rubber was unmistakeable. Likewise the smirk on Propaganda Chief Zheng's face, the gold microfibres clinging to the knees of his slacks, the mortified look on Sally Feng's face as she left the Chief's office brushing bits of carpet out of her hair.

Li Qi-han straightened himself and tried not to think about Sally Feng doing it with the Chief.

"What's to report?" Zheng gestured into the air with his cigarette.

Li stood to attention, feeling the hair on his shins crackle with static from the Chief's carpet – a brand-new red-and-gold creation interweaving the stars of the national flag with images of railways and construction cranes.

He clutched the intelligence file tight under his arm, fighting back nausea and dread.

"Nothing today, Chief."

Zheng, his feet crossed on the desk and head wreathed in smoke, wore his usual outfit: striped polo shirt, fawn slacks, tweed jacket and Playboy-logo belt, black-weave loafers and hair dyed the same colour as President Hu Jin-tao's: latex black.

Li himself was wearing a Nile green tennis shirt and caramel-coloured chinos: he despised designer belt-buckles but in preparation for his exam he had taken to wearing a cheap, milled-steel number with a rip-off of the Versace "V".

"You look a bit peaky today, Deputy Li," Zheng teased him.

"Peaky? Not me!" said Li. "Ready for action, Chief!"

Li's grandfather, a coalminer from Wuhan, had used to insist: a miner never misses work from being slaughtered with drink, as a point of honour. Li had arrived for work that morning slaughtered with drink but was not about to betray the family tradition.

"Nothing at all in the intelligence?" Zheng insisted.

"Squat." Li bullshitted; "We've got to organise a morality lecture at the High School because of what those kids keep doing on the Internet. After that, nothing until the," he angled his head and paused in the obligatory way, "twentieth anniversary..."

"Okay, get lost then." Zheng wafted a lazy circle of smoke in the direction of the door.

Li quit the room agitated. He'd spent most of last night at the Tang Lu branch of KTV, moving deftly through his Frank Sinatra repertoire into a medley of Chinese love duets with Sally Feng. Around 4am he had been kicked out of a taxi, alone, on the wrong side of the river in the brick-kiln suburb towards Wuhai, stumbling around in the shit-filled alleyways and being sick. He had stared tearfully at the Yellow River wondering whether its spirits were trying to communicate something. Now, six hours later, the throb of white alcohol behind his eyes was communicating the need to lie down.

He marched into the general office and slammed the day's orders onto the desk in front of his subordinate, Belinda Deng. She was related to some disgraced Shanghai party boss: wide-faced, supercilious, constantly trading shares via text message. Much of Li's workday was devoted to making Belinda Deng look down at her desk and not up, insolently, at himself.

"Different shit, same day," he said.

Her face barely registered his presence.

Li slouched over to the hot water machine, refreshing the leaves in yesterday's tea flask. Everything in the office smelled plastic. The air-conditioner was making his neck hairs stand on end and his brain ache. His under-arms reeked of aerosol. Everything was, in this sense, normal.

He studied Sally Feng's broad hips as she twisted in her seat to keep her phone conversation private. He studied the wall map of Ningxia Province, with marker-pen lines indicating areas of support for crazy imams in the south, where water had run out and Islamic fundamentalism had run in. An orange paper dot marked the location of Tang Lu Industrial Suburb. He would soon be out of there for good.

He felt shivery, bilious and weird. Usually when he got this paranoid after drinking it was because there was some kind of shit-storm on the political radar screen: an official visit, the upcoming trial of a mining boss. But the notes today said nothing. His computer screen said nothing, except for the usual "have-a-nice-day" from the Communist Party Discipline Section. There was nothing abnormal on the horizon at all.

"Oh my God, this is Mordor!"

Georgina's voice jerked him awake.

Brough could tell from the slant of the light that it was late afternoon. He had dribbled Coke-coloured spit onto his shirt. He desperately needed the toilet. They were at some kind of motorway toll, wedged into the middle of a long queue of coal trucks.

"D'you think they have a toilet here?" he muttered.

"No look, it's fucking Mordor! You ever seen anywhere like this?"

Brough craned his neck to follow the direction of Georgina's stare. It was the city he couldn't pronounce: Shizuishan. He let his eyes drift across the skyline, swathed in brown haze, arrayed with smokestacks, cooling towers, petro-chem rigs and blast furnaces. Implausibly vast, as if every industrial city in Britain had been cut and pasted into one mega-city.

"Yeah," said Brough, "Belgrade after the Septics bombed it. Listen, I'm desperate. Chun-li, d'you think I can just er, go to the toilet on the side of the road?"

"For urinating or defecating?"

"Urinating."

"Chinese men will do urinating under table at restaurant if nobody looking."

He lurched over the crash barrier and into the roadside scrub, stiff with jet-lag. The throb of diesel engines and the stench coming from the truck exhausts touched a childhood memory: his father had been a lorry driver. He unbuttoned his fly and relieved himself into the nettles.

"Smell that?" Carstairs was beside Brough now, legs braced, unzipping his trousers.

Brough let his nostrils flare against the smell of fresh coal.

"Fuck, that takes you back!"

Carstairs was pushing sixty: he'd been a long-lens snapper in Fleet Street, a cameraman in various wars and now made his money out of corporate videos plus–as he had put it to Brough on arrival–"shit like this".

"That's where all our bleedin' jobs went, innit?" he gestured with his chin to the skyline.

Brough nodded.

"What's up with that bird?" Carstairs ventured.

Georgina had once been breezily at home in the foreign correspondents' world of drink, late night bitterness and casual sex. But she'd quit, gone into the indy sector, made some money and now had a boyfriend in New York: hedge fund guy with a saltbox in Connecticut and a reconstructed septum.

"She's made a documentary about the Yangtse Dolphin," said Brough; "She knows all there is to know about China."

In the van, Chun-li was having a high-speed Mandarin conversation with her cellphone, which Georgina had learned to read as a sign of trouble.

"Slight problem with Shizuishan *wai-ban*," she announced.

"What?" Georgina began tugging at her handbag to fish out the schedule. The city's foreign affairs department, known as the *wai-ban*, were supposed to escort them to a three-star hotel, a banquet and the inevitable smoke-hazed drinking session to scope out tomorrow's interview with a senior party guy.

"Senior Party Guy will not receive interview."

"Why not?"

"Urgent business trip to Beijing."

"What do the *wai-ban* advise?"

"Move to next city."

Chun-li's voice betrayed that she knew how ridiculous it sounded. But that was what they'd said.

"So hold on a minute," Georgina's voice began to quaver slightly, "who's going to give us the interview about environmental policy?"

"Difficult to say," said Chun-li, as Brough and Carstairs swung themselves into the van. Georgina made her eyes bore through Chun-Li's tinted shades, searching for some kind of logical outcome.

"Are you telling me these guys can just cancel an interview we've taken six months to set up at half a day's notice?"

"Extremely possible," said Chun-li.

"For a major TV program specifically sponsored by the Chinese government?"

"Quite usual."

Channel Ninety-Nine had scheduled a special edition of its flagship talk show, *Live at Nine with Shireen Berkowitz,* to be filmed "as-live" from the top of a skyscraper in Shanghai. The aim was to mark the twentieth anniversary of the Tiananmen Square Massacre, or "Events" as they'd agreed to call them. "Let's do the issues that matter today – not twenny years ago," their boss, Twyla had told them. That meant everything except torture, democracy and human rights.

Brough's job was to front a seven-minute report about the Party's fight against environmental depredation in western China. They had to be in Beijing by Wednesday to edit and feed it to Shanghai. Brough's presence was not required in Shanghai; in fact his presence anywhere near a live broadcasting position had been actively discouraged.

Georgina flicked through her *Lonely Planet*:

"Let's get to the hotel, have a beer and work on it."

"Also another slight problem," it was Chun-li's voice quavering now. Brough, Carstairs and Georgina caught the quaver and began to stare at her intently:

"Three-star hotel in Shizuishan cancelled our reservation on advice of *wai-ban* chief."

"Well fuck the *wai-ban* chief let's rebook it ourselves," said Georgina.

"I already try that, they say: No Vacancies."

"Well book another one!" Georgina exploded.

"Already tried that also."

There was silence.

"No western-standard hotels apart from already-un-booked Three Star Beautiful Pagoda, No Vacancies. No other hotels at all listed."

"Where do the foreign businessmen stay?" said Brough.

"Not very often in Shizuishan."

Georgina screwed her eyebrows into a single eyebrow and studied her guidebook.

"See this? Where's this town here?" she tapped the page with her finger and thrust the book under Chun-li's nose; "It says there's a decent hotel in this place. But I can't find it on the map."

Chun-li produced a Chinese atlas and flicked through the pages, settling finally on one that showed only a blank expanse of desert and a precise, square grid of conurbation in the middle of it, with only one road in and out. It was a place she'd never heard of, about an hour's drive north.

4

A joke among steelworkers in Shizuishan runs: first prize in the trade union lottery is a week's holiday in Tang Lu, second prize two weeks. But that does not bother Tang Lu residents. They laugh at it out of a kind of pride.

Li Qi-han, who had clocked off and was headed for the massage parlour, hated Tang Lu. Despite his mining ancestry he was a Beijing boy to his core and the locals knew it: from the absence of that happy cynicism that Tang Lu folk carry around on their faces; from his lack of resignation.

Li's face was, in fact, permanently annoyed. Annoyed at Sally Feng, annoyed at the Chief, annoyed–above all and perpetually–at his dad.

Fair enough; in 2006 things had looked promising: there'd been talk in the Party newspapers about compensation for former "rightists". Grandfather Li had been a notorious rightist: jailed in 1956 for writing a wall poster against the Soviet invasion of Hungary–and never seen again. Li's dad had signed a petition requesting lump-sum compensation for the surviving relatives of persecuted rightists. But a year later, after working its way around the desks of various cadres, the whole rightist rehabilitation campaign had been deemed, itself, "rightist".

Li's dad, a leftist in the sixties but now running a self-help book imprint, had suddenly been hit with a massive tax demand. Li himself – who'd had no idea what his dad was up to – got called into the discipline section at the Beijing Olympics Propaganda Bureau and told to pack his bags for Ningxia Province.

So now, two years on, he wandered through the backstreets of Tang Lu, headed for the massage parlour: pissed off with the Chief, Sally Feng, his dad, life itself–and still suffering from this strange, unsettling apprehension.

Soon he would sit an exam in The Important Theory of Three Represents: "Just demonstrate some basic knowledge of Jiang Zemin's contribution to Marxism and you can fuck off back to Beijing," Zheng had told him. But studying the Three Represents had made Li become irritable, agitated: so agitated that, for weeks now, he'd needed to drink white alcohol to get to sleep.

On top of that he had, for some reason he did not care to rationalise, erected a shrine to Grandfather Li on the mantelpiece in his apartment, consisting of Grandfather's last known photograph, in PLA uniform, and his Type 51 pistol from the Korean War, a family heirloom. Li had been burning large handfuls of "spirit money" on this shrine most nights.

The backstreets of Tang Lu were teeming with that life you barely see in Beijing anymore. A woman lifted her toddler to pee into the gutter. The tea-seller smiled, beckoning Li to her table of gleaming steel pots: this one to calm his inner fire, this one to stoke it up. In the hairdresser's, one prostitute was combing the hair of another. Each had a Motorola flip-phone wedged between chin and shoulder: the one gossiping with her sister in Shenzhen, the other placing a bet on tonight's basketball game with an illegal bookmaker.

Kids wrestled in the street dirt; miners' wives engaged in

hard-faced, emotionless gossip. In an alley behind the hairdressers' stood the neon-lit frontage of the Happy Girl Massage Parlour. Li slipped silently through the door, barely nodding to its proprietor, Mrs. Ma.

He liked to keep his massage activities discreet and preferred the Happy Girl precisely because it was the kind of place party officials and local government stooges would avoid. Here it was mainly freelance mining engineers, Mongolian drug dealers with buzz-cut hair and other *nouveau riche* scum.

He killed his cellphone as the serving girl steered him into the booth. He had his shirt off, neatly folded on the chair, by the time she'd brought him a bottle of Snow beer and laid it respectfully on the side-table next to a basket of condoms and a basket of salted peanuts.

There was a mirror: he was in good shape for 27, if a little scrawny. His pudding-bowl haircut marked him out as a dutiful Communist. He waited for the girl to leave before getting his pants off and laying face down on the massage table. Who would Mrs. Ma send in? There was always the frisson of waiting to find out.

The door handle clicked. He could tell from the swish of her tunic, the clunk of her sandals that it was Long Tall Daisy; her breath, as always, a little bit rancid with catarrh but her fingers already trailing gently up his leg in compensation for that.

He would come back to Mrs. Ma's place for a full night with Long Tall Daisy before he left Tang Lu. He made a mental note of that as she started the CD – eerie, orchestral waves montaged with underwater whale noises – and lit an incense stick. Though his hangover had gone he still felt, for some reason, jumpy.

5

This is what they see on the tape when they finally get to view it:

Vertical spectrum-bars with a high-pitched whine, the word CARSTAIRS in a digital font, and timecode in the corner of the screen beginning 03.00.00. That means the start of tape three.

The opening shot shows the inside door of a Ruifeng van. The cameraman has hit the record button to run the camera up to speed as he mikes-up the reporter. Now the sound channels kick into life, jolting the graphic equaliser.

"Hold on David, I'm not really sure we have time for this." It is Georgina's voice, querulous but resigned.

"Maybe I get out first," Chun-li suggests, off camera. "Pollution very sensitive issue in towns like this."

"I'm not surprised!" It is Carstairs, his voice betraying that alert distraction that takes hold of cameramen as they begin checking their levels, their battery power, stashing extras of everything into the pockets of their trousers.

"I think I'd better stay with the van," Georgina suggests.

"Yeah, no worries. Just me and Chun-li." It is Brough's voice, calm and languid like it was when US Marines pointed a

.50 cal machine gun at him from a Blackhawk, deep to his groin in water, one humid afternoon in New Orleans.

The camera swings up as they bail out of the vehicle. Brough smoothing his sandy hair, his jacket crumpled; Chun-li wobbling around in the dirt on her unsuitable heels.

It's the very last light of the day: the colours are the warm rust of a traditional Chinese *hutong*. Low brick shacks topped with curved, medieval roof-tiles; an unpaved road where shaven-headed kids play stone-throwing games in bright yellow cardigans and acid blue T-shirts.

Chun-li leaves the frame and heads up the street but the camera stays on Brough, who keeps squinting at something in the distance, nervously, and whispering to himself: "Shit!"

There is, in the picture, a strange haze to do with more than just the fading light. The camera swings upwards; Carstairs' cockney grimace blocks the sky out and is in turn blocked out by a chamois leather as he tries to wipe dust off the lens.

"Yes they will talk," says Chun-li, at 03.02.27.

"Did you explain we are a Western documentary team?" says Brough.

"Yes they say no problem. They very angry."

The camera follows Brough and Chun-li up the street. Carstairs pulls a nice slow pan off them to a dirty kid, its smile revealing only half the normally allocated number of teeth.

Now Brough walks up to a group of local people who are looking a mixture of puzzled and wary:

"David Brough, Channel Ninety-Nine News."

Brough shakes a few hands while Chun-li does rapid-fire introductions, and then clears his throat:

"Is the air always as bad as this?"

Pause, translation.

They all start shouting at once. There is a woman in a Qing-dynasty silk jacket, an old man with a face the colour of lead, two middle-aged men and a yappy housewife. Kids skip around them to get into shot. Carstairs goes in tight, the lens out to its full wide-angle making the faces loom, distorted, at the edges. The camera mic picks up the sound of what they're saying and Chinese listeners will, later on, go pale once they make it out.

Man with grey face: "It's like this every night. During the day they switch it off so the sky looks blue. But every night at seven o'clock it comes over here. You can tell the time by it."

Woman with silk jacket: "We have to shut our doors and windows. Every night."

Yappy housewife: "You journalists should launch an investigation into it!"

Brough tells Chun-li to tell them to slow down and speak one at a time, then he has three goes at asking the same question, his voice tight with adrenaline:

"Have you not complained?"

Man, grey face: "We complained but nobody gives a shit! My chest is tight!"

Chun-li translates: "We have contacted the authorities but nobody seems to care." You can tell from the tremor in her voice she knows how close they are to saying something bad about local officials on camera.

Silk-jacket woman: "If you breathe this stuff you feel like vomiting and if its windy, your eyes burn."

And she clears a small space around herself and acts out the final agonies of her dead mother, coughing into her hands and struggling for breath.

Chun-li explains that it's a battery factory that's the problem.

"Where?" says Brough.

Everybody points into the distance. The camera – Carstairs is a genius – swings slowly round in a very useable one-eighty degree pan and pushes in, holding steady, to the flaring gas pipes that had made them stop the van in the first place.

It is a modern plant, big slabs of concrete wall and gross, concrete chimneys painted red and yellow, the whole base of the complex shrouded in white vapour.

Off-camera there is more uproar, the crowd shoving each other aside to present their case: "My kids are choking on this shit!" "My son is a dwarf!" "I ran the marathon once but look…"

"Chun-li what are you doing?" Brough asks.

"Just wait a minute. I need to type word into translator"

The camera goes tight on the small translation machine in her hands. Her nail job catches the last of the natural light.

"Chlor-," she says, then after a long pause: "ine". "Pollution contains chlorine."

Brough says:

"How do we know it's chlorine? It could be just steam."

Chun-li translates and the crowd – it has grown to a small crowd now–goes slightly wild. They shout at him in a cacophony of anger.

"This factory very notorious polluting factory owned by brother of local city mayor; whole cemetery is full of residents dying below age of 50," Chun-li translates.

Carstairs is getting cutaways now, of kids, dogs, crumble-walled shacks. A two-shot of Brough and the grey-faced man:

"What do you want the authorities to do?"

"They should move us like they promised," the man begins, but Carstairs whip-pans off him to a woman standing at the edge of the crowd who is staring coldly at Brough, barking questions at him that he is not hearing.

"This lady want to know who you are," Chun-li's voice conveys the clear subtext: "let's leave".

"Good evening madam: David Brough, Channel Ninety-Nine News–and whom do I have the pleasure of addressing?"

"Do you have permission to be here?" the woman asks.

It's Busybody Guo, head of the district management office.

She's been watching the 7 o'clock news bulletin, but luckily with the sound turned down or she would not have heard the commotion.

"Yes of course, we are here with the full permission of the Ningxia Province *wai-ban*," says Brough, using a supercilious form of English both he and Carstairs know they will cut out in the edit, especially when he adds: "We have been personally invited by Premier Wen Jia-bao to tell the story of the fine efforts of the Communist Party in the sphere of environmental protection."

Busybody Guo spins on her heel, flipping her mobile open as she stamps back into the alleyway.

"Ignore the bitch," somebody shouts.

"Piece to camera," Brough mutters and breaks away from the group, taking up position with his back to the factory, which is now spewing vapour, thick and greenish, towards them. It's already started to obscure some of the roofs and reduce the flames from the chimneys to a sickly yellow glow.

"Here in Western China, the official story is…"

"Wait ten seconds," says Carstairs.

Brough checks his reflection in the camera lens, sees the approaching cloud behind him and understands. He takes a breath, drops his shoulders and smiles wearily.

"Go" says Carstairs.

"Here in Western China the official line is that pollution's been outlawed. But the residents tell a different story. Every night, they say, a cloud like this comes over the fence and makes the air impossible to breathe. They say it contains chlorine. In the west they'd be able to call in scientists to test the air. Here all they've got is the Communist Party, and the local leadership seems more worried about *our* presence, than about this…"

He turns, with only mild theatricality, to the tsunami of vapour that is now a few yards away and then turns back to face the camera as the cloud engulfs him.

"David Brough, Channel Ninety-Nine, Western China."

"Wrap," says Carstairs. The camera drops to knee level and they walk quickly up the smog-wreathed alleyway towards a van with a blonde woman gesturing at them out of the side-door.

"What the fuck?" she is saying: "I'm choking to death here!"

The camera goes back to its starting position, the lens wedged up against the door. Slamming sounds are heard and the engine revs.

"What did you get?" Georgina's voice is a mixture of annoyance and excitement.

"The fucking works. This cloud is full of chlorine," says Brough.

"Is that dangerous?"

"No idea. Wait till you see the tape. Do you think that woman was pissed off enough to phone the pigs, Chun-li–I mean the police?"

"Pollution very sensitive in this part of China. Maybe she will not want trouble for herself. Better get away from area. Also switch tapes."

The screen goes blank. The timecode says 03.23.34: that's twenty-three and half minutes on tape. Two gigabytes on disc, max.

6

Xiao Lushan's eyelids were becoming soft under the damp flannel; on the stage the dirty-joke comedian had given way to a monologue artist. Xiao's feet were being massaged by a demure girl. And his cellphone was on vibrate.

Friday night, for Police Superintendent Xiao, was sauna night. Sprawled in the next armchair, snoozing in a pair of yellow-stripe pyjamas, was Zhou, Secretary of the Tang Lu chamber of commerce. On the other side, flashing a smarmy smile at the tea girl was Sheng, editor of the *Tang Lu Daily* (founded 1958), wrapped in a cotton robe.

Soon the monologue artist would give way to a drag act and, feigning distaste, the three men would put their slippers on and glide, cracking timeworn jokes, up the escalator to the cafeteria, where they would make menopausal small-talk with the waitress, slam dice cups on the table, shout chaotically for Chairman Mao's Red-braised Pork and slurp green tea.

This was Superintendent Xiao's routine. No other cops would dare show up at the Tang Lu Public Sauna Number One on a Friday night–except his driver, who was outside in the command vehicle, a BMW X5 with three digital comms antennae.

By Friday night all the drunks and fighters from the past weekend would have been processed to pre-trial detention centres; let somebody else take the rap if they got mistreated. Most strikes and industrial accidents happened, as every good cop knows, towards the beginning of the week. And any politically dodgy sermons at Friday prayers were a problem for the State Security Police, not Xiao.

Only "mopes" were the reason Xiao kept his cellphone on at all. "Set phasers on stun," the three men always joked on arrival.

"Mope" was a word he'd picked up from *The Wire–Series One*, which the command group at the station had been watching on pirate DVD with Chinese subtitles. It was satisfyingly close to the Mandarin word for con-man. Ningxia Province was home to all kinds of mopes, some driving SUVs, others zipping between the hairdressers, karaoke bars and acupuncture shops on little motorbikes. They would stare into space violently when the traffic cops busted them. Whether it was drugs, betting, prostitution – it was always executed with a profound failure of imagination: disorganised crime, Xiao called it.

He'd busted a whole gang of mopes last year, supplying trafficked women to a "ballroom" servicing the flint quarries in the Helan Shan. A spectacular bust – even rescued three of the girls alive and got a mention in the *People's Daily*.

He was one pip short of Commissioner and with his good connections–and bearing in mind the rule that says one out of every three officials in the Ningxia Hui Autonomous Province actually has to be a Hui Muslim, and not, like Xiao, Han Chinese– he would one day make it.

"Hey Spock, your tricorder is registering signs of life!" said Zhou.

Xiao's phone was a fat Nokia; its gold-lacquered fascia decorated with fake gemstones in the shape of the Taj Mahal. His daughter had given it to him when she'd left for Beijing and, though he knew it made other police officers snigger behind his back, he couldn't bear to change it. He had taped her photograph onto the back of the handset. Now, as he peeled the flannel off his forehead, it was her face he could see vibrating its way towards the edge of the table.

He leant wearily across, motioned the massage girl to leave his feet alone and grabbed the phone.

Xiao Lushan is a big man, so when he shot upright in string vest and shorts, purple-faced, neck veins protruding–like a giant walking penis–scattering pumpkin seeds and frightening the massage girl rigid, the whole room fell silent.

The duty officer had been too scared to call so had put the entire situation into a text message:

"Foreign media in Tang Lu East Village. Threat to social order. Await instructions."

Xiao's face went into the shape of a vengeful warlord's face, like in a TV shouting-drama:

"I'll give them a threat to social order," he said between clenched teeth.

"We will eat your portion of Chairman Mao's Red-braised Pork," Zhou chuckled.

"Somebody is going to regret that they were born," newspaper editor Sheng sniggered, reaching for what was left of the pumpkin seeds as Xiao strode–wordless and with fists clenched–toward the changing room.

7

At Tang Lu Police HQ he found the control room deserted apart from his deputy, Tong, and the riot-squad leader, Hard Man Han:

"Why were we not told the foreign media were in Tang Lu?" Xiao yelled.

Tong stood silently to attention, face like a show-trial convict. There was a metallic racket coming from somewhere in the depths of the building. It was Han who summoned up the courage to answer:

"We're onto the Propaganda Department now but nobody's picking up."

Han had a Kevlar vest draped loosely around his pectorals and was punching at the keyboard of a computer with one finger as he spoke, sweating slightly.

"Why did the East Village management office allow local people to talk to a foreign news crew?" said Xiao.

Hard Man Han cocked an eyebrow in the direction of Busybody Guo–who was standing, arms-crossed and furious, in a waiting room on the other side of a two-way mirror.

"Where are the journalists? Where are their Chinese minders?" Xiao let his face veer very close to Tong's.

Tong pulled his lips back to reveal mustard-coloured teeth and went into report mode:

"Three foreign journalists have been apprehended, accompanied by one Chinese female, Beijing registered, and one Chinese male, a driver, Yinchuan registered. All the journalists have English passports with valid visas. The driver has been questioned and released. He is in the van outside, smoking twenty cigarettes. Claims he's a casual informant for the State Security Police. We're checking that, discreetly. Says it all happened before he knew what they were up to."

"And the Chinese minder?"

"No minders. Decree Number 447."

"What?"

"It's a law they passed for the Olympics," Hard Man Han chipped in. "They don't need minders. They can go where they like as long as they tell the *wai-ban* their itinerary and stay away from sensitive installations. They brought their own copy."

He skimmed a sheet of A4 across the table. The words were in English but the State Council logo at the top of it looked real enough. Xiao had heard, vaguely, about Decree Number 447 but assumed it didn't apply to Ningxia Province, or had been rescinded.

"It's still in force." Hard Man Han was reading his thoughts.

"Where are we holding them?" Xiao checked his reflection in the glass of Chairman Mao's portrait and fiddled with the top button of his tunic.

"In the cafeteria, boss." Tong's voice betrayed nervousness.

"The cafeteria? Why not the cells?"

"That's the problem, boss," Hard Man Han was looking uncomfortable now. "Some of the lads were having a bit of fun with this mope; a drug dealer from Linhe. And it got… out of hand."

"What kind of fun?"

Xiao felt his face going mauve. He'd spent the whole car journey trying to calm himself, letting his head go heavy into the leather headrest and expelling his anxiety on outward breaths. He tried to keep his breathing steady now as Tong exploded, machine-like, at Han:

"Upside down! From the ceiling! Rubber truncheons! They get the cattle prod out! The mope has a coronary seizure!"

Xiao sank into the nearest swivel chair and let his fingers squeeze the bridge of his nose for a second, comb through his hair and then form into a fist. He punched the table half-heartedly and looked up, as if to the heavens, but actually at the words "Maintain Social Harmony, Promote Scientific Development" stencilled across the azure ceiling in gold leaf.

Then he stared a silent question at Hard Man Han, who responded:

"Alive, but in intensive care. But then the riot started. We've still got fifteen anti-social elements down there from last weekend because Pre-Trial is full. So it all kicked off. They got hold of some iron bars—we don't know how – and we've cornered them into the holding pen but they're as crazy as frogs in a napalm strike. Quarry workers mostly. Young lads. We were going to CS-gas the whole basement but then this happened!"

He jerked his head once again at Busybody Guo, through the mirror, her face crumpled with spite.

Xiao's mind searched for a course of action. Cell-block riots he had handled many times but he had never met a Western journalist. He knew the Standard Operating Procedures for dealing with them, but only the ones in place before Decree Number 447.

"What did they actually see?"

"Not much," Tong allowed himself to relax a little. He had

seen Xiao physically attack subordinates before now, but the moment had passed:

"The usual cloud of shit from Tang Lu Nickel Metal Hydride, bang on the stroke of seven. A bunch of idiots started mouthing off to them in the street. They legged it soon as Busybody Guo turned up. She's got a face like a carp."

"They get any evidence?"

"Only camera footage. Driver reckons they swapped the tape but he doesn't know which one it is. They've got three boxes of tapes at the hotel."

"You seized anything?"

Tong shook his head.

"Good. Where are the control room staff?"

Tong explained that, at the outbreak of the riot they had shut down communications with Provincial HQ, killed the station's video surveillance system and put the whole control-room team into Kevlar to reinforce the riot squad in the cell-block.

"Can we bring the cafeteria up on that?" Xiao gestured to the 30-foot video wall that dominated the control room. Hard Man Han hit a few keys on the computer and it flickered into life, heavily pixellated and bright grey.

They were sitting side by side, staring into space, silent. A Chinese girl, dressed nondescript. Skinny, bland, no Western bling about her; no Versace. Two washed-up looking Western men. One tanned and wrinkled, grey hair, chin on his chest, denim shirt, denim jeans, big wrist-watch. The other sandy-haired, balding, wind-burned, snipe-nosed; a gold chain around his neck: alert and fidgeting. Finally a glamorous blonde: no youngster, mid-thirties maybe. Plunging neckline, skin a little wrinkled at the eyes from too much sunshine. Annoyed.

The SOP says put the frighteners on the men, charm the women. Work on the Chinese citizen first, obviously, but nothing beyond threats and emotional blackmail. Work out who has most to lose. Get the tapes. Get a written apology and if possible a written self-criticism. This gets you out of the shit with Provincial HQ and avoids having to call in the State Security Police.

"Here's the plan," said Xiao. "Tong takes over the disturbance in the cell block. No gas. Negotiation. These are quarry boys right? Get the union down here, pronto. Get the imam down here too. I want them back in the cells by midnight and somewhere else by sun-up. Han," he paused to breathe, "one of your boys is going to take the rap for hospitalising that kid. Just like D'Angelo Barksdale, understand? And no more torturing on my sauna nights!"

Han bowed his head.

"For now, you handle the journalists and this ugly trout outside. Has she denounced them yet?"

Han shook his head.

"Me and you will do the questions. You go hard, I go soft. Soft on Sharon Stone, hard on these two losers. As for Supergirl here, the so-called Chinese citizen, we need to find out who she is and why she's helping foreigners to disgrace our country. But no calls to the opposition!" he meant the State Security Police. "We do everything with traffic records and residency: nothing political. If they hand the tape over, result. If not, we tear the hotel apart and stick them in solitary until we've watched every tape they've got. And remember: no calls to the opposition."

He looked Han and Tong in the eye, seeking their agreement, probing silently for any other details or transgressions they might have forgotten. Then he remembered something himself:

"And book me a call to that dog-fucker Zheng. How are you supposed to maintain social order when you've got foreign journalists – foreign journalists! – without any kind of…"

He shook his head and chuckled:

"Propaganda Chief Zheng's going to really enjoy Tibet."

"Yeah," said Hard Man Han: "or maybe Xinjiang. They really love the Communist Party there."

8

The digital clock said 05.15; Xiao, his jaw dark with stubble, blew the steam off a bowl of green tea and blinked at the video wall. Outside it was already 28 degrees and humid. The command centre was buzzing now; every workstation occupied by a day-shift cop with the night-shift crouching in the floor space amid discarded riot-vests and helmets, their chopsticks working on a delivery of steamed buns.

On the big screen, in pin-sharp colour, was a Ruifeng van, seen from a surveillance camera high on the side of the hotel.

At 05.16 the driver entered the vehicle, started the engine and stuck a techno-pop CD into the sound-system. Then he leapt out of the vehicle, scratched his balls, adjusted his aviators, puffed at his cigarette and took a sly glance up at the camera.

"You getting this?" Tong growled into the bud microphone nestling against his cheek.

"We see it," said a static-laden voice from the plainclothes surveillance car.

Next, Carstairs came out of the hotel lugging a trolley full of equipment, followed by Georgina and Brough, who were bickering. She was swigging mineral water and toting a large handbag, he was swigging from a can of Coke and carrying a day-sack. Chun-li came last, face obscured by sunglasses, scrolling absently through the emails on her phone.

By 05.32 the driver had come back from a corner shop with a six-pack of Coke, a bottle of Jack Daniels, some sachets of breakfast milk, an armful of stale cakes and a carton of *Zhongnanhai* cigarettes. The doors slammed shut and the van moved off.

It was a fine day in Tang Lu and the street life was beginning to stretch and yawn. Road sweepers were brushing at the night's grey dust. A dumpling seller was lounging against his greasy cart, having a smoke, waiting for the rush-hour to begin.

In the dormitory at the Happy Girl Massage Parlour, Long Tall Daisy was lying in her bunk, sleepy but awake, trying not to listen to the argument going on in Mrs. Ma's portakabin, out at the back. It was some young guy yelling at Mrs. Ma, and she was screaming back in her usual way and drumming the floor with her heels. Daisy caught the half-awake eye of Crystalmother, her colleague in the next bunk, who mouthed quietly: "go to sleep". And with the dawn filtering through the grey lace curtains, eventually, she did, dreaming of whales swimming deep in the green of the Southern Ocean.

On the banks of the Yellow River fishermen were digging for worms. They would fill a plastic box full of bait and go staggering off in the dawn to search for a stretch of river where the industrial scum was not so thick, and a bit of shade to sit in.

High in the Helan Shan an unmarked police coach full of detainees and riot cops–ratio 1:1–was chugging slowly up a mountain road, its air filled with relief and cheap tobacco smoke. The union had done a deal to relocate the cell-block rioters to a quarry on the Gobi Desert side.

At 05.40 the cameras above Tang Lu's main boulevard picked

up the van. In the control room everybody's eyes were on the video wall.

"Do you have visual contact?" Tong droned to the surveillance car.

Hard Man Han, who had shaved and put on a fresh uniform, fired up his own comms sub-net.

"They're five minutes from the intersection. They go anywhere near that factory again and we roadblock them at the corner of 19 and Shenyang. Full search and seizure."

"Got that," came the reply from the SWAT-team leader. They were lying-up in an alleyway: five SUVs, three motorbikes and an ambulance, with a team of ninja-clad female cops ready to deal with any histrionics from the blonde.

The control room's lead operator, a female sergeant with a punk hairstyle, frowned and pushed a button, whispering intently into her headset. She raised her hand:

"Superintendent Xiao. There's an urgent call from the proprietor of the Happy Girl Massage Parlour. She says she wants to speak to you in person."

"Tell Mrs. Ma I'm busy. I will take her urgent call in thirty minutes," said Xiao .

Xiao, Tong and Hard Man Han stiffened, faces lit by colours of the video screen. On the desk in front of them was a small grey plastic videotape: it had a white label with the word SONY printed on it, and a figure "3" scrawled in marker pen.

The tension in the room rose as the van neared a t-junction. Xiao heard the punk sergeant fobbing off Mrs. Ma for a second time, pleasant but firm.

And now the tension eased as the van swung east.

"They're going for it," Han whispered.

The screen switched to another camera. The van was approaching the main route back to the Yellow River.

"Stay back, don't spook them," Tong muttered.

Now the van was picking up speed. It was on a long, straight road that would take it to a bridge across the river, into Inner Mongolia and out of Xiao's jurisdiction.

"That's it, boss, yes?" Han breathed.

But Xiao's eyes were mesmerised by the screen, refusing to blink despite his exhaustion.

"Switch to the district camera network," he snapped.

The picture went grainy and monochrome but the van was there, a miniature vehicle in a fish-eye landscape of desert.

"Can we zoom that thing in?"

"Sir we can do a digital zoom, but it will be pixellated," said the punk sergeant, "and Mrs. Ma is insisting to be left on hold. She's quite disturbed,"

"Digital zoom!" Xiao yelled.

Now his cellphone was going off. It was Mrs. Ma trying to reach him on his personal number. He hit the fake, plastic ruby that functioned as the red button. Busy.

The digital zoom showed a camera lens protruding from the passenger window of the van as it coasted along.

"What are they doing?" said Xiao

"Taking skyline shots of Tang Lu Industrial Suburb," said Tong, picking up the tape and tapping it against a computer monitor, "famous throughout China for its strict adherence to ISO 9001 emissions standards."

The cops exchanged weary smiles. Only Georgina had kicked up any kind of trouble about the tape. She had banged the table, leaned across it with her shirt half-open, gone through the whole gamut of outrage, seduction, persuasion and then threats, including words that Xiao, even with no English, understood were profanities.

But eventually, around midnight, it had been Georgina who'd told them where to find the tape: in a box in her hotel room. Tape three.

Only Chun-li had puzzled them. PhD in genetics, freelance translator and life coach; single, owns a Lexus and a flat in central

Beijing, teaches *tai chi*; no known links with Falun Gong or democracy campaigners.

Skinny, deadpan, asexual: she'd refused to engage with Xiao's paternalistic banter. She had defiantly explained her right to help the journalists do their jobs. She'd demonstrated a thorough knowledge of Decree Number 477 and had mentioned other laws that Xiao had never heard of.

"People like that make me sick," Han had sneered, coming out of the interrogation room.

"If that's the new China, you can stuff it," Xiao had said.

"Sir it will be five minutes until the cameras at the bridge pick them up, do you want to take this call from Mrs. Ma?" said the punk sergeant.

"No I don't!" Xiao replied, petulantly. "I am starving. Who's got my breakfast?"

"Here chief," one of the riot squad piped up: "pork and shrimp."

Xiao grabbed some chopsticks and snatched a carton of bite-sized dumplings, still steaming, and ripped open a sachet of soy sauce, getting his mouth and fingers filmy. The pork calmed his mind and he forgot to be furious about Chun-li.

"This is it, boss," said the punk sergeant.

The camera system on the bridge was impressive, covering all angles, zoomable and in full colour.

"Let's have split-screen," Tong suggested, flirting with the punk sergeant now. But her face was creased with worry. She beckoned him closer with her eyes as she clicked and dragged the images:

"This Mrs. Ma is saying something really weird, involving violence. It's not clear. She keeps screaming at me to put her onto the Super."

"Put her through to that phone," Tong knocked a polystyrene bowl of soup across the desk as he reached for the handset.

"Hey boss, don't miss the moment," said Hard Man Han through a mouthful of pork.

Xiao watched as the van coasted slowly across the bridge. The cameraman was still taking shots out of the passenger window as a last gesture of defiance, but who in the control room gave a shit? The Yellow River is a beautiful sight at dawn.

"That's not our car is it?" said Xiao.

There was a black Honda bearing the blue number plates of an official vehicle creeping onto the bridge behind the van.

"Nope," Han punched the comms button to make sure. "You guys are not trying to follow over the bridge?"

"No, Sir," came the answer.

"Boss!" It was Tong, looking pale now.

Han ordered: "Operator: go in tight on that Honda and gimme a scan of the number plate."

"It's a P-number," said the punk sergeant, "Propaganda Department."

"Five, four, three, two…" Somebody in the room had started a jovial countdown as the van sped towards the provincial border, which turned into a group handclap as Xiao took the videotape between thumb and forefinger, flipped it open, snapped out the tape and wound it into a ball around his fist.

He took his lighter and struck a flame beneath the knot of tape. It went up with a "whuum", triggering the fire alarm and making flames flicker for a moment up the arm of his tunic. He patted them out, clowning around, and there was a bigger, less ironic, cheer.

"Kill that fire alarm right now!" Tong yelled, leaping up from his seat, white with anger: "Stop the alarm and seal the premises!"

He was shaking.

"What's the matter?" said Xiao, rubbing the hair on the back of his hand where the fire had singed it.

"You," Tong bawled at Hard Man Han: "Get that SWAT

team on the road. You!" to Xiao's driver, munching dumplings in the corner, "Get an unmarked vehicle."

"What's the matter?" Xiao grabbed Tong by the epaulettes and shook him hard. Tong went into that robot voice cops use to deliver bad reports:

"Shortly before daybreak, Mrs. Ma, proprietor of the Happy Girl Massage Parlour, was approached by a male, late twenties, Han Chinese, to organise the murder of three Western journalists and two Chinese, plus the retrieval of specified items of video and computer equipment. Mrs. Ma's team of bodyguards were importuned to perpetrate the crime."

Some light went out of Xiao's eyes that moment that would never return. Tong continued:

"Mrs. Ma, a loyal citizen, refused, ordering her security team to resist all entreaties from this male, which during the next hour they did. This male…"

Tong's breast sagged as he summoned up the effort to continue,

"…climbed to the roof of the Happy Girl Massage Parlour, where he waved a pistol, engaged imaginary persons in conversation and threatened to shoot himself. At this point Mrs. Ma attempted to call the control room but our lines were busy. He has now disappeared."

"Get me that blue-plate Honda back on screen!" Han yelled at the punk sergeant.

She dragged an mpeg into the workspace.

"Have you run the number?" said Xiao.

"Registered to Propaganda and allocated to the departmental deputy. Male, 27. Birthplace Beijing. Resident Peach Garden Loft Apartments, Tang Lu Industrial Suburb. Two drunk-driving offences…"

But Xiao was already striding through the door, buckling on his holster. A cloud of white dumpling cartons, seized from the hands of his colleagues and thrown into the air, seemed for a second frozen, static in the space behind his head.

PART TWO

"There are deities just a few feet above our heads."
Chinese folk-saying

1

Grandfather Li could not be physically in the car – borne by it or propelled–so in order to be there in the passenger seat, at the edge of Li Qi-han's peripheral vision, he had to adopt a sitting position and fly himself along independently at the same speed, anticipating his grandson's every gear change, swerve, and braking manoeuvre in order to stay within speaking distance.

Grandfather's Type 51 from the Korean War was wedged beneath the dashboard, together with two clips of vintage 7.62mm ammunition, which Li had bought on the black market. Grandfather was looking at the Type 51 as if he would like to pick it up for one more time, though he could not. He had shot three American prisoners with it at the Battle of the Changjin Reservoir; in the head – according to Li family folklore.

Grandfather Li didn't know whether he was supposed to speak to Li Qi-han; whether it was in the rules of the afterlife or not. Li Qi-han didn't know whether the voice he was hearing was from the spirit world or from some part of his brain he had never before encountered. They were both, in this sense, in uncharted territory.

Added to that, Grandfather Li did not know what to say. Being a restless spirit he had the right to intervene to prevent his

grandson from fucking things up. Spirits who've already passed
into the underworld can just relax–back to the mountain, feet to
the river–and watch the passage of events in the world, like going
to a movie. But the unquiet dead, though not exactly allowed
to be in the movie, can hover in the aisles like peanut vendors,
occasionally casting their shadows onto the screen.

What Grandfather Li should have said is "Stop, don't do it!"
But he could see that Li Qi-han, like himself, had a hardness in the
eye that, notwithstanding the modern obsession with maintaining
social order, you do not want to mess with. So he said:

"You should drive more carefully and back off a little or they
will spot you. There's only one road across the desert; you will
not lose them."

"It's because of you they named me Li Qi-han!" Li snapped;
"If I wasn't named after a famous revolutionary…"

He'd been picked on and ridiculed since nursery school.

"Li Qi-han was a great Communist. That's why nobody
remembers him. Get over it. What you want them to call you?
Bruce?"

Li sniggered and yanked the steering wheel to overtake a
swaying truck, dangerously overloaded with sacks of metal ore.
This made Grandfather shoot, ethereally, through the back seat
and outside the car, forcing him to adopt a Superman-style flying
position in order to catch up.

"Sorry," Li murmured, as Grandfather drifted back into vision.

"These westerners are going to kill my career. They've made
the Propaganda Department look like idiots. It's supposed to be
my fault. The cops confiscated the tape–but Western journalists
are clever like rats. They had two hours to make copies – maybe
onto a laptop or a disc. Should have grabbed the lot. But no, the
dick-head cops go dewy-eyed over some blonde and just take the
tape. Zheng says the whole department will go to Tibet unless I
sort it out."

"I know," said Grandfather Li.

"You know everything?"

Grandfather laughed: the bitter laugh of somebody who's done fifteen years' hard labour in a bauxite quarry and then been, summarily, shot.

"We only know what we see in real time. We have no advance knowledge."

"So you were there with me in the office? With Zheng?"

"Logically, Zheng should just let this thing blow over. Maybe Beijing even *wants* that factory to get its ass kicked for environmental damage. Otherwise why did they let Western journalists go roaming around there?"

Li had been weighing these options since Zheng had called him to the office after midnight. They had both been struggling to sober up but had quickly found the Provincial *wai-ban* missive, buried in an unread file–apparently signed off by Li Qi-han and countersigned by Propaganda Chief Zheng, but in fact just rubber-stamped by Belinda Deng–warning them, as a matter of courtesy, that a Western news crew would be visiting Shizuishan and that all surveillance contacts should be put on alert, especially around sites of a sensitive nature.

Busybody Guo, who would get an award for spotting the news crew, had already made a statement saying she was not alerted. The only solution was to get the tapes, the laptops and all kinds of digital storage media, find the rushes and destroy them. That was an order, Zheng had stated.

"I need to see it on there," Zheng had pointed to the 42-inch Samsung TV on his office wall. "If we can get the tapes and do a deal with Xiao, we can plaster the whole thing over. The cops nearly killed some drug dealer overnight, so we can use that as leverage. Make no mistake," Zheng had said, using the old negotiator's trick of looking Li straight in the eye and putting his fist right under Li's cheekbone, "don't come back and tell me it's all sorted. Come back with tapes, laptops and any sneaky storage devices you find in that van. Or do not come back at all."

It was only after he had drunk one third of a bottle of *Wuliangye* spirit, burned a fistful of ancestor money and contemplated suicide with the Type 51 that the logical option of killing the news crew had come to him. It had thrown him when Mrs. Ma refused to put her door team on the case, but now that his brain was clearing he could appreciate the risks to her.

Li Qi-han would do the job himself. He'd been hoping Grandfather Li might show up and was not surprised to be seeing him now, much older but still dressed in the same shabby PLA uniform as in the photo, right there at his side, the colours distorted by – presumably – his status as a deity.

2

The road beyond the Yellow River levelled off into a dawn-lit sprawl of truck-stops and road-houses: white-tiled shops fronted by dogs and diesel-spill.

The van sped past a *hutong* nestling in a hollow, its passageways the colour of ginger cake, the shacks huddled up against a colonial-era Methodist church topped by a neon cross.

A few human forms were visible; a lone truck driver with his vest pulled up to his nipples to let his belly catch the sun; a weary prostitute hobbling out of the all-night café to resume her job as checkout girl at the petrol station.

Now the Ordos Desert began to stretch and undulate to the horizon. Scrub thinned out to semi-scrub, the patches of clay between the spindly shrubs got larger. In the distance a few dilapidated Bactrian camels chewed the wild alfalfa. The terrain was bent into gullies and hills, parts of it still cool with shadow.

Bird life was zero. Pedestrian life was zero. Only the trucks gave the landscape movement, cycling through a medley of digital siren wails and honks as they formed up into unofficial convoys at a steady 55 miles per hour.

Now coal mines and power stations began to smear the

landscape; some visible only from a sky-stain and a gas flare where the heavens met the sand; others towering right beside the highway, swaddled in high blue netting to thwart the prying eyes of inspectors, intellectual property thieves and compensation lawyers.

Brough, sprawled across the back seat, had been drifting in and out of sleep to the sound of Georgina and Chun-li bickering. Carstairs, in the passenger seat up front, snored, oblivious to sight and sound.

"After Olympic Year, not really normal to give up tapes to Public Security Police on request," said Chun-li.

"Problem is, if we don't they mess us around for a day and mess up our entire schedule."

Georgina had adopted a managerial tone towards Chun-li– remembering that foreign fixers, like dressage mounts, would take charge unless you told them exactly what you wanted.

"Should at least have tried to give fake tape."

"Wasn't time. They viewed it anyway didn't they? That's why they started bawling at you, isn't it?"

"Yes, maybe. I think so." She seemed suddenly capable of turning vagueness on and off at will.

The road signs had become bilingual, in Mongolian and Chinese.

"How far to Ordos?" said Brough.

"Driver says 350 kilometres. He's never been this far away from home," said Chun-li.

"Can we stop at one of these truck stops?"

"Truck stops unhygienic. Also rife with criminal elements and those transporting so-called unofficial cargo."

"That's why I want to stop there. See if any of them is carrying stuff that produces chlorine or anything that goes to that battery factory."

"What!" Georgina's yelp was loud enough to wake Carstairs: "Turn that fucking music off!"

She jabbed the driver in the shoulder with her finger and blew strands of hair out of her eyes. Overnight she'd ditched the cambric skirt for jeans and the Birkenstocks for a pair of battered Aussie stockyard boots. She'd been expecting some kind of delayed outrage from Brough and Carstairs, who'd merely snorted sardonically after she'd given up the tape. Now she said:

"Look, they were going to turn us over. It was a good spot; it could have worked in the film; it's gone. Let it go – when we get to Baotou we can…"

"It's not gone," Brough smirked.

"What do you mean it's not gone?"

"I mean that Jimmy, here, and me, over a glass of warm beer, digitised it shortly before the boys in blue arrived."

Georgina had spent the half hour before dawn explaining to Twyla in London that she had "sorted out" a potential incident, skimming over the details of their arrest and the written apology she'd signed, but logging the fact of having to surrender footage to cover herself in case things went haywire. Twyla had reminded her of the basic aim of the broadcast from Shanghai– "constructive engagement" with the Chinese government–and that the Channel had long-term plans to get onto the Chinese satellite system.

"Where is it?"

Georgina put on that face that managers adopt to signal they are no longer your work buddy but are about to assume command.

"I think we should keep it on a need-to-know basis," Brough shot a glance at Chun-li. "Love, did we ever get the name of that factory?"

Chun-li shook her head. "Something like a metal element, I never had chance to write it down."

"I don't care what the name of the fucking factory is because we're not …"

Georgina trailed off, realising she would have to confront

Brough later, in a hotel room, threaten him with the sack. Or get him so drunk that he would commit some kind of sackable offence. She was first in line for the New York bureau job at Channel Ninety-Nine after this, and had already begun looking at apartments in the newly gentrified district under the Manhattan Bridge Overpass.

"Is it on your laptop?" she scowled at Carstairs, who shook his head and replied flatly:

"It's safe."

"Chun-li-eee," Georgina went into name-stroking mode. "There's no chance that the police would plant a bug in this van is there?"

"Police chief probably just happy to see us go. Propaganda Department in deep trouble. Normally local propaganda guys and *wai-ban* and undercover cops are incessantly tailing foreign news crews, and know their itinerary. Normally, foreign media don't just stop van and begin interviewing residents. David very clever I think. And normally residents don't just talk to foreign media…"

"So why did they?"

"Don't know. CCP constantly saying it will crack down and prosecute polluting factories."

Georgina wedged her boot against the wheel arch and swigged her milk, which tasted like a liquid version of Kellog's Frosties. Her original plan had been to tone down the footage and work it into a wider theme: good China, bad China. It would be worth a watch, as they say, despite the presence of a has-been hack with his Yorkshire accent from twenty years ago.

But Twyla had sounded extra wary. She had not exactly said "thank God the cops took the tape," but the whole tenor of the conversation had conveyed that meaning, together with the subtler message of "forget the district under the Manhattan Bridge Overpass" should any more panicked calls to London become necessary.

What Georgina needed now was "content": colourful footage to fill seven minutes' worth of airtime. She needed an interview with a senior Party guy, and some pretty landscape shots. And to take control.

"What's Ordos famous for?" she snapped at Chun-li.

"Ordos a boom town. Driver says if you only have one million RMB in Ordos you are poor."

"What's the boom? I thought there was economic downturn?"

"Land under this desert is very rich in minerals. Coal mines everywhere, also iron ore. Also Rare Earth. Lots of people get rich during the privatisation of state-owned enterprises and come to Ordos to take part in brand new, private sector mining ventures."

"What will we see?"

"Don't know, never been. This desert very fragile – very beautiful. Early Mongol culture is known as Ordos Culture…"

"What the fuck is Rare Earth?" said Brough.

"Rare Earth a kind of metal," Chun-li began.

"Yes but what's the English translation for it? Rare Earth sounds like some weird Chinese concept like inner fire or–Fuck! Why is that car following us? That's not the cops is it?"

Brough's voice signalled a rising panic.

"And what the fuck is he doing now?"

3

Xiao hit the siren and set the lights flashing out of instinct. He had no jurisdiction in Inner Mongolia but an accident is an accident.

He strode out from the SUV, motioning his driver to initiate a roadblock. Hard Man Han leapt out of the car and sprinted over to the nearest casualty, a businessman slumped against the wreckage of a metallic-green Audi Q7. Xiao had his pistol out, held against his thigh like a movie gunslinger.

There were the limbs and bowels of a horse smeared and scattered across both lanes of the highway, together with the remnants of a horse-box. There were flight cases, camera lenses, videotapes, aspirin tablets, stale cakes, spotlights and rolls of coloured gelatin filter. There was the black Honda, which had skidded round and hit a road sign sideways-on. Its doors were open and its seats empty. There was the grey Ruifeng van, on its roof, wheels still spinning. It was a mess of blood, broken glass, airbags and women's hair.

Both women were hanging upside down, pinned by their seatbelts. The Chinese girl was gabbling into her mobile trying to call an ambulance; the blonde, face caked with dirt and glass, was screaming English obscenities at the driver, who was dead.

The cameraman was moving: crawling out of the wreckage using one arm.

The reporter was lying in the road amid the luggage, at Xiao's feet: eyes glazed like a dead fish, a day sack wrapped around his neck. There was a damp patch on the sun-seared ashphalt beneath his body that smelled like whisky.

There was the odour of clay, alfalfa, liquorice, diesel, tarmac, blood, horse-flesh and Jack Daniels.

It occurred to Superintendent Xiao that this was a neat conclusion to the entire episode, if not exactly welcome. Dead lunatic propaganda guy; dead foreign reporter; scratch one lowly informant for the State Security Police; film crew neutralised.

Then he saw Li Qi-han stagger up from a ditch at the roadside, hands gripping a pistol. The pistol seemed to have a life of its own: it seemed to be pulling Li in a crouching run towards the wreckage of the van.

Xiao's brain kicked into gear. "Ah-ha," he said to himself: "this little shit has caused the accident and is intending to put bullets into the survivors."

There was no chance of hitting him from this distance but Xiao knelt down, levelled his own pistol and fired. He was out of breath. Years since he'd done this. The shot had got the punk's attention. He was young, scrawny: sensible haircut, scowling face. The kid ducked back down behind the Honda.

Xiao strode past Brough's body. He saw Carstairs make a weird, disoriented grab for his camera in the wreckage, following the cameraman's instinct to film everything, and then collapse to the floor. Georgina's screams were getting louder. She had worked out that she was still alive, but had heard the gunshot.

Xiao saw Li Qi-han stagger up to the top of the roadside embankment to stand, legs akimbo and with blood seeping from a head wound, the sun behind him.

"Please send an ambulance to the National Road, east of Tang Lu about 50 kilometres," Chun-li was saying to her cellphone.

A bullet grazed the tarmac next to Xiao's feet and the report boomed across the desert. Shit, he should have put the Kevlar on! Georgina's screaming suddenly stopped.

"I demand the posthumous rehabilitation of Li Rui-dong, veteran of the PLA, unjustly jailed during the anti-rightist purge of 1956," Li shouted, bringing the pistol up to aim at Xiao in a cool tai-chi-like arc.

"Enough of this, son. Give yourself up!"

There was a brief moment of eye contact over the sights of their pistols but then Li crumpled to the sand. Hard Man Han, creeping like a wraith across the desert, had tasered him from a range of less than 10 feet.

"Good," Xiao grunted. "Let's get him back to base. That other guy alright?"

"Mad as a firework, boss" Han hiked up a huge, green snot into his mouth and spat it into the sand. "On the phone to his lawyer already. Very upset about the horse."

There was a small crowd of truckers forming about fifty yards beyond the crash site, where the traffic had backed up. They watched the two cops haul Li to the unmarked SUV and throw him into a dog cage in the back. Meanwhile the SWAT team had arrived and were trying to sort out a chaotic detour that the truckers had begun to make into the desert. One truck was already stuck and others were inching their way around it, kicking up a dust cloud to above head height.

"Think we can dump this lot on the Inner Mongolian Ambulance Service?" Han jerked a thumb at the van.

"Better help them," said Xiao. "Witnesses. Snap a couple of photos of me giving first aid."

Xiao made a laboured jog over to the upturned van while Han fiddled with the controls on his digital camera. There was a nice shot of Xiao using his Leatherman tool to slice through the seatbelt holding Georgina upside down. Another showed him cradling the Englishwoman as he dragged her carefully through the broken window. Chun-li, once they'd cut her free, managed to slither out by herself. As she checked the driver for signs of life, Han snapped him for the record and retrieved his cellphone. Then they all turned away, leaving his smashed face to dry in the desert sun.

"Hold on a minute, where's the other one?" said Xiao.

Xiao and Han stood squinting at wet patch on the tarmac, where Brough's body had been spread-eagled a moment ago.

"That guy was dead, right?" said Hard Man Han.

"Eyes wide open," said Xiao.

4

They had shot Georgina, shot Carstairs and if they had not shot
the driver and Chun-li that was probably because they were dead
already–or police informers. Anyway Brough had counted two
shots. He still had the USB stick wedged inside his anus, wrapped
in a condom. If he could survive he now had a massive story on
his hands. He owed it to his colleagues to survive.

Brough had learned that the best thing to do when something
happens is to accept the fact: the story has changed. One minute
you are cracking jokes with a street kid in some barrio south of
the equator, the next minute the kid is lying sprawled in the shit,
life draining away through a gunshot wound. One minute you
are staring at the computer screen in London, trying to decide
between cappuccino and latte, the next minute a wire drops
saying "FLASH: CONGO. JOURNALIST KILLED" and in
the pit of your stomach you already know which journalist it is
because your bosses are on the phone asking if you happen to
know the name of the private school his kids attend.

With death, but also with a host of less permanent reversals,
the ordinary human response is denial. Carry on as normal for a
few hours, days, and in the case of some people, forever. Brough

had learned to do the opposite of this. He had learned to sense the worst of the situation, accept it and formulate a plan. Even, if truth be told, to welcome the onset of danger–just as a Pavlovian dog welcomes the arrival of an electric shock.

So when he'd spotted the black Honda overtake them, slam its brakes on, force the van to swerve into the path of an SUV pulling some kind of trailer, his brain had registered this as a hostile act. When he'd woken up on the tarmac and seen the police chief from Tang Lu looming above him with a handgun he'd realised the Chinese cops were trying to kill him. So he'd played dead.

He had swapped, drunkenly with other hacks in the dim-lit bars of various Sheratons, the usual "what would you do?" bullshit: what would you do if Al Qaeda stopped you at a roadblock in Iraq claiming to be cops?

"Run", is always the answer. If they are real cops they won't open fire. If it's AQ you are dead anyway and harder to hit while moving.

So when he'd heard the first shot he had leapt to his feet and started running. His blood had gone cold. He had heard Georgina screaming so he'd assumed they had shot Carstairs. Then, boom. Another shot and Georgina's screaming had stopped.

So now he sprinted, legs the consistency of oyster flesh, towards a ditch where he flung himself face down, panting into the dust. He checked himself for blood, wiggled his fingers and held his hand in front of his face to test for concussion. His entire body felt punched and scraped.

Now truck tyres came popping over the gravel and into the ditch behind him. There was a commotion – drivers shouting and engines revving. He stumbled through a dust cloud and found himself in the middle of a queue of trucks edging into the desert. One truck revved out of the dust and nearly flattened him. The driver braked hard and swore at him through the sand-caked windscreen. When the truck restarted, Brough was clinging to its high metal sides, whimpering.

The truck bounced around crazily on the desert until, after a couple of hundred yards, it veered back towards the road.

He jumped off, electrifying his neck nerves with an inept commando roll through vegetation that smelled like a drink from the 1970s called Dandelion & Burdock. He picked up his day sack and jogged–in that comical way shot people do when they are trying to run away from their own gunshot wounds–to a gully, where he threw himself to the ground.

He scrabbled in the bag. There was a litre of water and three cans of warm Coke. All the other stuff he religiously carried round was there: packet of condoms, one missing; roll of duct tape; first-aid kit; Wrigley's Juicy Fruit; passport; a foot-long piece of coat-hanger wire for prodding his way out of a minefield.

The whisky bottle was just shards. His muesli bars were there, squashed and sodden. Sun cream he had. Missing from its usual hook was the USB stick, presented to him on a visit to the Conn-Selmer Corporation of Elkhart, Indiana, from which he had removed all the hi-res jpegs of the company's famous trumpets and uploaded, in their place, two gigabytes of digital video in the .mov format. Twenty-three minutes and a bit.

Something unspoken between Brough and Carstairs had made them avoid telling Georgina about the USB stick. The same journalistic sixth sense had prompted Brough to wrap the thing in a Durex and plug it into his anus the moment he'd heard police radios crackling in the stairway of the hotel.

He could feel the sun scorching his neck and it was only, what, nine o'clock? He grappled in his jeans for his Blackberry. Fully charged. The time was 08.47.

He would head into the desert and then call London. Or Shanghai. Did he have any numbers in Shanghai? No matter. He would survive. The story had changed: the action had to change.

They had killed Western journalists. If this pollution footage was enough to make them kill, then he had a major scoop in progress.

Overweight people can survive in the desert, because that's the way veteran SAS guys always go in. He opened the water and took a deep swig, scraped the shards of the whisky bottle out of the bag and then set off, at a crouch, along the bottom of a gully, under a sky of eggshell blue.

5

"Why have the English decided to send a war reporter to Ningxia? Could they be expecting some kind of social upheaval we had not anticipated?" That had been the mission-defining statement given to Cai Chun-li by her personal mentor, General Guo.

Two days ago she'd known the answer: coincidence; just a drunken hack tasked with producing eye-candy for some second-rate TV channel, approaching the end of his career.

Both Brough and Carstairs had registered a mild "beep" on China's intelligence radar. Both had passports plastered with entry visas into conflict zones. They'd been processed, noted and the Ningxia *wai-ban* alerted to their presence.

General Guo, however, ran his own bureau supplying *ad hoc*, instinct-driven product to an unofficial unit of the PLA's Military Intelligence Department. This unit was currently obsessed with potential conflicts within the higher echelons of the Communist Party, where relations between the pro-market "Princelings" and the more social-democratic "Youth League Faction" had been getting spiky since they'd each started to jail rival city mayors on corruption charges.

Chun-li was one of those Chinese women who was just

trying to live her life without lies and ideology, and with a bare minimum of lip gloss; to conduct her life, as the *Tao Te Ching* says, "without regrets" and to realise her full potential.

Realising her full potential had, since she left Peking University, involved life-coaching various wannabe dotcom millionaires, translating for Western business delegations and, when she felt like a challenge, the foreign media. Out of pure devotion to General Guo she kept an eye on various things and various people, some of whom believed she was their informant.

So Guo had pushed Chun-li into the Channel Ninety-Nine assignment, like a black stone into a white-held corner of the *wei-qi* board, as an intuitive move. He had seen no possibilities in the targets themselves, but hoped to discern patterns in the lines of inquiry of those who routinely badgered Chun-li for information– officials, spies, crooks and Chinese investigative journalists.

Now, with Brough headed for certain death in the desert, and some crazy Propaganda kid trying to kill her, Chun-li was having to revise the initial sit-rep. She also suspected there was a bit of ancestral intervention going on, for which – as she'd joked with General Guo many times – neither the Party nor the PLA has any Standard Operating Procedure.

She handed Georgina and Carstairs each a bottle of water and made them sit in the shade. She fired up the GPS on her cellphone and marked the exact position where Brough had been lying. Her hair, which had been caked in breakfast milk and windscreen fragments, she twisted between her fingers into a shape; it had been shapeless and without life before. Her eyes, which had up to now been droopy, came to life like somebody had thrown neat gin into them. She started snapping pictures of the crash scene on her phone.

"Georgina, David's gone. Did you see him?"

Georgina shook her head.

"He's escaped into the desert."

"Don't make me laugh 'cos me rib is killing me," Carstairs groaned.

Chun-li's English, which she had not bothered to lace with definitive articles before, became perfect.

"Am I correct in thinking David has a copy of the video rushes with him?" she asked Carstairs.

Silence. Chun-li sighed:

"You think I am some kind of agent?"

Silence.

"Just trying to live my life…" she muttered, under her breath but audible.

Georgina's adrenaline made her gabble:

"Gotta phone Shanghai, and London. The insurance. It's a private medical system here, correct? We're all entitled to treatment – including you. He," she motioned to the driver, "will be entitled to a lot of compensation. His family I mean. Do you know them?"

Chun-li shook her head.

She had spotted a blood-caked man walking towards them, swatting at the space around his head as if dodging a swarm of invisible insects. He was smoking a black cigarette, wearing a black v-neck sweater and black Evisu jeans, with black leather flip-flops. His roof-shaped eyebrows, square face and buzz-cut hair marked him out as Mongolian. Above forty years old.

"You guys have killed the odds-on favourite to win the 2010 Wuhan Derby. I hope you have good insurance," he said in English, with a slight European accent.

"Channel Ninety-Nine," Chun-li declined the Sobranie Black Russian he held out to her: "I thought horse-racing was illegal outside Hong Kong?"

"We're actually trialling it on a controlled basis." He extended one shaky hand with a business card:

"Come and visit my club. They'll be taking you to Ordos

General Hospital shortly, I imagine. Can I get insurance details from you?"

Chun-li flashed a row of teeth, which nobody had noticed up to now were white and perfect. She became hippy and bone-shouldered, like a teenager negotiating her first drug purchase at some summer music festival in an English field.

"We're terribly sorry," Georgina butted in. "Obviously any damage caused by our vehicle will be paid for but the question is what the driver of that," she swished her hair towards the Honda, "was trying to do."

"Kill you, I imagine," the Mongolian horse owner ran his palm over his skull and staggered backwards:

"Sorry I am a little bit concussed. As far as I could tell that car is Propaganda Department, Tang Lu plates. And the cops very keen to retreat over the provincial border, not taking you guys but taking the driver. We're into all kinds of jurisdiction problems here but the fact remains I have to cite you guys for the collision and the Propaganda Department for dangerous driving. The excess on these Audis is unbelievable."

Chun-li rummaged in her bag and pulled out her own business card, which the SUV guy studied for a moment and slipped into the back pocket of his jeans. Then she hit him with a wacky, clueless grin:

"Do you by any chance have access to a helicopter?"

6

Brough's plan was to walk south, turn east, walk parallel with the highway and then rendezvous with the rescue team back at the road towards nightfall. For now, as a precaution, he had killed his Blackberry in case they were using scanners to find him.

He would make a call to London later. His mind had been subconsciously computing the chances of the Chinese having an agent inside Channel Ninety-Nine, or somebody they'd put the burn on. That plus the correspondent's instinct to avoid all contact with his superiors had dictated the course of action: become invisible and unpredictable.

It would mean spending a day in the desert but, now he was out there, he could see it was not exactly the Sahara. There was low, sparse scrub everywhere and as the sun got higher clouds were forming. With the Coke and water he had two and a half litres of liquid. He had survived on less in hotter places. He covered his neck and face with sun cream and his nose and eyebrows, like a cricketer, with white zinc.

He squatted down in the sand, pants around his ankles, and squeezed the USB stick out of his anus; removed the condom, blew a few grains of sand from the object itself, mentally thanking the Conn-Selmer Corporation for choosing the smooth, bullet-shaped profile of the stick. He looped his gold neckchain through an eyehole on the stick: people were always taking the piss out of his gold neckchain but it always came in useful.

He'd been trying to stop his mind composing lush obituaries for Georgina. It was his fault the poor kid had got blown away. Jimmy Carstairs? Well he knew the score: been to the edge of the diving board a few times and looked over. In a deeper layer of Brough's brain there was a parallel process of obituary composition going on, for himself.

It was getting humid. He needed to get a good five miles south of the road – well out of visual range. That would take two hours. By then it would be 11 – that was 3am in London and the worst time for finding journalists awake other than lonely and dishevelled ones slumped across the bar towels at the Basra Lounge, in need of a rescue party themselves.

He would get to where the mobile phone signal was weak, reducing the chance of them triangulating his position off two masts, send a text to Twyla and then shut down again; then find shade and rest for a couple of hours to give London time to alert the British Embassy.

He shouldered his bag, rolled his shirt-sleeves down to his wrists, pulled his collar up against the sun and started walking.

He'd been calm up to now but soon found himself shaking with fear and fury as he swung along. A little bit later he was wiping snot off his upper lip because he had begun to cry.

Thirst made him sit down amid the liquorice bushes and open a can of Coke. He gulped it down, wiped his face and immediately wanted to piss. While he was pissing he fired up the Blackberry. It took forever.

The time was only just before 10am. He fired up the GPS map system and it came up: a lat-long reading but no map. He waited minutes for a local map to download. When the red line of the National Road appeared it was startlingly close to where the position marker said he was standing. On the scale of a major desert he'd gone nowhere, basically.

He saved his position into the handset as a waypoint and set another one, due east ten kilometres. A low hum started in the distance.

He pointed the top of the Blackberry in the direction of the next waypoint and scrambled to the crest of a small hill to try and find a landmark to head for. In the very far distance there was a glint, just half a glint, like a truck mirror flashing in the sun. A glint surrounded by a huge dustcloud.

It was a helicopter landing near the road.

The panic that had been trying to claw its way out for the last hour, through twenty years' worth of learned insouciance, finally won.

They were tracking the Blackberry. Turn it off. He was already thumbing the red button as he started sprinting – where? Anywhere he could find cover. Shallow breathing and the Coke turned his spit acidic.

What would an SAS guy do? Anything that moves can be seen, anything that can be seen can be killed. Where had he learned that? In a bar in Beirut? In a watchtower in South Armagh?

He limped to the top of a small rise, out of breath. The other side was a shallow ravine. There came the sudden flaring of the chopper's rotor noise as it banked to take off. He yanked two shrubs up by the roots and ran with them to the edge of the ravine. There was a tiny overhang and he leapt down under it.

Must keep still. He sat on his bag to obscure the fluorescent decals and squatted with the bushes over his head. He smeared his face with desert earth, earth sticking to the sun cream. He poured a handful of desert over each boot and scrubbed more into his hair. The earth was grainy, quartzy, coarse, metallic.

The chopper made a low pass parallel with the road. Clatter-clatter. It was turning.

He began to tremble. Why was life, which had been treating him so decently, and to which he had been starting to feel so attached again–after months of not being–getting ready to dump on him for one last time? He heard himself whimpering quietly that he did not want to die and that he would hand over the rushes if captured.

On the kidnap-survival course they teach you to look your executioner in the eye. They can't shoot a human being, is the logic; they have to dehumanise you. The first time he'd done that course, Brough had been tripped into a zone of total panic: the pheromone-laden Zulu language of the South African mercenaries playing the kidnappers had freaked him out so badly he had started screaming once they put the bag over his head. Inwardly he was screaming now.

If the Chinese cops found Brough now he would plead with them, look them in the eye. But these people were inhuman. He had decided that in the police station: stone faces; no eye contact, not even over a cigarette.

The helicopter had turned and was making a slow hover back towards him. He would be hidden by the ravine if they'd only pass right over him.

With a deafening roar and a backdraft of dust that filled his nostrils, that's what they did. He could feel the overpressure punching at the ground beneath him.

He watched the chopper fly away: fifty yards, one hundred. Now it had stopped and was turning on its rotor axle. He buried his head as it hovered, stationary, blasting sand straight at him.

He let one eye slant half-open. Did he see Chun-li's face peering out of the porthole? Did she see him? He thought the answer to both questions was yes, but then, with a final blast of grit into his face, the chopper banked and veered and cackled off into the distance. Its noise subsided into a drone as it picked up height and speed.

Brough, not stopping to dust himself off or clear his hair of debris, was already running. If they'd seen him, they would be back in force. If they hadn't, then this was his chance to escape and tell the world about these murdering bastards and their chlorine cloud.

He slept in an ancient clay watchtower, its walls two feet thick, until the sun dropped low enough to shine through the doorway and wake him up. He decided, while asleep, not to phone or text London. London would order him to contact the nearest police station. London would send private security contractors hired in the nearest city to come and "protect" him, gaining total control over his actions. London would tell him to ditch the report – "everything's changed now David", the quiet menace in the voices of people who pay your wages. He decided to get to Beijing with the footage, and pitch the story directly to his old mates in the newsroom, bypassing Twyla.

He could see from the map on his Blackberry that the nearest city with an airport was called Baotou. To get there he would have to get out of the desert and hire a driver. That meant getting to the nearest city without an airport, which was Ordos, 200 kilometres away.

He stood up, spat, raked dirt out of his hair with his fingers, checked the direction of the sun, positioned his face looking directly into it, held the Blackberry at arm's length, pressed a button and began speaking:

"Shortly after those pictures were taken the police arrested us and seized our tape. Later, as we tried to leave the city, an official car rammed us off the road and a senior local police officer opened fire. Producer Georgina Wyndham and cameraman James Carstairs…"

His brain faltered, scrabbling for some final thought to end the piece-to-camera, but it was not there. He flipped the Blackberry around and took a couple of static panoramas of the desert. Whatever needed to be said could be said over those pictures.

He set off across the rolling scrub, knowing that if he followed his shadow as the sun set that should take him northeast.

What did he know about China? Not much. He had no Chinese contact numbers other than for Chun-li. He knew the basic facts about Tiananmen Square in 1989; he knew that Deng Xiao-ping had started the market reforms, that Jiang Zemin was a corrupt arsehole and Hu Jin Tao was supposed to be a bit better. What he knew about Chairman Mao he had learned from a brown-eyed female cadet of the Colombian EPL who'd used his hotel room as a place to hide from a death squad tailing her across Bogota, trading sex for safety. He had followed the rise of China's economy with the same fascinated fatalism as most Westerners.

Brough had no reference points for China. His reference points began at Heathrow Terminal Five and extended mainly to places that offered conflict, alcohol and journalistic bonhomie. At the *Lichfield Guardian* they had put him third on the list of reporters volunteering to be "embedded" – it was a new word back in 1990 – with the Staffordshire Regiment deploying to Saudi Arabia. The first two guys on the list had dropped out when, to the astonishment of everybody, all requests for access were immediately granted.

He'd watched the start of Desert Storm, like everybody else in the world, on CNN: over the top of a can of Holsten Pils.

He'd watched the end of it in a sweaty tent near Basra with a bunch of elated squaddies again drinking Holsten Pils. By then he'd got the bug: for war and television.

The *Western Mail* had given him a stringer's job in Moscow because he could speak Russian (or so he'd told them) and in 1993 he'd been called up by ITN to do a live "phono" interview while an alliance of Communists and neo-Nazi nutters were trying to storm the Duma. And then by the BBC, CNN and ABC.

Somewhere between that and Srebrenica he had realised that the fall of the Berlin Wall, far from bringing about universal peace and global harmony, had unleashed a world where class and ideology would simply be replaced by ethnicity, crime and precision-guided firepower.

The best thing to do (once his dad had died and his last live-in girlfriend packed her Virago novels into a big plastic crate and said goodbye) was to stand at the edge of the spectacle and watch–always near enough to the action to work up a thirst, always far enough away from moral commitment that it was no great wrench to leave the victims bleeding in the street and head for the hotel bar.

And suddenly he had a family again. In the soul-draining softlights of the Abuja Hilton, the Nairobi Norfolk, the Hotel Tequendama Bogota there were always to be found, clustered around the reception desk and demanding by the middle of the 1990s something called Internet Access, people just like David Brough. Only ten percent more.

There'd been a brief moment of doubt at the end of the 1990s when kids all over the place started to hurl stones through the windows of Gap and Nike. But then, sure enough, it turned out the new century would not bring a return to class warfare: the small wars of the nineties would turn out be just the warm-up act for something bigger.

He had watched 9/11 happen live on a CNN feed in the

Reuters office in Mexico City ("Fuck, was that a second plane?")
He had been deployed to Afghanistan early, when the Taliban
were still giving press conferences; then to Iraq at a time the
Americans were not giving press conferences. Then the West
Bank, Afghanistan, Lebanon, Katrina, the tsunami – and in-
between all those low level conflict zones they send you to when
things are quiet, in the hope that something will kick off just as
you pass through customs.

A technology journalist had once told him, waving a brick-
sized mobile phone over the bar at Sheremetyevo airport: "I will
write about these things 'til I retire. They will not change; they
will only get more complicated." After 9/11, Brough knew it
would be the same with wars: power-crazed assholery, like mobile
handsets, would conquer the world, offering–live or pre-rec, take
your choice–graphic footage of blood, police tape and starvation
all the way through to oblivion.

"You should never have let that Elaine lass go," a voice from
within began to chide him.

Weird what the desert could do, because normally these guilt
trips would happen to Brough when he was drunk and alone.
Now he was sober and alone, although maybe getting high off
the liquorice aroma of the foliage.

He knew, because it was part of the pattern, that he would
soon start having an imaginary conversation with his dad.

"I know," he muttered.

He was already shedding tears. Thinking about his father
made him cry instantly when not in public.

"You've got yourself into a right mess," said the voice. He
trudged along, mentally agreeing.

"You've caused all this malarkey … and now you're trying to
get yourself lost in the desert!"

He stamped up a slope, head down and the world closing in
on him. It was getting towards twilight. There was an electric

energy to the sky; the shrubs were becoming skeletal, projecting their shadows like a crackle-glaze across the dirt. Clouds were boiling up, tall cumulus, their lighted undersides stretching across the sky forever.

"You're acting like a bloody idiot." It was a bit sharp sounding, even for his dad and his subconscious. At the very edge of his vision Brough thought he actually saw somebody.

He shook his head like a puddled boxer and swigged the last inch of water. There was just one more Coke can left, and that made him shiver a bit. A firefighter had once told him that the colour of your urine and the capabilities of your brain are precisely correlated – on a scale from clear to stenching ochre.

Now, on the brow of the next slope, he could see the silhouette of his father, arms outstretched just like they'd been one Christmas Eve, sometime during the seventies, with the snow falling, when Brough had run to meet him walking home from work.

"I would sling that gadget away if I were you," said his dad.

Brough, remembering how badly he had failed his father, and how many beer-stale nights he had wept over all the unsaid things between them, said simply:

"I'm sorry."

"Sling the gadget. Get yourself to a hospital. Look at you!"

Imaginary conversations with his dad were not usually so abrasive or visual.

"This is my chance. I've got myself a scoop," Brough began; "I can't just give it up now."

There was a long silence as they stumbled through the desert together, side by side.

"No story is worth it, son," said his father's spirit.

It was only the continuation of the debate he'd been having with himself for the past hour, knowing how little liquid he had left and how far he had to go, so he was not surprised that his dad had started to persuade him.

"Alright," he said, "I'll probably just give it to them. I'll have to call London and get myself evac-ed out of here first. I'll just see how far I can get with this," and he held a Coke can up against the last of the sunlight.

"No, lad! Do it now! Sling the sodding thing away right now!"

His father's tone shocked him. It seemed real and insistent, somehow malevolent.

"Hold on," Brough said, squinting at the figure, which was trying to hover just beyond his peripheral vision. He put a hand up to shade his eyes:

"Dad. I don't want to sound funny or anything, but how long have you been Chinese?"

8

The ground surveillance radar was Vietnam-era, or not much later. The entire sidecar of her motorbike was filled by the radar and its related gizmos: banana-shaped dish, clunky tripod and then the electronics, all reassuringly analog.

The rider pulled her combat jacket tight against the desert cold and twiddled the dials. She'd rewired the monitor screen to sit just above the mirror on her handlebars so that – although it was pointless operating a PPS-5 radar in anything but static mode–she could run the Chiang-Jiang's engine, sit on the bike gaining warmth from it as she ran the search patterns.

There'd been some crackle over the network about an incident. High-pitched bullshit on the CB radios of the truckers, chopper sightings by jumpy miners that turned out to be just the sparkle of lightning from a far-off storm. Still, she'd pulled the recce shift tonight and had cranked up the PPS-5 as ordered: its tripod slick with Valvoline, its surfaces lovingly re-painted with the unit's regulation tiger-stripe camo.

She'd got the valves warm on the monitor and set the dish on an arc to spot anything moving to or from the road. Ten kilometres was the maximum range for vehicles, six for human beings. But at the end of the day you will struggle to hit anything beyond 500 metres with a Type 56 – the raw Chinese copy of the AK–and in the strictly retro culture of the Ordos Snow Leopards Motorcycle Club nothing with better accuracy was allowed.

The radar was just a giant microphone, and its brain an analog computer. It could filter out the rustling of wind and the clatter of falling stones. When it heard a pair of size 42 Lucchese cowboy boots crunching through the dirtstone at about 4750 metres it gave a brief "ping" of recognition. It had once been a perimeter sensor at Aviano airbase and there was a whole collection of cowboy boot sounds stored in its memory on account of the Texas Air Guard, stationed there with their A-10s.

She was onto the trace already, tweaking the knobs to tighten the signal, nudging the dish ten degrees to centre it on the contact. She would not engage without support. There was an SOP to follow – plus the fact that sending a Chiang-Jiang out into the desert on its own, given the age and provenance of most of the unit's bikes, was not a good idea...

Brough, traipsing along, oblivious to the racket he was making, was exhausted. The moon had risen, silver white. The cold enveloped him with a numb, ascetic clarity. He had got rid of the hallucination by telling it to fuck off, several hours ago. He had drunk the last of the Coke but was insisting to himself that he could make it to the road by morning.

He flicked the Blackberry on again to check direction. For the third time since midnight a whole bunch of text messages dropped, the notification ping echoing across the sand. The texts were mainly about a crisis in the British government: his mates in London were swapping cruel and sexist jokes about this; the departing ministers were mainly female and had mainly messed up the simplest of tasks. One had to apologise because her husband had claimed porn films on her government expense account. That was the gist of Brough's text messages, and their casual profanity renewed his feeling of confidence.

Plus there was a message from Chun-li: "David RU OK? Pls get in touch!" This meant she wasn't dead.

He scanned the subject lines of his emails, still dropping relentlessly into his inbox, here in the middle of nowhere: Viagra, Cialis; press releases from moderate Muslim groups slagging off others allegedly infiltrated by terrorists; hassle from the HR department at Channel Ninety-Nine; more British deaths in Afghanistan; some black kid stabbed in Newham; the usual expense queries from his last trip haunting him deep into the desert.

Presently he sensed a throb coming from somewhere out in the dark. A deep throb: not a helicopter. Maybe a light plane? The question was: run or stop? He stopped.

"He's stopped," the motorcyclist barked into her radio. She could now see the rest of the unit's bikes as a thick red trail of contacts on the radar screen and Brough as a small red dotted line.

"Forty two degrees, about five clicks East of your location," she said.

"You certain?" came the response.

Pling. A text message. Brough hit the "Quiet" key but too late.

"Certain," said the motorcycle radar operator.

The unit now closed in: the bikes broke into an arc formation about two clicks from the target, the flankers forging ahead to make a semicircle they could easily close around him if he tried to make a break for it. Headlights off: every rider and sidecar passenger was wearing night vision goggles: Soviet era, naturally. As they closed in, they could see the target frantically thumbing something into his mobile phone.

"Halt!" said a voice from the tannoy rigged to one of the sidecars. "Drop the phone!"

Brough saw the red dot of a laser gunsight juddering around

on his sternum. He skimmed the Blackberry to the floor and it broke into its constituent parts on impact. Now everything happened fast.

Two motorbikes throbbed out of the darkness towards him, each with a sidecar passenger, each passenger training a light carbine in his direction. They were giant bikes out of another era, the sidecars and fuel tanks bearing the sabre-toothed face of a big cat stencilled in day-glo white against a tiger-stripe paint job; each bike flying a large red Chinese flag from its radio antenna.

As they circled him, tightening the trap, staring at him through their NV goggles, one of the riders pulled out some kind of pistol and levelled it at his chest.

Brough saw, for a moment, straight through to the other side of death. He pictured himself joining a restless queue of teenage squaddies from Afghanistan, their trauma wounds packed and wrapped; stabbed young black guys from East London with diamond earrings and gold teeth, each with an embarrassed smile on his face asking: "why me?"

Weirdly, amid the odour of the desert, the smell of gasoline and fear, Brough caught the sickly top notes of a perfume, something like Kenzo Amour Florale, just as a projectile punched him in the chest.

PART THREE

"Saudi Arabia has oil. China has Rare Earth."
Deng Xiao-ping

1

"When's the last time you saw a porn movie where a Chinese man with a giant dick is giving it to some li'l English lady?"

It was a tough first question and not one Brough had prepared himself for in any interrogation he had ever imagined.

"Okay," the woman slapping his face had a Californian accent; "lemme put it another way. When was the last time you saw a porn movie where a Western guy is screwing some little Chinese girl?"

"These exist," Brough croaked.

She looked angry, her face was strong and pure, her hair dyed chestnut brown. She had pulled up a chair so she could sit knee-to-knee with him and slap him back to consciousness.

"First thing you need to get straight, Mister Brough is: show some respect!"

"Yeah, due respect!'

That was another woman, pacing around behind him, pronouncing "due" as in "do", agitated.

He was in a yurt furnished Kasbah-style with cushions and rugs, with a heavy emphasis on animal skin. They had dressed him in a white paper jumpsuit and speedcuffed his wrists behind his back. The USB stick was missing from his neck, together with his chain.

"You prolly don't realise," the woman behind him leant close to his ear; "because you only been in China less than a week, that every Western guy that comes here comes – subliminally – to fuck Chinese women. This is hard-wired in your genes but totally forgotten by your culture."

"Ever *seen* Piccadilly?" said the woman in front of him. She had a NATO-style name-patch velcroed to her flying jacket, drawn in smudgy marker-pen: Chi.

Brough stared at her, his brain struggling.

The other woman strode around the tent, her shoulders giving off menace as she messed with the sticky chamber of an AK carbine. She had that fine, fragile bone structure and blue-veined skin that Brough – if he'd had any cultural reference points at all – would have recognised as the "Four Young Dan" film actress look.

"It's, like, a movie," she chipped in, pronouncing the sentence like a question and in a midtown Manhattan accent. "*Piccadilly*. Nineteen twennynine. White man fucks Chinese lady?"

Her name patch was stencilled with the word "Lai". Miss Chi and Miss Lai.

"Where's my stuff?" Brough looked past them, through the tent doorway. It was pre-dawn and he could hear a generator growling, bike engines revving and the clink of spanners on spark plugs.

"Relax honey." Miss Chi had that full, knowing, so-many-gay-male-friends way of speaking that you can default to if you spend any time in California. Her voice ran up and down the Aeolian scale, one note for each word; "we're not gonna kill you. We dripped you, dit'n we?"

He looked down at his left hand; there was still a plastic

cannula slotted into a vein there, but the saline drip had been removed.

"What did you shoot me with?"

"You got a lotta nerve mister." Miss Lai had slung the AK over her shoulder and was flicking through his passport:

"You arrive in China, three days later you tryin' to drag our country's reputation into the shit!"

They were wearing identical gold embossed T-shirts under their leather bike-jackets, depicting a manga girl throwing a hand-grenade.

"An' stop lookin at my boobs, motherfucker!" said Miss Lai. "Stop objectifying us!"

"Where am I?"

He decided to go on being dazed.

"Technically," Miss Lai skimmed his passport through the air to hit him in the chest, "you are detained by us. But you should be grateful. There's a freakin' manhunt under way by law enforcement and you, Mister Brough – cool name by the way, same as the bike T.E. Lawrence rode–anyway, like I say, you're better off detained by us right now. Off the radar."

"Who are you?"

"Knocked you down with a zoo dart. It'd take out a big cat for a few hours," said Miss Chi.

Miss Lai interjected:

"Getting back to the subject, you gotta respec' the fact there will be no sex, no flirting, no freakin' slimy compliments by you, no lookin' at people's boobs or nuttin'…"

"Sounds ideal," said Brough, "can I have some water?"

"See this?"

Miss Lai twirled the carbine around her finger like a gunslinger and did a Suzi Quatro pose with the stock against her knee: "It's fuckin' real!"

"So no escape attempts!" Miss Chi seemed to lighten up marginally. "No Steve McQueen-style exploits."

Brough's jaw hurt as he tried to smile.

"I'm serious," said Miss Chi, pulling a bayonet out of her boot and slicing the speedcuffs off him. "We seen the movies: you English guys spent the whole o' World War Two constantly escaping. But not from here, buster."

Miss Lai dumped his sweat-stained clothes in a bundle at his feet. Both of them, despite their beauty, had the dry-calloused knuckles of the martial artist and their muscles seemed to contain a whip-like energy.

"Can you take me to Ordos?"

"Sure," Miss Chi pulled a parkerized Colt pistol from her belt and thrust it into his face:

"We can take you to Ordos where you can go fuck some teenage girl in a hotel room for twenny dollars and then carry on your slander campaign against the PRC!"

Her hand was shaking.

"Lotta evil mo-fos out here in the desert, Mister Brough," said Miss Lai, behind her, sniggering.

2

"We're basically a private military and security company," Miss Chi led him through the camp under a chrome cloudscape. She'd calmed down now but was sullen: subcutaneously angry.

The wind was snapping at the guy-ropes of several camo-patterned yurts. There were maybe two-dozen bike-and-sidecar combinations parked in a rank. At each bike women clad in a motley collection of vintage military gear were busy with wire wool, ratchet spanners or pouring icy quarts of mineral water into the battery. From each bike flapped a metre-wide Chinese flag.

"Emphasis on military?" Brough's mouth was too dry for humour.

Not every woman was packing a firearm, but there were enough in evidence: the old, short Chinese AK carbines – as seen from the Niger Delta to Kabul – plus the odd RPG slung over a slender shoulder. They shouted college-kid jokes in Chinese at Chi as she led him past. He wasn't sure if it was his altered consciousness but they all seemed tall and, if not exactly beautiful, fine looking; brimming with hope and righteousness.

There was a lot of Nam-era paraphernalia on display too: 101st Airborne patches, graffiti-covered M1 helmets, embroidered

Ranger tabs. One kid was, disarmingly, sporting a WW2 German helmet with a swastika spray-canned fuchsia pink against the grey.

"Would it be impolite to ask what you guys actually do with all this hardware?"

"We off the record?" said Miss Chi with eyes slit, a sideways glance, chin angled to the sky.

"Deep background."

"Sign a non-disclosure agreement?"

"I never sign NDAs."

"You're gettin' Grade A access here, mister, so I'd be obliged if you'd stick to the journalist's code of conduct. For your information only, not to be quoted, even without attribution, and purely on background, the Ordos Snow Leopards Motorcycle Club provides, basically, mobile security for various mining operations out here in the desert."

"What kind of mining?"

"Rare Earth mostly. Some iron ore to keep an eye on."

"I keep hearing about this Rare Earth," Brough said. "What is it?"

"Oh boy! You're in a Rare Earth hypermarket and you don't know what it is?"

She stared at him and kicked the sand.

"This here is the Walmart of Rare Earth. It's like turning up in Saudi Arabia and saying er, like, what *is* this stuff, o-yi-lll?"

Brough could only think of the medicinal clay called Fuller's Earth.

"What does it look like?"

"Okay," Chi pulled a glass vial full of silver powder out of her combat trousers, which she held up to his gaze.

"Like, Rare Earth 101 would take, maybe, an hour which we don't really have time for but the for-dummies version is: this here is Neodymium. Feel."

She snapped the vial and poured a tiny speck of the powder into Brough's outstretched hand, which began to tingle.

"It's only mildly toxic," she grinned. "And only radioactive for about seventy seconds. It's oxidising right now."

He peered at the crystals, which were turning white and beginning to stick together.

"Try *not* to breathe it in," she added. "There's seventeen rare earth elements, know what an element is?"

A lightbulb lit dimly in Brough's brain. She continued:

"Scandium, yttrium and the fifteen different lanthanoids. This is one of the lanthanoids. Neo-dym-ium. Nd. Number 60 on the Periodic Table."

Last time he'd encountered the Periodic Table he'd been throwing darts at it in the common room at university, the other side of an entire adult life lived in fear and ignorance of science except where it could combat liver failure or sexually transmitted disease.

"So this is a kind of metal?"

"Found – in – the – Chi–nese – des – yourt," Chi mocked him.

"And is it precious?"

She scattered the contents of the vial into the wind for an answer, flapping the speck off his hand with her Air-Cav scarf.

"Is it, by any chance then, actually rare?"

"Not even that," she snorted. "There's, like, eight million tonnes of Neodymium on the planet. Problem is you gotta dig up huge chunks of ore to find a tiny speck of it. Then process it. Then avoid oxidation. Global production is about seven thousand tons a year. There's plenty left."

They'd reached the edge of an escarpment and Brough realised that he'd been hearing, but not exactly comprehending, the sound of a backhoe loader at work. The hydraulic howl and the scrape of metal claw against hard surface, familiar from every building site on earth, came to him from somewhere below them.

"This is the mine here," Chi gestured with her boot. "Hey!"

A couple of scrawny guys in hard hats came scurrying, half bent, from a man-made cave in the side of the ravine below them; they flashed teeth the colour of corroded brass out of sun-dried faces and gave a friendly wave. There were a couple of grimy tents for sleeping quarters, a tea-kettle steaming on a wood fire and a bright yellow tipper truck with massive tyres and a stone-crusher attachment.

Brough watched as the miners, cigarettes trailing from dry lips, coaxed the digger backwards out of a tunnel shored up with timber, guiding it with a cacophony of whistles, shouts and handslaps. It dumped a shovel full of rock into the crusher, which shot it out as gravel into the truck, creating a spume of red dust.

"If it's not rare or precious, why the security?"

A radio at Chi's collar-bone crackled. She spoke back to it in dead-face military Mandarin.

"We've gotta ship out in the next hour. There could be trouble soon but I think, given all that shit you were saying under the Haloperidol, you're probably safer with us."

She shouted something at the miners, who started running around and spitting up dust. Then she pushed Brough back down towards the camp, whose tents were being collapsed and compressed into sidecar-portable lots, while a small team deregularised the sand with twig brooms and moved bits of scrub back into place to foil aerial surveillance.

"The security is needed, Mister Brough, because these mining operations exist in–what you call in the West–the informal sector."

"They're illegal?"

"The grey economy is quite large in this country," Miss Chi shrugged:

"They'll seal the entrance in a minute: half a stick of dynamite does it. Leave only footprints, take only three tonnes of Rare Earth ore, as the saying goes. Find it again on GPS."

"I still don't get it," Brough stared at the fading red weal on his palm. "If that stuff is not rare or precious, and presuming it's not some kind of high explosive, and bearing in mind the fact that I have never heard of it…"

But they were already at the line of motorbikes, engines idling. Miss Lai, insect-faced behind a pair of mirrored Ray-Bans, beckoned him over to her machine, which dwarfed her.

"Ever ride a motorbike?"

"Had a trials bike when I was…"

"Never," she cut off his wind by hitting him in the gut with a spare helmet, "have you ridden a motorcycle, Mister Brough, until you have ridden the Chiang-Jiang 750."

3

"Stop throwin' these Anglo-Saxon preconceptions in my ear, will ya! And keep them hands around my waist, not on my ass!"

They were bumping through the dust at a steady 40mph. Brough, riding pillion–the sidecar was cluttered with Miss Lai's radar gear – had made the mistake of questioning the Chinese Communist Party's legitimacy. Now she, gabby with biker adrenaline, was delivering a monologue into his helmet's intercom at the speed of a Charlie Parker solo.

"When I turned up at the Stern School it was, like, you know: typical Chinese girl. Joined the Chinese Student Society, goin' on demonstrations against the Dalai Lama and freakin' Falun Gong. My dad's a general in the PLA and we got this, kinda, property thing goin' on, and so there's a whole bunch o' places on the Upper East Side to pick from but I think, No, live the life, dream the dream, do the right thing, so I move into a very nice duplex on Bleecker, facing south, lotsa sunshine and meanwhile my English is, you know, pretty good, and I got a good sense for the body language and the nuances and after a while I'm thinking – shit! these people are just seein' straight through me.

Straight through. Even un-Americans. Even Africans. It's hey Joe ya comin' to the Mets game – just like in *Friends*, the Mets – or hey Idris you wanna come to a hip-hop event ay-at the Brecht Forum... and always the conversation is goin' on... here!"

She waved her hand to indicate the space above her head.

"White guy, African guy, Somali lesbian girl, Eye-talian chick who turns out to have a dick; one thing unites 'em: No See Chinese Lady. And I check it out with the others and it's the same. You put on a pair o' jeans from Gap they don't see you. You put on a pair o' jeans from Escada plastered with Swarovski crystal and they still don't see you. You put on a tartan skirt, pastel headband and a pair o' knee-length socks and, yeah, then they see you: Chinese student girl. Typical ugly Chinese girl. You think I'm ugly?"

Brough had already imagined Miss Lai draped across the saddle of the bike in poses subliminally recalled from the March 1978 issue of *Fiesta* magazine.

"Point is, one day, we're in class and the professor is explaining the Efficient Markets Hypothesis and suddenly these smartass kids start, like, *questioning* it? I mean really ripping it apart. And, like, at Tsinghua University you do that you get marched out of the door but this prof he just laughs and rips into them back, calling 'em anarchists, neo-freakin-Ricardians? And afterwards this kind of frisson as if they've all achieved something."

"So I go to the laundromat and there's some guy bitching with his girlfriend, right after I mean they have obviously just fucked each other OK, but there is this black cloud hanging between their faces and they are, you know, enjoying the whole thing. Then I realise what they're all getting off-of on *is* conflict. You guys just *think* conflict is good!"

She drew breath. They were in a flying V, twelve bikes each side, throwing up dirt and stones. The Chiang-Jiang was hot: Brough's calves were burning. Lai had loaned him a leather flight jacket, which despite the heat he was glad to have between himself and the gritstorm they were throwing up.

"You go out with a guy," Lai picked up, "what you're lookin' forward to is breaking up with him. You elect a President what you're majorly lookin' forward to is that moment they come on *Good Morning America* and say the guy's a fuckin' war criminal. There is," she squeezed the clutch and flared the throttle open to vent her anger, "just this unfathomable desire for conflict and abrasion and I'm suppose to relate to it? And because I can't I'm spose to feel like, autistic?"

"Didn't they have a point?"

"What?"

"About the economy? Markets are not efficient. Look what happened to Lehman Brothers."

"Now *you're* doin' it!"

"What?"

"Arguing, bitching, disputing – what the fuck do you know about the Efficient Markets Hypothesis? Anything? Look, fella, this economic crisis is just a blip – OK, it's big signal that America is fucked long-term, but a blip for capitalism, believe me. I graduated from Tsinghua – that's like the MIT of China; and the Stern School is the number five B-School in the world. Think they're gonna teach you a bunch of dumb shit on purpose? Efficient Markets is right!"

"So why did you come back?"

She waved her hand at the flying wedge of motorcycles and dust.

"The money is here. The future is here. Don't get me wrong: we love your system. The free market, the rule o' law, separation of church and state – Oh Boy! do we love that one. Basketball, securitised finance, independent regulation and central banking. We love it all. It's just you guys are determined to fuck it up with all this conflict shit!"

"Capitalism doesn't work without freedom and conflict. Didn't they teach you that at NYU?"

"They teach it but they don't mean it. Look I know you never been to Beijing, Shanghai–but believe me those places are swarming with Western business guys. Goldman, Citi, the London School of Economics, Deutsche; every shyster law firm you ever heard of and every shyster consultancy firm. You think they give a shit about freedom?"

"So this is Chinese capitalism in action?" Brough gestured to the grit-hazed squadron.

"I had you down as smart, Mister. No, this is Chinese Communism. We're Communists till we die!"

"But you operate outside the law!"

"There is no law says you can't have a motorcycle club. Listen – half of these girls been fucked-over by the Party: Chi had a dotcom fashion startup until some motherfucker in the Shanghai Party made a forced acquisition under threat of a wire fraud prosecution. But in the end Marxism is all-powerful because it is true! The CCP is essential to the peaceful transition to a market economy. The CCP will ensure social order from here to eternity."

He could feel, through the joy in her shoulders, that she was elated.

"What makes you so sure?"

He had twenty years' start on Miss Lai in the processing of ruling-party bullshit.

She dropped a shoulder to glance back at him:

"Ever seen the inside of a Chinese jail?"

4

Li Qi-han's arms were still shuddering from the brick-hod torture
and his left eye had swollen from where Hard Man Han hit him
in the face a few seconds after he'd regained consciousness. His
ribs were stinging from where they'd yanked the taser barbs out
and his trousers reeked because, at the point of being tasered, he
had let go both shit and urine. But he was in a strange way happy.

They had not, despite verbal threats to do so, shoved a cattle
prod into his anus, nor smothered him, nor hung him upside
down and flailed him. These were the standard tortures Li had
always fantasised about inflicting upon Tang Lu's petty criminals;
indeed they were the standard tortures, full stop. So he was
getting away lightly and, at the same time, impressing the hell
out of Grandfather Li, who was hovering in the corner of the cell.

Grandfather had been answering every insult the two-man
beating squad threw at Li with his own highly surreal and comical
ripostes, which had at one point made Li laugh out loud–but not
the beating squad, who couldn't hear him.

Now the squad had gone: some kind of meal-break or shift
change. Li had no way of knowing the time of day. They had kept
him awake with forcible squatting half the night, then a tape loop

of *Without The Communist Party There Is No New China* played so many times that, for an hour after it stopped, Li felt like his entire body, blood, heart rate and breathing were happening in time to the Mao-era marching song. Then, finally, Grandfather Li had showed up.

"You think this is harsh?" Grandfather said, once they were alone. "It's nothing. Should have seen what they did to us in the bauxite mine! Should have seen what we did to the Americans in Korea! You caved in or something? You confessed?"

Li wanted to say no but his throat was swollen. He'd had no water for the last six hours. They'd taken his shoes and belt. It felt like the temperature in the cell was up around 40 Centigrade. Presently he'd summoned the energy to shake his head. No.

"Listen carefully. They think you're some kind of Communist princeling with Beijing connections."

"Li Qi-han," Li Qi-han said hoarsely. Venerable communist name.

"My father idolised Li Qi-han, that's why I left instructions – to give you Qi-han's name." Grandfather Li leaned forward and peered into Li's eyes.

"Great-grandfather knew him?" Li croaked.

"No – glimpsed him. Wuhan in 1926. Big speech. Big crowd. Great-Grandfather Li was there. Wipe your nose, you have snot and blood on your lip. The real Li Qi-han was a workerist, just like my father. Never wanted to go–to the countryside with Mao I mean. When the Long March began, father left us in the pit village: just me and mother. We had a dog but it died."

"Those journalists have destroyed my life," Li moaned.

"Not yet…" Grandfather Li closed one eye and made the other fizz as if a wasp was hovering inside it; and he pulled a face signifying, with just a subtle tightening of his paper-cool skin, wisdom from beyond the grave:

"Two of them have been taken to the hospital in Ordos by the Chinese assistant. She is wily and has seven senses. The third one is still in the desert. I watched him shit a little plastic thing out of his backside."

"USB stick," Li whispered.

"What is that?"

"Memory stick. You can save information from something called a computer,"

"Think I don't know what a computer is!" Grandfather Li snapped.

"The camera footage will be on the USB stick. He take anything else away from the crash site – the foreigner I mean?"

Grandfather shook his head. Xiao's team had scooped the whole scattered contents of the van–socks, tampons, laptops, camera lights, tapes, stale cakes–into plastic bags, working fast to beat the Inner Mongolian cops to the evidence.

"This memory stick," Grandfather Li seemed to play with the concept of a stick with memory, mentally holding it up before his eyes like a kid with Asperger's, turning it around and around, " – the stuff that's on it, the memories, can they be copied onto another stick?"

"Only with a computer."

"So if we get it off him before he copies it onto a computer, then the Westerners can't make their news report?"

Li nodded and started laughing with pain.

"Apart from that, no problem! I've only killed one shitty-assed police informer and a pedigree racehorse, written off a Honda belonging to the People's Republic of China, totalled some gangster's Audi and opened fire on a police officer..."

"Plus you have threatened suicide in a public place, importuned the owner of a brothel to commit premeditated murder, and they have got you in possession of a firearm technically still belonging to the PLA," Grandfather chuckled. "You have a true Li family charge sheet there!"

"What shall I do?"

Grandfather squinted at him and said:

"Today the Communist Party is just a fascist party in disguise, you know that? Fascist methods of control. Fascist levels of surveillance. Fascist police tactics. Even under Mao – even during the anti-rightist campaign – it was never as bad as this. And remember you're talking here to a victim of grave injustice."

Li scowled: "That's Rightism talking! No wonder they put you in a bauxite mine!"

"Rightism, leftism? It doesn't matter to them. When they need to fill the jails they just go along through the party scooping up everybody with a brain, like those lucky shoppers who win the lottery and get to raid the supermarket for sixty seconds without paying."

Li placed his fingers in his ears. The Communist Party was, to him, a given. With its order and hierarchy it was the world. It was a perfect mechanism and it was only idiots like his dad, with his stupid petition, that made it malfunction. And now Grandfather was talking dangerous bullshit.

"Outside they are planning what to do," Grandfather butted in to Li's thoughts:

"That big one, Xiao, he's scared. Han, the one with the bull neck, he wants Xiao's job. Both of them are crapping it about the State Security Police. Can you believe it? Three Western journalists on the loose and they never told the secret police? Zheng, your boss…" Grandfather shook his head, "he's going to Tibet unless we get the memory stick thing. You–you, they will either execute or let go free."

Li's eyes betrayed total incomprehension.

"Look. The unquiet dead can't physically interact with the world. I can't touch anything or move it, otherwise I would slice Hard Man Han's balls into the shape of an origami goldfish, I promise you. All I can do is give advice and collect intelligence – and right now I am going to listen to them plotting their interrogation campaign. In the meantime, don't sign anything. When Xiao comes in he will be playing the soft cop. You just listen to me and start out angry. Angry and outraged. Believe me, power is the only language these fascists understand."

5

When the beating team returned, they limbered up by making him squat for ten minutes with his arms outstretched, holding the brick hod again, shouting insults into his face. When he collapsed, they kicked him in the ribs and one urinated over him. Then they left him, sodden, on the floor.

After a while the door burst open and Hard Man Han swaggered through it, still in his stab vest and twirling a cattle prod around his forefinger by its leather strap. Next came Xiao in full Superintendent's uniform, a red Communist Party pennant fixed to his sleeve with four safety pins. Then came Grandfather Li floating along at head height in the lotus position, eyes closed, taking the piss out of authority as usual.

"Li Qi-han, you have committed murder, conspiracy to murder, attempted murder of a police officer, wanton destruction of property, theft of a firearm from the People's Liberation Army and dangerous driving," Xiao began, using that tone of voice they use in soap operas when pronouncing the death sentence.

"In addition, you have called into question the legitimacy of Communist Party Rule in China, advocated Rightism and procured ammunition from an arms-dealing network linked to Al Qaeda."

"Just let them do the act," Grandfather muttered, his eyes still closed.

"If you do not sign a confession in the next five minutes, four minutes fifty-nine seconds, fifty-eight, fifty seven," Hard Man Han yelled at him, like a robot, "we will be forced to hand you over to the State Security Police, giving them a full list of your political misdemeanours. Also sexual harassment of colleagues and derogatory attitudes to the Hui minority and the religion of Islam."

Li stayed silent and looked at the floor.

Han leapt to his feet and kicked the plastic chair from under him, grabbing Li's flailing arm and twisting it to breaking point so that he let out a scream.

"Hold on!" Xiao shouted, pulling Han away and pushing his own face into Li's. "Hey, little boy, it's hot in here and you smell."

Xiao fixed the chair back into place and sat Li down on it.

"Go and get me some tea," he ordered Han. "And get some water for this little idiot."

When the door closed Xiao drew up his chair knee-to-knee with Li and thrust a clipboard under his nose. On it, Li noticed, was a typed confession by himself admitting to threatening suicide on the roof at Mrs. Ma's, causing the car crash, and possession of the Type 51. There was no mention of shots fired, no mention of Western journalists, and nothing about crimes against the state.

"This is a plea bargain," Grandfather, hovering two feet above Xiao, sneered over his shoulder. "They threaten you with political crimes and get you to sign for the ordinary criminal stuff in return for leniency."

"Tang Lu people stick together," Xiao's voice was full of menace. "Tang Lu's reputation for social order is second to none.

Sign this and your crimes against the state will be overlooked as the actions of a mental case."

Now Han burst through the door, agitated, hyperventilating, his eyes deranged.

"What? He has refused to sign?"

Han ripped his pistol out of its holster and jerked Li's head back by the hair. He thrust the muzzle of the gun inside Li's mouth, shouting wildly while Xiao screamed for him to stop and maintain self-control. Meanwhile Grandfather Li shouted wildly too – a full litany of Mao-era political insults – so there was cacophony.

When it ended, Li found himself sitting once again on his plastic chair and the two men staring at him, with evil faces. Grandfather was at his side now, feeding him lines in a whisper:

"You two provincial dick-heads really do not get it do you?" Li sneered through a film of snot.

Han raised his fist and Xiao caught it; this time neither of them was play-acting.

"Get what?" Xiao gasped at him, becoming flushed.

"I, Li Qi-han, graduate of Beijing Party School and great-grandson of a Long March Veteran, solemnly declare that in pursuing a team of unauthorised Western journalists, posing an acute threat to social order and in possession of state secrets, I was sabotaged by members of the Tang Lu Public Security Police, operating beyond their jurisdiction inside the Inner Mongolia Autonomous Province."

"I will kill him now, slowly," Han hissed, but Xiao's mouth stayed open, silent.

"Furthermore, one senior officer, Superintendent Xiao," Li glanced at Xiao's name badge as if to check, "opened fire without provocation while I was in the process of apprehending evidence vital to national security!"

Li spat the last words out with genuine venom, beginning now to see where Grandfather Li was taking this.

"You little shit, you were going to kill them!" Xiao exploded.

"Maybe I was going to rescue them from you? Where are your witnesses? Ordos General Hospital? Or maybe five unauthorised carloads of Ningxia Province cops fresh from – oh yes did I forget? – the attempted murder of a petty criminal in the cell block of Tang Lu Police HQ?"

Xiao and Han tried not to stare at each other in amazement, but failed.

"Think we're going to let you go?" said Xiao.

"He's kidding right?" Han shook his head, as if hallucinating.

"I will sign a receipt for the return of the Type 51. It's a family heirloom. My grandfather was a war hero in Korea. *Famous* war hero. I will sign for dangerous driving if you need it to clear things up with the Mongolian cops."

There was a moment of silence while everybody in the room struggled to comprehend what was going on.

"Finally, I urge you to expedite my release and return to duty. Because," here his delivery faltered as the statement was totally false: "I know what's really going on inside Tang Lu Nickel Metal Hydride."

Han, who did not, blinked. Xiao, who did, put his head in his hands and groaned.

6

It was late afternoon by the time the Snow Leopards GPS-ed their way to a supply dump. Miss Chi waved them into a circle where, after a bit of prodding with tent poles in the sand, and a lot of gratuitous throttle revs, they began digging up jerry cans of gasoline. At 40mph and eight hours on the move, Brough – a habitual calculator of mileage and headings–knew they must be somewhere close to Ordos now.

Soon there was a charcoal fire and the smell of lamb sizzling. Somebody handed Brough an inexplicably cold bottle of Rolling Rock, and a few minutes later he was slouching against the still-warm fuselage of a Chiang-Jiang surrounded by a handful of women cradling canapé-sized burgers and sipping from old, scarred-glass bottles of Pepsi.

"Why all this vintage stuff?"

"It's our youth subculture, Mister Brough," said one, wearing a green silk flying jacket with the name "Terry" embroidered in loopy writing next to a USAF patch.

"But what does it signify?"

"What it signifies is," another began, pushing her fringe off her face and straightening herself as if to make a statement, "our love of the free market. Free market is the new Chinese religion!"

"Also the open road. The motorcycle is a symbol of freedom," announced a third, the one with cool sunglasses and the pink-stencilled swastika: "Freedom and democracy."

"I thought you were opposed to democracy," said Brough.

They giggled in near unison.

"No, Mister Brough." said the Statement Girl. "The Communist Party supports democracy, only we need an extended transition and not necessarily towards the Western style of democracy."

They all had perfect, colloquial English learned in some other part of the world.

"This guy tryin' to indoctrinate you against Communism ladies?" It was Miss Lai, holding a frankfurter and a jar of Cheez Whiz.

They giggled again.

"Want some Cheez Whiz?"

Brough shook his head. His neck was beginning to ache from looking up at them:

"So how did it develop, this subculture?"

"Started when we were in high school I guess," said the Statement Girl.

"You all went to school together?"

"Ha! This guy never stops!" said Miss Lai, at his elbow. A flicker of concern crossed their perfectly plucked eyebrows. Lai guffawed:

"No, really, go ahead, tell the guy. Get some practice!"

The whites of their eyes glistened as they waited for Brough's next question.

"Are you," he took a swig of beer, "all from the same place?"

"Xuanpu District, Beijing," said Statement Girl.

"We're still off the record by the way." Miss Lai chipped in: "Chatham House rules."

"Your English is very good–have you studied abroad?" said Brough.

"Paris," said Swastika Girl, "but then I moved back to Beijing to continue my studies."

"MBA?" said Brough.

"Actually fashion," she blushed.

"And yourself?" Brough angled his head to the Statement Girl in an excessively kindly way.

"Dance!" she laughed, "at the Northwest Indiana Conservatory. Now I'm doing an MPhil at Beijing Women's Fashion University."

"So what brought you back here?"

A wave of silence and consternation seemed to pass across their faces again and they looked intently at Miss Lai.

"Okay Mister Brough," said Miss Lai. "you know what is the big anniversary this year? And no, not your shitty little Western-inspired coup twenty years ago! Zero-nine is the sixtieth anniversary of…" she spiralled a finger near his head.

He wracked his brain. There was a fact there at the edge of it he could not reach.

"Ding! Time's up. The foundation of the People's Republic of China!"

"Shit, I did know that."

"See," Lai lectured the others: "They come to our country aided by unreliable elements and kick the shit out of our reputation; fuck our little village girls in their hotel rooms and go away knowing nothing of our history. Or of their own role in our exploitation."

The women surrounding him suddenly looked very

displeased; indeed struggling with their displeasure to appear polite. Miss Lai continued:

"Okay so in the big parade, October time, the district of Xuanpu is getting a major honour." She cocked an eyebrow at the Swastika Girl, who began speaking into the space above Brough's head, in a voice similar to that you hear in a recorded elevator announcement:

"In November 2008 the higher authorities urged the Xuanpu District to set up a female militia group."

"Responding to this great honour," Statement Girl picked up, "selection was quickly conducted among business, civil service bodies and higher education establishments in order to create the Militia Square Array."

"However," Flying Jacket Girl joined in, breathless with excitement, "it quickly became clear that the Square Array of the Xuanpu District could not be assembled without calling on forces from beyond the initial pool of volunteers..."

"Therefore," Swastika Girl continued, "many highly educated female entrepreneurs who had temporarily moved abroad to study, realising that they met the physical requirements, immediately volunteered."

"Ah, I get it, you're all above a certain height. I was wondering about that..."

"Not above, Mister Brough," said Miss Lai, "to get into the Steel Fuchsia Number One Female Militia Square Array you have to be exactly one metre seventy-eight, which with the army boots brings you to one metre eighty-three, which is six feet."

"That's some kind of army boots," said Brough.

"White leather – Prada's makin' em on special commission," said Miss Lai.

"And the rest of the uniform? Let me guess..."

"It's a kinda skirt they had, popular back in the sixties- maybe there was a fabric shortage? A historic reference I guess," said Miss Lai, feigning bashfulness.

"What colour?"

"Fuckin' fuchsia, of course."

Brough snorted beer down his nose and laughed until his eyes watered.

"Sorry, you had me there for a while. Very funny."

"I'm not joking!" said Miss Lai.

"To wear the uniform of the Steel Fuchsias is a proud opportunity for the patriotic women volunteers of Xuanpu District," said Statement Girl, throwing her shoulders back.

Brough drained the dregs of his beer. As the sun dipped low the desert breeze had begun to whip into their faces.

"And what did you make of Western democracy while you were out there preparing for this unique honour?"

"I found it kinda degenerate," said the Statement Girl, after a few seconds' thought.

"Lack of social harmony is a major problem," said Swastika Girl, adopting that dull, modulated tone Chinese newscasters use: "but also political fragmentation. America has strong political factions based on strongly competing ideologies of liberalism and neo-conservatism. Communist Party's senior theorists believe this leads to renewed civil warfare within twenty-five years."

"But without democracy..." his thoughts trailed off.

He'd stood on the campus at Trent Poly arguing with Trotskyist newspaper-sellers just after the miners' strike, their largactil gaze unflinching in the face of logic. But at least it had been an argument: this was much weirder.

"China's commitment to democracy is unparalleled," said the Swastika Girl, breaking into his reverie.

Brough had talked philosophy with psychopathic Bosnian Serbs, discussed Islam with pro-Taliban clerics, and the finer points of Aymara separatism in the backstreets of El Alto, in each case at gunpoint. In Brough's experience you could reason even with indoctrinated nut-jobs. Even with Islamists you have some kind of shared logic system to start with – not just about good and evil but about development and contradiction. But he sensed, behind these pretty eyes, blinking pleasantly at him now, a totally different philosophy.

For a few seconds the long doom of Western civilisation played out in a rapid-fire montage inside his brain. There was a cloud of red sand whipping off the horizon.

"Lemme show you your bivouac, Mister Brough," Miss Lai grabbed him by the arm and led him away from the smiling group, who flipped their mobile phones open and began chatting in giddy Mandarin about their investment portfolios.

She steered him to a pup tent at the edge of the encampment.

"Can you get me to Ordos by tomorrow?"

"We gotta deliver you personally. There's a lot of radio traffic following your, er, incident and a lot of jumpiness. Get you there tomorrow night."

"What happens if I just get up and leave?"

"We shoot you, maybe not with a dart either. Anyway, tonight's a lockdown: storm's about an hour away. Prolly have to dig ourselves out in the morning."

Brough unzipped the tent.

"Is everybody here a member of this Steel Fuchsia thing?"

"Heck no, just those guys! We're lookin after them – getting them into shape. We got all kindsa people in the Snow Leopards; dotcom kids who flipped their companies, nuclear science geeks on R&R from Bushehr: day traders sitting out the stock market slump. Just gotta show some commitment to free enterprise! And motorcycles!"

"And they're really going to march in pink mini-skirts on your National Day parade?" said Brough.

"Well, not exactly marching – it's a kind of special marching style, kind of a retro thing again, where you keep your leg straight and make a lotta noise with your heel as it hits the tarmac? I think you guys in Europe invented it, way back when…"

She threw her insouciance into his face. Brough had run out of things to say.

"What happened to feminism?"

"Raising women out of the status of domestic sex slavery is a key objective of Chinese Communism," Miss Lai's voice flipped into an irony-laden monotone: "And is 98.7% complete."

7

Chun-li's achievement had been to get the doctors to sedate Georgina for twenty-four hours. Carstairs, once his shoulder had been jerked back into place and papers shown to him certifying the injury had been sustained in a Channel Ninety-Nine vehicle, was happy to lie back and ogle the bottoms of the nurses, high on acupuncture and intravenous painkillers.

He had not made any phone calls. Technically it was Georgina's shout whether and when to let the Channel know their driver had been killed, cameraman injured and that they had a reporter missing in the desert. But she was asleep and beeping in the next bed.

Chun-li, meanwhile, had been busy. She had caused a minor spike in the spot price of digibeta tape in Western China by buying up as much as three separate audio-visual stores in Ordos could supply, together with the heaviest tripod she could find, and a set of lights procured from an amateur photography club.

While interfacing with this world of high-spec Western electrical goods sold from darkened retail spaces she was inevitably offered, and given the circumstances had accepted, the chance to purchase other forms of Western hardware, opting in the end for a compact Beretta 8000 pistol with two clips of 9mm negative energy to go with it.

Then she meditated. She stood in her hotel room in her pants and bra, emptied her brain of worries and made her mind the mirror of heaven and the glass of all things. She made slow, circular defensive blocks against an imaginary foe; stretched her feet into the long stances of Wu-style tai-chi, which her mother had practiced, surreptitiously, in defiance of the compulsory simplified Yang style, in a labour camp during the 1960s.

Next, she contemplated the primacy of the objective circumstances over subjective will in Marxist theory. She let herself say, out loud, all kinds of crazy shit until, as the Tao suggests, her mind no longer dwelt on right and wrong.

It all came down, in the end, to the same principle: *wu-wei*, the action of non-action, performed with the profound conviction that no harm could ever come to her since she really did not exist.

Then, on the dot of 11pm, having secured a new driver and an identical Ruifeng van, she arrived at the smoke-glass doorway of the *Club Prix de l'Arc* just in time for Happy Hour. She had put on a halter-neck top that, while not completely shapeless, would give off clear floral signals that she was not – well, at least not in the same way as every other woman in the black-lit interior of the club – for sale.

She spotted Oktyabr Khünbish immediately: he was posed beneath a silver gelatin print of a racehorse, taken at Longchamp sometime in the 1920s. He looked only slightly deranged from his concussion, and was able to flash a smile at her before slouching over to meet her at the bar:

"What are you drinking, Miss Cai?"

Chun-li ordered her usual – Blue Cat date juice with a single ice cube–and perched herself on a bar stool.

"Oktyabr's a cool name," she ventured in teach-yourself Mongolian.

"Actually," he glanced at the floor, "these days it's not really seen as politically correct to speak Mongolian to foreigners, so if you don't mind..." He switched to Mandarin, "Yeah... Oktyabr. It's somewhere out there in the family history. Ardent communists. But my clan name is Jalayir. Not acceptable on a Chinese passport so I went for Oktyabr. Just writing 'X.X.X.' looks so needlessly confrontational, hey?"

"What was the horse called?"

"Er, Jalayir," he sighed. "My sub-clan runs the syndicate."

He was balancing a glass of Chardonnay by the base, between forefinger and thumb, and took a noisy slurp.

"And, just so I am not making any more cultural fuck-ups, the name Khünbish means what I think it means?"

"Too right!" he laughed. "Not A Human Being! They were torn between that and Wolfbite. My sister died of–well, you know, the usual stuff during the Cultural Revolution–at the age of three months, so my folks weren't taking any chances."

Chun-li knew all about this Mongol ritual of giving babies taboo names to ward off premature death at the hands of evil spirits. She knew, too, all about this Communist elite ritual of engaging in total meaningless bullshit until you worked out which faction, corporation or niche interest within the Party might be playing them.

"I am presuming, since you're approved as a guide for the foreign media, that you are a loyal, decent and upstanding Chinese citizen?"

She nodded.

"Me too," he grinned. "Lots of cultural nationalism out here in the Party – tolerated too, like horse-racing. There's a hundred flowers blooming out here in the West, if you know where to look."

She made a goofy gesture at the club decor, as if to say "Clearly!"

The walls of the club were of polished chestnut with mahogany used for the rails and details. Doric columns stretched to the tin-tiled ceiling, salvaged from a shirt-waist factory in Manhattan. Out of the Art Deco picture frames Clark Gable flashed his brilliantine smile at Myrna Loy, Cary Grant slouched against the rails of the ballroom on the *SS Bremen*, Harold Arlen tinkled the ivories alongside Frank Sinatra in the wee small hours of the morning.

There were lush palms at every corner, a waiter poised within fifteen feet of any customer, and, apart from that, wall-to-wall Mongolian prostitutes and their clients, who, Chun-li noted, were mainly Han Chinese and, from their attire, superbly rich.

"The aim is to become the de facto Jockey Club of the Chinese racing scene, once it's fully legalised," Khünbish explained.

He was wearing a black shirt with collar open to reveal greying chest hair and a horse medallion; Armani trousers, a belt with the RL Polo symbol discreetly etched into the buckle and a pair of black cowboy boots with white tooling and Cuban heels. This made Chun-li think for a second about Brough and check her phone in case he'd replied to her text message. He had not.

"How's your concussion?" she ventured.

"The better for this," Khünbish held up the wine glass. "Been fielding calls about you guys all day so I could use some answers."

"Me too," Chun-li was an expert *wei-qi* player and knew that one of them would soon have to go beyond the initial tactic of placing random stones on meaningless points across the board, and attempt to encircle the other, which involves going out on a limb and embracing risk.

She explained about the pollution they'd accidentally discovered at Tang Lu, stressing the randomness of their arrival there and the low ambition of Brough's team. Khünbish in response tended to probe in the direction of Brough: his background and intent. He went straight to the same issue that General Guo had gone to: why do the British send a war correspondent to China on the eve of the twentieth anniversary of those unfortunate events in Tiananmen? She returned to the same conclusion as originally formed: a pure accident. Brough's mission was designed to do what English journalists call a "snow job" on the CCP over environmental issues. What she could not understand, she stressed, was the response of the local Propaganda Department, as endangering life seemed like an overreaction.

Khünbish countered with a second line of inquiry, wondering why a highly-educated and apparently *well connected* – he artlessly stressed those words – professional lady such as Chun-li would be wasting her time on media-fixing jobs if somebody somewhere did not have a higher agenda? He had also, she noticed, placed his hand in a friendly manner on her knee.

"Why so much money in Ordos?" she gave him a stupid, gone-out stare from under her hair, and sucked the last of her date juice up with the straw, making it gurgle. He understood it as a time-out signal.

"You got one million in the bank here and you're classed as poor!" he laughed a cheesy laugh.

"Yes but where from?"

"Well, technically it's from mining. When the mines were privatised, anybody with any connection to mining got rich. Except the miners, of course – poor bastards. Talk to any mining engineer, surveyor, coal haulier, geologist and it's the same story. Right after privatisation–well, guess what? – clapped-out old mines with no reserves suddenly struck new seams. Guys who didn't want to work there anymore were paid out for their shares at ten times market value: I mean ten times market, not IPO, and that can literally mean a million – yuan of course. Then the property boom started. As you may have noticed, it's hit a slight hiatus now…"

She'd seen Ordos from the air as they'd choppered in: a grid pattern resembling the computer game *Second Life*, in which everybody is engaged in buying land and building unfeasibly tall, egotistically designed skyscrapers. But like *Second Life*, deserted.

Most of the tower cranes were static, caked in desert dust. There were migrants hanging around in builders' overalls, hard-hats slung from their belts: mean, confused and hungry; or huddled into dirt-faced groups gambling for matches on the pavement right next to rows of chauffeur-parked SUVs.

"It's an absence of working capital," Khünbish shrugged. "Because of the fiscal stimulus, the banks have been ordered to start throwing money at infrastructure, not real estate. There's even a speculative bubble in infrastructure land right now, but actual cash to pay builders on apartment blocks and office space?"

He shook his head ruefully.

"And beyond technically?"

He looked at her with his relentless smile. She shifted herself about one millimetre in a way that signified she was probably going to sleep with him.

"Where does the money really come from?"

"Well," he ordered them two more drinks with a flick of his eyebrow, "you sure you don't want anything stronger in that?"

"No thanks; you were saying?"

"Well, actually a lot of people did make money out of coal-mining but then, right after the dotcom crash, the Rare Earth boom began. So we've had this unprecedented raw materials boom here, and when you consider what happened in the commodity markets in financial year 07…"

"Ah but," she smiled politely, "didn't the central government place severe restrictions on the production of Rare Earth in 2005? Because of the environmental damage? Don't I remember that?"

"Yes, how very environmentally responsible the Communist Party became that year," Khünbish took a slurp of wine. "And if supply goes down, as all those Western textbooks tell us, and demand is inelastic, price must go up."

"And is demand inelastic?" She let her eyes shine into his for a moment.

"Who wants to know?" His face hardened. "I've been getting calls about your news crew from–you want a list? – Okay: the Inner Mongolian cops who're not happy with this policing incursion from Tang Lu. Top of that, the *wai-ban* here are very concerned about your well-being – particularly because you seem to be missing a member of your team."

She knew this already because Carstairs had been sending her texts about bedside visits from rancid-breathed officials, during which he had feigned sleep or sedative-induced idiocy.

"Finally, some gentlemen in the Rare Earth processing business have been very keen to know about your future itinerary."

"Would these gentlemen be from something like an industry body perhaps? A chamber of commerce?"

"More like a cartel," he breathed, adjusting his stance to try and conceal the mountain his erection was making in his pants.

8

Oktyabr Khünbish's apartment was an endless penthouse decorated in that mind-softening beige and grey popular with the super-rich. The *objets d'art* were 14th century Mongol, the spirits in his cocktail cabinet mid-20th: Cutty Sark, Stolichnaya. The surround-sound was playing something lush and heart-rending from the soundtrack of an Almodovar movie, though to Chun-li, who had never seen one, it just oozed–like Khünbish himself–sleaze.

Khünbish had entered the room already grappling with the straps of her floral top and stumbling over his own erection. Chun-li was by this time well down the path of *wu-wei*, using circular mental blocking patterns to turn Khünbish's sex-monologue back and around again to various details she needed to clarify:

"Why does the Rare Earth cartel have a problem with my team? We're not covering the resources issue, only the pollution issue?"

"Ah," his breath was a mixture of Chardonnay and Sobranie smoke, "that's because probably everybody in the metal mining business right now is very touchy about the connection. There is some trouble out along the river. Heavy squads stocking up with weaponry and cash. Last thing anyone wants, little doll, is the arrival of news cameras – or a white guy lost in the desert."

She breathed hot into his neck and he plunged three rough fingers down the front of her jeans, making her squeak. She had never tried *wu-wei* in this situation before and Khünbish, hairy and slightly paunchy, she noticed now that he had his shirt off, was generating slightly more karmic energy than she had anticipated.

A minute later they were both standing naked on a white sheepskin rug, silhouetted against a skyline of unfinished office towers. She bent backwards, mussing her hair up with soft wrists and revealing her unshaved armpits.

"I am a bit traditional," she murmured. "I don't like to shave my body hair. Hope you don't mind."

Khünbish whacked her in the face with the back of his hand, hard as steel. She blinked back the flashing stars and wiped tears off her face.

"I am also a bit traditional," he said.

She forced herself to run her fingertips along his balls and shaft.

"Ha!" he grabbed her hair. "I've just taken two thousand milligrams of Man's Treasure so my little brother is good for ninety minutes before he even thinks about ejaculation. Your cunt will be raw! Your chrysanthemum will change shape permanently!"

Chun-li shuddered. She had had three boyfriends since university, all of them shy, romantic types. None had shown any particular interest in her chrysanthemum. She had only schoolkid fables and ethnic stereotypes to go off for handling an *hombre* like Khünbish, and he was living up to all of them.

"What's the problem in the desert?" she whispered, working hard to maintain the action-of-non-action as he sunk his teeth into her breast.

"Ha! Too much information, not enough fucking. Let's fuck first and do information later."

She shivered. Khünbish undug his fingernails from her ass and picked up a remote control. A whole wall of the apartment began to slide back revealing, spotlit on a dais, a lifesize replica of a – no, in fact an actually deceased and stuffed – pinto horse. The horse was frozen in the moment of rearing up on its hind legs, revealing what looked like a steel replica of an erect horse penis glinting beneath its belly. As she stared at it, horrorstruck, Khünbish approached, flipping the pages of an ancient manuscript, suddenly transformed from sex pervert to antiquarian book enthusiast:

"This is the famous erotic tract by Danzan Ravjaa," he whispered reverentially. "Genuine early copy. It contains all of Ravjaa's 108 tantric sex positions: tonight we're going to attempt number 103."

His thick finger traced the outlines of a black-and-white lithograph showing what they had to do. It did not look much fun but, she was relieved to see, it put the female participant well away from the penis of the horse.

She swung her right foot into the left stirrup, mounting the horse backwards and, as the drawing indicated, positioned her ass high in the air, her head down over its haunches. The horsehair was rough and the stirrups made her feet cold.

Khünbish swung himself athletically – as the drawing instructed–into a position she had last seen performed by an Olympic gymnast on the rings: head to the floor, feet pointing to the sky, body rigid and braced against the side of the horse, one arm clutching the antique Mongolian saddle for support and the other clutching – ah, now she understood – the horse's rigid metal thing.

Khünbish hit a remote control button in the saddle and the Almodovar slush music gave way to a grassland soundtrack of jingling reins and horses' hooves.

"Who buys the Rare Earth that is illegally produced? Who is

the cartel's main customer?" Chun-li demanded, feeling that the action-of-non-action may have gone far enough.

"No more impudent questions, bitch!"

He began thrusting wildly in the general direction of her chrysanthemum, but missing–his paunchy frame shuddering with the effort of remaining rigid and upside down.

Chun-li–who had read about this trick in the classical Chinese novel "Plum in Golden Vase"–spat on her palm and cupped it just at the entrance of the hole Khünbish was aiming at.

"Whore! Bitch! Nobody!" his voice rose to a yodel as he made what he thought was an entrance.

At the touch of another button the sound of weird tribal yells, bells and drums pushed the speaker system to distortion point.

"The cartel, sells, to the global market," he panted. "The price is inflated because production has been capped!"

She began to pant in unison with him, allowing her face to remain in that bored, quizzical expression she imagined the 17th century concubines had worn in "Plum in Golden Vase". In her mind she recited couplets from it.

"Cartel... evades export controls. Market capitalisation of Western miners stays low. Massive, one-way, bet. All... depends" his penis was jerking around wildly in her hand now and she began yelping to encourage his flow of thought.

"All. Depends. On."

He switched to some ancient steppe language as he ejaculated, blubbering and incoherent. Chun-li faked an orgasm, keeping her mind focused on an eighth-century lyric of sadness, and her face still as a lake in winter.

Khünbish collapsed below the neck of the horse, where he clung now, like a forlorn circus rider, as the steppe cacophony segued seamlessly into the kind of trickling-stream-plus-birdsong music they play in mental hospitals to calm things down.

He put on a gallant show of helping her down from the horse

and then socked her in the face again, making a high-pitched whistle start in her ear, before throwing her over his shoulder and dumping her onto a purple-grey Ligne Roset sofa.

"It all depends on what happens with GM," he panted.

"The crops?"

"The automobile company, idiot!"

He grabbed her hair and twisted it. She had a chilling premonition that he was intent on killing her.

"Wait," she whispered, feeling his thumb probing up into a region she had hoped he was done obsessing with.

"You are too hasty. The *tao* of Danzan Ravjaa will work better if you slow down."

She wriggled off the sofa and grabbed the neck of a champagne bottle from a bucket of ice, pushing him in the chest so that he sank back, sweating, onto the upholstery. She flicked her own hair back, slick with perspiration, and climbed slowly on top of him.

"Close your eyes," she promised, hoarsely. He did.

Chun-li rubbed herself against his thigh, tipped the bottle vertical and took a mouthful of icy bubbles. She bent her head to his and kissed him, dribbling the cold champagne between his lips, which he began to swallow eagerly.

"Maybe this will cure your concussion," she stroked his hair. He smiled cruelly, forming the intent to whack her in the face one more time and mulling over the alternatives of killing her or selling her across the border to some casino guys in Macao. He would...

But the Rohypnol was taking effect now, sending long, deep Delta waves across his brain while the Russian truth drug, SP-17, was also working fast, making him feel like telling her lots of other stuff he had planned not to. She had cracked open the capsule hidden in her false tooth and spat the whole (she hoped) contents into his, together with about 250 ml of Crystal.

She felt his dick shrivel and his body temperature plummet.

She found a cashmere throw to cover him and stroked his brow a little while he began to burble about GM, Toyota, scandium, yttrium and the fifteen lanthanoids, and the assholes of the cartel, and the bitches at the club who were never grateful even if you let them go free after three years' indentured labour, and had she ever thought of hospitality work? And his horse Jalayir, and there was gonna be trouble, and, and …

Five minutes later, showered and fragile, Chun-li slipped through the fire door into a concrete passage linking the penthouse to the building's emergency stairs. It would trigger an alarm somewhere and a call from security to Khünbish but he was stone cold and comatose.

She clattered down one flight of steps. There was the sound of distant shouting deep below. She kicked open the fire door to the 19th floor and left it swinging, the velvet corridor beyond it empty, except for a few trays of room service trash. She slalomed to the 17th floor, quietly jimmied the fire-door open and slipped through, closing it gently to the echo of Khunbish's bodyguards sprinting up the stairs.

The corridor was dim-lit, black, its walls lined with lamb's fur. There was an expertly faked equestrian oil painting in the distance, more room-service detritus, some Qing dynasty porcelain in the wall sconces. Several of the doors were open, emitting pools of harsh top-light, raucous laughter and wedges of cake-thick smoke that gave away their occupants' profession: Communist officials on a business trip.

Chun-li edged her way along the corridor, adopting the persona of a hotel functionary and allowing *wu-wei* to make her seem unremarkable to those who caught sight of her.

Two men in business suits came staggering out of a room, marching a woman on tiptoe between them by means of fingers pushed vertically beneath her jaw. Her face was red with stress. They were young men, slightly handsome. At the door of another room stood a garishly made-up woman, her hair in a pile on her head and her bare arms clutching the doorpost to retain balance, vomit trickling from her mouth. Behind another door there were sounds of a card game fuelled by white liquor, just at the moment of hollow-faced shame when somebody has fleeced somebody else.

At the last door before the elevator there was a mixed crowd gathered to watch, and place bets on, four middle-aged men attempting to jerk themselves off onto the face of a waitress. The floor was scattered with 50-yuan bills, popcorn, the men's pants, some towels, discarded beer bottles. The crowd was firing jokes at the jerking-off team, mainly concerning their inability to ejaculate on target, and Chun-li, as she slid past, recited to herself the last lines of the Liang-chou Prelude:

"By icy peaks and snowy balustrades prepare to feast; how many people live to see such times of peace?"

The fire door burst open and two security goons hit the corridor with high-powered flashlights and chewing gum breath. The Bukkake-spectating group scattered to their rooms. But Chun-li was already gone, swooshing silently past sixteen floors of shimmering, soul-less architecture in the capsule elevator.

The driver had filled the van with the smoke from cheap cigarettes and the stench of sweat. Dawn was filtering into the blackened sky. It was thirty-two degrees. Her jaw ached and her pussy tingled, but at least now she knew what was going on.

9

"You like Oreos?" Miss Lai zipped the tent shut behind her, throwing a pack of biscuits in Brough's direction. It was pitch dark.

"I figured you're probably a whisky guy. All I could find was this." She swung a plastic half-bottle of Yamazaki between finger and thumb.

He was struggling to see through the cloud of sand the wind had hurled in behind her. She had an LED light strapped to her forehead, which was blinding him. She poked him in the stomach through his sleeping bag.

"You could lose some weight, Brough."

She shuffled herself next to him, kicking him with her boots as she struggled to extract two battered paper cups from her knee pocket. Brough, on one elbow and blinking against the light, managed to get the whisky open with his teeth and pour two shots.

"You try exercising when you spend most of your life in a hotel. Er. What are you doing?"

She had slid down beside him and slipped the jacket off her shoulders, downing the whisky with the same deft movement as she tossed her hair back.

"You know how many AA batteries this unit gets through in one week?"

He blinked.

"You know? AA batteries. Bzzzzz." She mimed switching on a vibrator.

They were close enough to taste each other's breath. He reached out, instinctively, to stroke her hair but she clamped the flat of his hand between her fingers and bent it backwards so it felt like his elbow was tearing out of its socket.

"You are breakin' the rules, Mister. No sex allowed. No lookin' at people's boobs. No objectification."

"Alright." His face was a scribble of agony. She let go.

"So you drinkin' that or not? Don't tell me you're racist against the Japs as well?"

He tipped the whole cup of Yamazaki into his throat. She said:

"Here's the deal: I fuck you. You don't fuck me. I come first. You come before I come, no deal. I come before you come, you get your li'l USB stick returned and I tell Chi to let you go."

"What about the rules. What if your mates find out?"

"Everything's battened down. Nearly choked on sandstorm shit getting here. Nothing's moving. Only the wind howling. Nobody vill hear you screeee-am. What're you waiting for?"

She pulled her T-shirt over her head. He licked her breasts while she kicked her way out of her pants. He took a gulp of whisky out of the bottle. She killed the beam on the LED light and grabbed his balls. Fifty-nine seconds later she was sitting astride his chest punching him in the face: vindictive, out of control.

"I said you come after I come. What part of 'I come first then you' did you not understand? You're a shit person, Brough. Useless."

She looked for something to hit him with but could only find the Oreos, which she smashed and crumbled into his face

and then collapsed, hiding her sobs behind her rigid, bony and–
Brough suddenly thought–beautiful shoulders.

"I could…"

She hit him in the cheek with her elbow. Five minutes later
she turned around and buried her nose into the crook of his
neck, which he took as an unspoken apology.

"Let me," he began.

"What?"

Five minutes later, after he had accidentally ejaculated in her
mouth, she had him cowering in the end of the tent, kicking him
with her heels, screaming muffled Chinese swear words at him.

"Will you please stop kicking me! It's not fair!"

She stopped.

"Now listen, this is not going to work. Maybe we just don't
match each other. Sometimes, two people–they just don't get on."

"You want your USB stick?" She was peevish, snot-nosed,
fragile. He nodded.

They tried it doggy style but while it worked for him it didn't
work for her. They tried it with Miss Lai crouching on top,
dictating tempo, and Brough below–but by now fear of getting
seriously harmed kept making his penis go limp.

Finally, his jaw electrified by another kung-fu jab, Brough
sighed: "There is one more thing to try."

She was breathing hard and blowing her fringe off her face
and frowning:

"Be my guest."

10

Mrs. Ma's face blenched as she spotted Li Qi-han, marooned in a pool of light out in the alleyway. She shrieked, dropping Crystalmother's baby onto the floor and totally losing her place in an online game of *Match-It!*

Li pushed through the door. He had looked better: one eye was bugged out, his lip was broken and liver-coloured; he had that "just-tortured" look you see a lot around police stations. It was common for detainees to hit the massage parlour on release – common even for them to come just for the human touch of the massage.

By the time Li managed to croak that he had been released without charge and present ten thousand yuan in new 100s as compensation, wedged between the third and fourth fingers of his lacerated left hand, the sound of boots thudding down a wooden staircase reminded Mrs. Ma she had pressed the panic button.

"It's alright," she trilled as two guards emerged from a hidden doorway, jackets hissing with static, and grabbed Li around the neck:

"He is nuts, but they've let him go."

At this point Grandfather Li should have let out some disgusting wisecrack but–after Li Qi-han had been released and taken a shower, smoked a full packet of *Yun-Yans*, returned the Type 51 to its place on the mantelpiece shrine, drunk three warm cans of Snow and slept – Grandfather had disappeared.

On waking, a calm silence had broken out in Li's mind. The pain in his joints felt sweet not sour; extreme fatigue made him serene. It was evening. The sun, which sets over the Helan Shan hours before it touches the horizon on the desert floor, was burning an orange hole through the dust. In the distance, a muezzin's call was meandering upwards and upwards, close to the official limits of permitted ecstasy. He'd felt lonely without Grandfather Li. He'd decided to go and see Long Tall Daisy and sort things out at Mrs. Ma's.

"Long Tall Daisy's busy. In fact they're all busy. Crystalmother is free in about five minutes," Mrs. Ma snapped, one hand switching the computer screen to a grainy CCTV feed of the relevant cubicle, the other scooping up Crystalmother's baby from the floor. "Daisy's still got ten minutes left with another client and needs downtime afterwards but since it's you–and you are too criminally insane to be around this place for long–I will hurry things up."

Mrs. Ma's false fingernails slid and cracked against her cellphone as she texted instructions to Daisy.

A few minutes later Daisy wandered sleepily into the reception, rubbing her hands on an alcohol wipe. Whenever Li had bothered to look at Daisy's face before, the face had been unmemorable. It was her legs, long and perfect as a high-jumper's, which mesmerised the clientele and allowed Mrs. Ma to bump Daisy's price into the "three-and-three" bracket: three hundred yuan for tea, sympathy and masturbation; three hundred more for sex.

The other girls called her "the long-three" after a domino with a three on both sides.

Once they were in the cubicle, with the whale music playing, Li blurted out:

"What do you charge for anal sex?"

He was angry and wanted to do something cruel to Daisy, like in a porn movie. She answered:

"That request has never been made."

Her voice was soft, flat, betraying her constant bewilderment at the fact she was not still on a farm in Zhejiang Province and about to be sold to a toothless halfwit for the bride price of a television.

She texted Mrs. Ma and, a few seconds later, held up her mobile phone mutely to Li's gaze. Another three hundred plus tip.

"It's OK, I have gone off the idea," Li stripped his shirt off, sulking.

"You had a fight with a herd of sheep?"

His ribs were covered in tight, round bruises from the batons. He tried to laugh but it hurt.

"Wow, you struggled with a vampire?" Daisy peered at the holes, still raw and proud, where the taser barbs had been pulled out.

Her voice lilted and swished like that of a sleepy child saying goodnight. She stroked Li's neck and went into the sign language she'd had to invent when she first came to Mrs. Ma's, on account of her first language being Wu, not Mandarin, and not even official Wu but mountain Wu—unintelligible to anybody beyond the next valley.

She pointed to Li's pants, which he removed. She pointed to the massage couch and Li lay back on it, letting out a separate moan and shudder for each vertebra as it touched the surface. She opened her tatty robe to reveal breasts the shape of steamed buns tweaked to a point. She had trimmed her pubic hair to a heart shape and was soon naked except for her light-blue cotton socks and a pair of white operating-theatre sandals she'd been given by a nurse after her miscarriage.

She kicked these off with what may have passed in the mountains of Zhejiang as seductiveness—and then, long and slow, began to massage Li Qi-han's feet.

Li's penis became electric hard. The rest of his body could barely summon muscle tone but his cock, tuned to the frequencies of life and freedom, throbbed like a magnet.

He saw a long, blue-socked foot arch like a swan's neck above his face. The massage bed was narrow and wobbled as she knelt astride him. Balancing on her toes she lowered her vagina onto his face and he found his tongue licking her in a manner that his conscious mind, if it had not been consumed by happiness, would have found disgusting.

A few minutes later they were still wrapped in the sixty-nine position, which Li had never done before, but were now on a small sofa and in the dark. At some point they had fallen off the table and bounced off the tiled floor but neither of them could remember it. The whale music had finished; only the hum of the CD player and the hiss of joss sticks remained.

Li drew a breath of her skin and hair. He threw his arms around her ass and clung to her, upside down, as if to a lifebuoy. When he looked up, the glow of her cellphone was lighting her face, like a Degas ballet dancer. He found himself smiling.

"Don't worry vampire-boy: your time is up but I'm not throwing you out. Mrs. Ma is accepting your ten thousand as a credit line so you can keep going for exactly sixteen hours and forty minutes if you feel like it."

"Where are you from?"

"I come from Zhejiang," she went into a singsong formula; "My family are poor. I have never had a disease. My police file is spotless. Acupressure is an ancient Chinese art." Then, switching to English:

"You want fuck me in hotel room? You like younger girl? I can find."

"Hey you speak English!" Li laughed and it felt like a hydraulic drill inside his chest was doing the laughing.

Soon they were cuddling, nose to nose, each appearing to the other in that weird perspective lovers achieve that makes the other look like a giant ant. Long Tall Daisy cradled Li's head in her fingers and breathed into his hair.

"Why did they kick your head in?"

"It was a mistake. Cops thought I was trying to kill some journalists when I was only trying to help the police do their job."

"Yeah but you *did* try and kill them. It's all over Tang Lu. Why did they let you go?"

Grandfather Li had disappeared without ever telling Li what was actually going on at Tang Lu Nickel Metal Hydride, intimating only that it was a city-wide conspiracy involving the usual cast of deputy this-and-thats–and that Xiao was scared shitless. Li had meant to probe Grandfather for the full story – but in the back of his mind he knew probing Grandfather for information was ludicrously ambitious and had assumed he would be told in due course.

"It's all to do with that factory, Tang Lu Nickel Metal Hydride."

"Ah." She was silent for a moment. Li slid four swollen knuckles between her legs and began to rub there. She giggled and squirmed out of the way.

"We get a lot of those Hydride workers in here. Their wages must be three times normal. All they want to do is drink and fuck," she sniggered uncontrollably.

"They ever talk about what goes on in there?"

"All the time, vampire boy."

A shiver drifted up Li's spine.

"What do they say?"

"It's hot in there. They wear spacesuits and big gloves. They make batteries."

"Yes but what's the secret? What do they really make?"

"It's a big joke. They're always telling it. They have to live in a dorm and get the irises of their eyes scanned coming in and out; get searched inside their anus, have a cellphone issued to them by the company, and their whole lives are recorded on closed-circuit TV. They come here on a bus and a whole security team looks after them, in and out."

"What's the joke?"

"The joke is, it's just a battery plant. It's not what they do that's secret, it's who they do it for."

"And who do they do it for?"

She let out a surly "huh", from the pit of her stomach, and blew her sweaty hair out of her eyes.

"You ask that question they start strangling you and dump your body in the desert."

"They threaten you with death?"

"Those guys *smell* like death. Iron filings, magnets, bad breath, machine oil, clothes washed in a toilet, acid – all of that stuff; but most of all they smell like death. Some have to wear wigs made like out of wire wool or rat fur."

"Tell me who they do it for?" He put his tongue inside her ear. But she burst into tears and hid her face in her hands.

"When I think of what they do to the whales I can hardly bear to say it!"

PART FOUR

"Hand in hand, march forward!
Even if we do not see any light!"
Migrant workers' song

1

Superintendent Xiao scowled at himself in the mirror of the lavatory at Tang Lu Railway Station. The bags under his eyes looked darker than usual, the wrinkles in his face more persistent; the white chalk his wife had patted into his hair at the temples was going sticky in the heat, stretching his scalp taut.

She'd forced him to change out of his slacks and smoking jacket. He'd said:

"I'm on a plainclothes mission!"

She'd sneered:

"Ha! All you look like is a plainclothes cop!"

Xiao's wife could conduct an entire drum orchestra of middle-aged ladies with a single eyebrow, and she'd used that eyebrow to denounce his Armani leather belt and force him to rehabilitate his old plastic one, from the 1990s, with a tin buckle. She had swapped his smoking jacket for an ancient windbreaker, confiscated his tasselled loafers and Longines watch and ordered him to wear a pair of old gym shoes, completing the look by making his hair look grey with chalk.

"There, now you're just another loser from Ningxia Province," she'd declared.

Studying the man peering out from the cracks and stains of the mirror amid the yellow smoke, the urine reek and the sound of guys retching up snot, Xiao was inclined to agree. He let his cigarette trail like an uneaten noodle from his bottom lip and made his face go blank, like the hero of a French gangster movie.

The bitch had even confiscated his *Zhongnanhais* and replaced them with smuggled *555s*, which disintegrate between your teeth. He hoiked a half-ounce of snot and tobacco dust from the back of his throat, let fly onto the grubby marble floor and shuffled out onto the concourse.

When Tang Lu was founded, during the Great Leap Forward, it had a railway but no station. Coal would be loaded out of handcarts beside the gleaming tracks, by railway workers who slept in canvas-covered pits. There'd been a grey concrete lump of a terminus dumped there sometime during the early 1970s which had, during the market reforms, suddenly swarmed with people trying to migrate East.

Under Jiang Zemin, the concrete slab had been replaced by a steel and glass slab of equal dinginess, its interior lit by an expansive LED display showing the punctual arrival and departure of six trains a day to Shizuishan and one, the Helan Mountain Express, direct from Tang Lu to Baotou. Railway workers had renamed it the "Swiss Mountain Express" following the attempted flight of a local party boss in late 2001, anxious to exchange two suitcases full of used deutschemarks for the coveted new euro 500 notes.

Xiao stilled the impulse to barge to the front of the queue. It was years since he'd travelled anywhere by train. He would go sleeper class – no sense pretending to be a complete bum, since he'd probably have to mix with money people at the other end. He made a mental note of the faces of ticket touts lurking next to the snack bar; he shuffled, looked at his wrist where his watch should have been and tried to avoid the glances of other passengers, which – though it was surely paranoia – seemed all to be focused on him.

"Hi Chief, what's happening – fishing season started?"

He gazed, startled, at the cashier.

"Where are you travelling to today? Do you want a police discount?"

"Keep quiet woman, I am in plain clothes," he hissed. "Baotou, one way, Soft Sleeper."

She cast her eyes down at the abacus and issued the ticket, fingers trembling slightly as she handled the banknotes.

Xiao barged his way through several queues, trying to remember his plainclothes training. Problem is, Chinese plainclothes cops operate so as to be noticed. The idea is not to blend but to intimidate. Only foreigners and Gansu peasants can't spot a plainclothes cop, runs the police academy joke: foreigners because they have never seen China, Gansu peasants because they have never seen clothes.

"Hey Chief, the fish biting today?"

It was the newspaper seller. Everybody knew Superintendent Xiao wore this grubby, cream windbreaker only once a year: to judge the Tang Lu Workers' Fishing Club championship (before it was discontinued during the mutant bream scandal of 2006). He put his head down and headed for the ticket barrier. Maybe he would buy a baseball cap in Baotou.

As he reached the platform he noticed a clutch of railway officials running towards him, buttoning tunics, hoisting up laddered tights, some attempting fake mobile phone conversations with fake superiors, all looking as if they'd been dragged out of an all-night–maybe all-decade–session of card games, blow jobs, snoozing and white liquor. The stationmaster halted in front of him and attempted a bleary-eyed salute.

"Good morning, Police Superintendent Xiao. To what do

we owe the honour? Please join us in the special waiting room where…"

"Shut up!" Xiao bawled, his big body arched with fury. "Go away or I will put colour in your cheeks! You are sabotaging a crucial police operation!"

He watched the stationmaster's face drain.

"Perhaps," said that little shit the Railway Party Secretary, peering out from behind the Stationmaster, epaulettes covered in dandruff and his shirt buttoned wrong, "…perhaps, er, you need some help with your luggage? Do you have any more bags?"

"Don't worry, I'm not headed to Geneva," Xiao sneered, indicating the scruffy holdall that was his only luggage. "This is important business and you are compromising my immunity. Please disperse."

He strode away from the Railway Team, resuming his disguise. But they huddled obstinately in a group on the platform, craning their necks after him like a family of Helan Pikas, which are like meerkats only more suspicious. The ragtag group of bored teenagers, old women and seedy bums milling about on the platform made a space around him as he walked, its circumference bigger than if he had swine flu.

"Hey Chief!" It was a group of retired coal miners with broad grins, waving their wooden chopsticks out of the open window of a Hard Class carriage.

"Come and join us: we are eating bream. Only one head per fish this year!"

2

He slept through Shizuishan and woke up in a world of starched white linen, plastic flowers, sunlight slanting through frosted windows. The sky outside was hyacinth blue. He had fugged-up the carriage with cigarette smoke, stale gym shoes and surreptitious farts. The tannoy was warbling a light-orchestral number that took his mind back to the seventies, Tibet and sentry duty.

After a while Xiao slid the door open with his toe and bawled into the corridor for green tea. When nobody answered he stuck his head out and shouted at the concierge, who was lolling, bored, against the fire extinguisher:

"Hey, *xiao-jie*! Get me some tea and pumpkin seeds and be quick about it before I kick your fat arse!"

She slouched out of vision but no tea arrived. Instead a Mongolian train guard arrived and rapped on the door.

"Hey you! Show me your ticket!"

Xiao fumbled in his shoulder bag; his wife usually handled tickets. He fetched it out eventually, crumpled.

"Tickets remain state property," the guard snapped after studying it, and studying Xiao. "Please take care in future."

"Where is that waitress?" Xiao began, affecting matey-ness.

"In the train Discipline Section writing a complaint against you on the grounds of gender stereotyping and racial abuse," the guard said curtly, turning on his heel.

Xiao had heard that the traditional Chinese term for waitress, "*xiao-jie*", technically synonymous with "prostitute", had become politically incorrect east of the Yellow River, and that the correct term now was *fuwuyuen*, serving person. But he'd always dismissed it as an urban myth.

When the train pulled in to Linhe, Xiao noticed the crowd was ignoring the platform guards; the queues for the Hard Class carriages, always formed and orderly back in Tang Lu, were straggling and rowdy here. He lit a cigarette and slammed the door: there was no-one else in any of the three Soft Sleeper compartments and he was damned if he could think of anybody in Linhe who'd be able to afford a ticket.

But now the cacophony of platform attendants shouting into their tiny megaphones was drowned out by a small crowd of hard-voiced women arguing and complaining in Mongolian and clacking their high heels down the corridor of the train. After they'd filled up the other sleeper carriages, Xiao's door slid open to reveal five moon faces, each female, each plastered with makeup, each wearing looks of disdain for Xiao and flaring their nostrils at the smell of his shoes. He scowled at them, and they slid the door shut again, chattering to each other now not just in Mongolian but what sounded like Russian.

Presently the door slid open again to reveal the train guard and a squat Mongolian kid wearing Oakley sunglasses, an oversize basketball shirt, plus a pair of jeans that seemed to be falling off his backside and gathering at the ankles around his gold-flecked training shoes.

"This carriage," the guard began, deadpan, "has been re-booked."

"What do you mean re-booked?"

"Show me your ticket."

"I already showed it to you."

"I have concerns about your ticket; I suspect it may be fraudulent. Did you buy it from the station or from a ticket tout? It looks crumpled."

Xiao leapt to his feet, red and angry.

"This ticket," he held it up so close to the guard's face that it was impossible for him to see beyond it, "was issued by the Tang Lu Station booking office of the People's Republic of China and you are talking to..." he dropped his shoulders "to, to a decent, respectable, upright citizen."

The guard grabbed the ticket and thrust it back into Xiao's face, which had turned purple.

"Well citizen, you've got to obey the rules. This is a standby ticket. If a full-fare passenger requires the space, you have to vacate."

"I will not," Xiao muttered.

"It's alright, man," drawled the kid in the Oakleys. "I'll just stand here in the corridor. It's smelly in there."

The Oakleys Kid started herding the girls in. They tutted and pulled the kind of face you pull if you have burning diarrhoea. They lit up pastel cigarettes with gold filters and dug into their tartan handbags for bottles of fake Western perfume to spray into the air.

Xiao wedged himself in the corner behind a copy of the *Beijing Daily Messenger* (five-column headline – "Japanese Cartoon Film Steals Ancient Chinese Sun God") and pretended to read the personal ads, which were mostly placed by young women who had money to transfer to older men as a marriage incentive, if they would simply send their bank details.

The girls traded jokes and comments at each other in Mongolian and Russian, lapsing into Mandarin only to imitate sexual requests thrown at them by Chinese clients. Beneath the makeup their faces looked bitter, strained. Xiao noticed one had self-harm scars on her wrist. When they started swapping insults about each other's private parts, tattoos and childhood sexual experiences Xiao decided it was time for lunch.

He grabbed his suitcase and clambered over their sprawled legs, cracked toenails and Vuitton luggage. The Oakleys Kid was leaning against the window in the corridor, having a cellphone conversation that required him to place his hand over his mouth.

Xiao took a seat in the restaurant car, now filling up with railway workers slurping tea and flicking ash onto the paper tablecloths. Two stewards settled next to him, taking their break. He ordered chicken and rice. They ordered chicken and rice. Theirs came. His didn't.

"Hey *fuwuyuen*," he pronounced it carefully, "where is my chicken?"

"Your ticket is forged, or standby, and you have insulted our colleague!" she shouted back. "You have to wait until the second serving!"

The stewards got him a paper plate and shared their dinner with him.

"D'you see those Mongolian ponies getting into the Soft Sleeper?" Xiao began, doing a good imitation now of a leery drifter. But they buried their noses in their rice.

"What's the country coming to when that kind of…"

"What's your game, pal?" one of the stewards interrupted. "You trying to spread rumours or something? Keep yourself to yourself!"

The stewards edged half a foot along the bench away from Xiao and started a loud conversation about how great Hu Jin-tao was, and how lucky they felt to be living in a mediumly developed social-market economy.

He toyed with the idea of revealing his true identity and busting the Oakleys Kid, but a tiny bowl of chicken and rice arrived at last and he ate it in a haze of cigarette smoke, staring at the blue-lit mountains flashing past and spitting bits of tobacco.

At Baotou station there was a police ID check at the exit barrier; Xiao watched as the Kid paid a bribe to get the girls through. Xiao's own ID was marked with his police rank and he wanted to stay undercover, so he hung around for twenty minutes in the men's toilet, where ghostly heroin addicts started coming in and out doing their jerky shuffle in the hope that he was a dealer. There was blood on the walls plus graffiti: mostly offering fake ID, some requests for homosexual sex, some insults about a foreman on a building site plus, as in every male toilet in the world, a crudely drawn picture of a man's cock with sperm coming out of the end.

He took a taxi to the coach station. Did the taxi driver know where he could buy a fake ID?

"Mate, I can get you a Glock, a thirteen year old girl, a diplomatic passport or a PhD in materials fuckin' science. Fake ID is no problem whatsoever – what do you wanna be? Mongolian?" He flipped open the glovebox. There was a thick wad of frayed and bent plastic ID cards, held together with a rubber band.

"I can tell you ain't in construction, mate: what line are you in?"

"Fishing tackle." The phrase came into Xiao's brain a nanosecond after his mouth had said it.

"Ha! Ye'r on the wrong river pal – I used to go fishing here when I was a kid but its buggered up now. If you're not trying to get a contractor's licence you won't need a Mongolian ethnicity – pity, 'cos I've got plenty your age and size." He threw the bundle of cards over his shoulder, yanking the car into a dangerous overtake with the other hand.

"Flip through these, mate: three thousand standard, five for police, army or medical."

"You can buy police ID?"

"Har, har," the driver cackled like a fifties-era comedian. "Where've you come in from pal? Gansu Province? Welcome to the 21st century! I can even get you a party card! You need a new cellphone? My brother's got an unlocking shop right by the terminus. Hey, d'you hear about the Japs stealing one of our ancient gods for a fuckin' cartoon? Fuckin' ridiculous, eh?"

Xiao was mesmerised by the wad of ID cards, too thick to hold in one hand. There was an Anhui migrant with a curled lip, a surly student from Beijing, a widefaced docker from Tianjin Port, a migrant bricklayer from Gansu, a PLA corporal from Shenynang. Lots of pretty girls, too; always young, always with that just-out-of-school fringe that makes their photos look so similar to each other and so different to the actual girls plying their trade out of hotel rooms in Hohhot, adobe shacks in Erenhot, porn cinemas in Shenzhen. These are the photos you see in the papers when they disappear.

All of China was there. Frayed at its plastic edge, ripped off, impersonated, discarded. The thought occurred to Xiao to abandon going after Brough and simply bust this taxi driver's ass into long-term detention, or better still, play along and get evidence to bust the whole gang that must be behind all this. A deeper worry played at the edges of his mind: there were IDs from public officials here–cops, soldiers, local government guys. Had they really all been lost or stolen? Or had they been sold?

And if it was this easy to get fake ID in Baotou, what about Tang Lu? Xiao had always made sure the only graffiti offering fake ID in Tang Lu was put up by undercover cops. They led straight to phone lines operated by Hard Man Han's division, and from there to a kicking in the cells or pre-trial, depending on what kind of low-life you were dealing with.

"You found one yet? We're nearly there."

The biggest batch of cards was of middle-aged Han Chinese guys with dyed-black comb-over hairstyles and doleful faces. Put them in a row and you could collect the whole Politburo. He selected one at random – ha! decent likeness and – huh? – same surname! "Xiao Yi-ming, dotcom entrepreneur," right age too, give or take five years.

"That'll be three thousand mate and, hey look out, we're here and the cops are fucking sticklers for parking in this place, so come on fella, hurry up!"

Xiao struggled to extract one of the wads of money he'd stashed inside his vest. There were horns blaring in the dense traffic around the coach station and the taxi cab's sound system had begun a digital announcement in Mongolian, Mandarin and English wishing Xiao a safe onward journey and urging him to avoid spitting in a public place.

The crowd outside the station was full of faces just like the ones on the fake IDs: confused and powerless, pushing in many directions at once, slipping off the pavement, losing their offspring, spitting phlegm into the gutter. The cops were blowing whistles and banging on the roofs of taxis with their white-gloved hands to move them on.

"How do you get the police ID? It must take some doing?" Xiao said, handing over three thousand in 100 notes as the cab jerked to a stop.

"Har, har, if only I knew mate. I'm just the middle man, mind your back!"

As Xiao opened the door he managed to knock an old geezer off his bike, which had a cage full of live chickens balanced on the back. Xiao tried his usual apology routine: he pulled a sycophantic smile and patted the old geezer on the head. But a passing streetsweeper remonstrated with Xiao and pushed him. Xiao was going to push him back when a pretty girl stepped in and grabbed his arm. The taxi screeched away from the curb as the cops approached and the girl hissed at him to scatter because the cops were on an arrest quota due to the twentieth anniversary of "those unfortunate events".

Only when he was out of the crush and in the ticket hall, his blood pressure back to normal and methodically checking his pockets, did he realise something was wrong. He'd slipped the fake ID into his wallet and his real ID into the back pocket of his trousers. The wallet was still there. The real ID card of Superintendent Xiao Lushan had disappeared.

He let out an expletive towards the roof of the bus terminal then pushed his way back to the taxi stand, but the man with the chickens was gone; also the pretty girl and the streetsweeper. Instead of chaotic, the scene seemed calm. Instead of blaring horns, he could hear only announcements and peaceful music. One cop remained, and he cast a cold glare at Xiao, the only person betraying agitation in a scene of otherwise perfect social harmony.

3

A ticket taker shoved Xiao onto the coach headed for Ordos. Half the seats had been bought by a construction team on their way to break somebody's strike. They sat at the back, having a raucous smoking session, playing dice for each other's future wages. There were slovenly mothers staring out of the window and demure daughters fussing with shopping bags. One old man had a bucket of fresh-water lampreys balanced on his knee, their black tails flopping occasionally through the frothy scum.

The passengers were wedged up together, closer than necessary, because three massive guys had decided to take up two seats each, crashing out exhausted. They lay slumped, their sleeping heads rattling against the coach windows as the engine throbbed, legs splayed untidily into the aisle.

Xiao, who'd become sulky, resisted the urge to kick them and slid silently onto a half-vacant seat next to one of the sleeping slobs. This one had stubble, a fat belly showing from under his polo shirt and a Bluetooth headset wedged into his ear. When the coach set off, the slob woke up, yawned, farted, looked straight at Xiao and began speaking, as if in mid-sentence:

"Yeah and, then, last night we missed you mate, ha, down the Iced Nipple, your girlfriend was there, askin' after you she was." After a beat of incomprehension, Xiao realised this fat slob was talking to somebody else, through the earpiece.

Because the phone did not ring, but only made a tiny blue light in the earpiece blink, and because the calls always began in mid-sentence and never ended with goodbye, it took Xiao a few minutes to work out that it was not one person but a series of people calling up Fat Slob. Xiao also noticed that whenever they were awake, Fat Slob and his two slob companions caused the volume of the babble between the other passengers to go down a notch, out of respect:

"Blink, blink. Yeah, I do. But not individual items... Is it boxed? Sorry, going through an underpass. Is it boxed? Yeah well then...blink, blink...So yeah we were down the Iced Nipple club and your girlfriend was askin' after you... you know! Yeah, you do, you cheeky bastard...blink, blink ... Oh, yeah, hello it's Mister Han speaking actually. Yes that's right, Flat 696 on the sixth floor. Nah, mate. Three hundred thousand is my maximum offer...blink, blink... Yeah, if it's boxed: I'm not really in that business but I know somebody who might... wha'? At that price? Gotta be kidding, yeah...blink, blink...Hello love we're on the fuckin' coach! Yeah the fuckin coach! Is she? Is she there? Hello darlin' – how was your trip to the Peach Festival? Have you been good? Put your mummy on again...blink, blink ...Yeah he's just been onto me. What will they do if we just throw the keys at them and walk away? Huh-huh, huh-huh. Three hundred thousand. Let's give it till next week ... blink, blink...Yeah well, she ended up fuckin' lap-dancing for 1000 kwai note-rolls. Lumpfish put three of 'em up her fanny! Ha, ha – said to give her a call next time! ...blink, blink...Nah, the fuckin' car got impounded and the cops have whipped all our licences. Get the driver round to the coach station for half past three with the Merc, will ya, darling?"

Where was this outrage coming from, that was boiling up inside Xiao's guts? He knew how much human scum the market reforms had brought to the surface; he knew the way they talked – he'd listened to enough surveillance tapes. But out of uniform, and invisible to hoodlums, he suddenly felt like a time-traveller.

He remembered coming home from Tibet in the late 1970s. It had felt like time-travel then, too. He had signed up for the PLA and, right there in basic training, they'd made them chant slogans against Deng Xiao-ping. "Criticise Deng and oppose the rehabilitation of right-leaning elements!"–combined with twenty jumping jacks–had been the sergeant's favourite.

Within a year, he'd been on the Indian border, freezing his bollocks off at a listening post high in the Himalayas, and a sergeant now himself. Chairman Mao's funeral had come on the radio and Sergeant Xiao had sat on his bunk bed, sobbing uncontrollably. The "Criticise Deng" campaign had reached a peak and then subsided, and everybody had assumed Deng was a goner.

Then one day the unit commander had come into the mess hut, stamped the snow off his boots and nailed a framed photograph of – what the fuck?–Deng Xiao-ping into the breeze block wall, right next to Mao. And he'd coughed politely and said, in a low voice:

"Would anyone like to criticise any excesses within the party leadership?"

Xiao knew what happened to people who'd fallen for this during the Hundred Flowers Campaign, back in the 1950s, so kept shtum. But gradually–when was it, October '77? – sometime in 1977 anyway – they'd actually started denouncing Madame Mao on the radio, and by the time Xiao had been demobbed, a year later, and turned up at Tang Lu in his double-thick snow fatigues and a fur hat in the middle of summer, ribs skinnier than a mountain goat–it was already the Deng Xiao-ping Era.

There'd been a small Democracy Wall set up on the corner of Tang Lu Boulevard back then–just where the Deng Xiao-ping statue is now; there'd been underground journals circulating on street corners; sneaky little business types whose fathers had collaborated with the Japs had gotten themselves party cards.

Xiao had sensed what was happening: a historic shift, not forwards but backwards, towards order and respect. Around the same time, people had quietly begun to burn ancestor money and to buy fireworks again, read horoscopes, perform *qi-gong* on the streets, even if back then you had to struggle to find your *qi* amid the smog and squalor.

Xiao, braced against the pitch and roll of the coach along the desert road, felt now like he'd felt then: the shock of new details, the guilty realisation that things are going on that should not be–but nobody cares. The feeling that the world has changed and you have not.

"You come on these buses regular?" Fat Slob nudged Xiao in the ribs.

"No way," Xiao said. "Crawling with coppers these stations, always on the take, and–look at it! – filthy. Shunted my SUV and I've got this urgent deal to do in Ordos, want a fag?"

"Nah," Fat Slob said, "Trying to cut down. What business you in?"

"Bit o' this, bit o'that. Lanthanum one day, Neodymium the next, know what I mean? Can't afford to get too specialist. These cunts," Xiao lowered his voice, surprising himself with his own fluency in the underworld argot; "these cunts in Ordos are world famous for ripping people off."

"Hey, you cheeky twat," Fat Slob chucked Xiao under the chin with a friendly fist, "I am one of the biggest cunts in Ordos and I've never ripped anybody off, hey fellas?" He swivelled in his seat. "This guy's in the Fifty Seven business!" Dropping his own voice, he leant his head towards Xiao's; "Lots of Fifty Seven on the market right now, mate; Sixty too, if you know who to talk to."

Xiao summoned a stone-like look of indifference copied from Jean-Paul Belmondo and lit a 555.

"I do, mate, I do."

4

By this time the Cancer Village Commune had been clearly visible from space for three days.

For twenty-four hours it was even there on Google Earth, until the People's Internet Police hacked into the servers at Mountain View and replaced the relevant tile with an exact image of how things had been the day before, and indeed how they would be again, once the Commune was crushed. ("Those anti-social elements are messing with one of the world's most reliable information tools," the Internet Police commander fumed, "We're actually doing Sergey and Larry a favour!")

It had all started with Leon Wu's middle finger. Scrawny kid with a wide smile, he'd been caught one night fumbling around inside the pants of the day-shift foreman's seventeen-year-old daughter. As Leon Wu himself was only fifteen, his dad, Big Wu, thought this was a brilliant achievement and shouted so at the security guards, who'd locked Leon Wu inside the company's piss-fumed cells. If anybody should be charged with molestation, it was the girl herself, Big Wu reasoned.

By then Leon Wu had scrawled two Chinese characters on the wall of the cell with a penknife the guards always left there, just in case somebody felt like committing suicide. One, shaped like a man without a head, said "six"; the other, a box with two panda eyes at the top corners, stood for "four". Leon Wu had seen a lot of hip-hop graffiti on the Internet and developed a Basquiat-influenced style; the guards had a profoundly conservative attitude to calligraphy. That plus the fact that Six-Four is the symbol for June Fourth, date of the Tiananmen Square massacre, forced the guards to call in the management. While waiting for them to arrive, they beat Leon Wu around the head until blood ran from his ears and nose, and stamped on his fingers.

Shortly afterwards, Big Wu arrived with a delegation of smelters, who freed Leon from the cells using iron crowbars and the weight of numbers.

Then Frank "Lloyd" Wu, who'd led the architecture students to Tiananmen Square back in '89, and spent the last twenty years as a smelter's mate in Cancer Village in recompense, decided to make a point.

He commandeered a Komatsu super-dozer, tracks twice as high as a man and shovel wider than a house, and headed into the barren plateau surrounding the village. Within three hours he had managed to etch the characters "June Fourth" into the desert: each character a kilometre across; each stroke waist-deep into the earth, the whole pictogram perfectly aligned north-south. Frank had bickered constantly with his cousin, Middle Wu, who was operating the GPS and had tried to insist on making the letters in the correct calligraphic stroke order.

They'd finished around dusk and headed for the social club to gently take the piss out of Leon, and his now-slightly-crushed middle finger, over a beer.

It was only when two members of the State Security Police arrived at the smelting plant towards lunchtime the next day that the Cancer Village management office knew anything about Frank's stunt. The cops had zoomed here in their Honda, stirring up clouds of dust, because of a face-melting phone call from Beijing and a grainy fax showing the June Fourth characters mysteriously apparent on a satellite image, right next to Cancer River, a meandering seasonal tributary to the Yellow River, about thirty kilometres east of Ordos.

As they led the cops into the plant to arrest Big and Frank, the managers were shaking with fear. Big was in favour of going quietly. He'd been in the workers' tent at Tiananmen in '89 and felt, around this time of year, just lucky to be alive: he'd spent one out of every three Tiananmen anniversaries in preventive detention anyway. But Frank stood his ground and gave the cops a mouthful of abuse in the form of an anti-bureaucratic Dadaist poem he'd been composing in his head.

The morning shift, who'd viewed all this as comedy up to now, through a haze of weak beer, went crazy when one of the security cops struck Frank across the face.

"What are you going to do? Jail us? What does it look like here? Freedom?" Frank gestured at the iron landscape of the smelting shed, only the sunlight filtering through cracks in the roof to remind them they were not in hell. Then he ripped his shirt open to display the colostomy bag attached to his side.

"Yeah, Pig! What you gonna do? Kill us?" It was Middle Wu. He'd done five years in a penal factory after Tiananmen, before finding his way back to Cancer Village; "Feel free! My oesophageal tissue looks like black-bean sauce! You will be doing me a favour."

"Yeah," a decrepit iron-puddler removed his hard hat and the bandanna beneath it; "Look at this!" Chemotherapy had turned the few last hairs on his scalp into fluffy wisps.

"You want blood?" a hunch-backed forklift-driver spat, "Take mine. I get a body-full at the clinic every week until the myeloma goes into remission!"

To spare the State Security Police any further embarrassment, the management deployed the security guards. But the guards in Cancer Village have lungs that whistle and bones that are fragile; they move better – like many of the workforce – if they've been hooked up to a saline-morphine drip for a couple of hours.

The workers hurled pig-iron pellets at the guards; the guards tasered a couple of workers, whacked a few more with side-handled truncheons, and it was petering out to a draw when a crowd of women wearing protective gloves broke into the factory and pelted the guards with pork dumplings, microwaved to explode like napalm. The guards, the management and the secret police left the village in a convoy of blue-plate Hondas, chased by a pack of melanoma-mottled dogs.

That's how Leon Wu, with his middle finger, had summoned the Cancer Village Commune into existence. They'd held a mass meeting to formulate demands. It had started out from specifics like conditions in the plant, moved in a syndicalist direction – Frank and Big had been clandestinely reading Antonio Gramsci – and then veered, finally and inevitably, to the place everybody knew it would.

"Immediate rehabilitation for those convicted after the massacre of June Fourth 1989," said the email they sent to the All-China Federation of Trade Unions. "Plus immediate and free provision of healthcare facilities for those suffering from pollution-related cancers due to the lax standards and *unofficial production activities* at the Glorious Dawn Metallurgy Plant, Cancer Village, Cancer River County."

Frank reminded the meeting that it was the 138th anniversary of the defeat of the Paris Commune, so they voted to change the name from 'strike committee' to 'Commune' in its honour. At the same time, they wired the cartel, informing them of an immediate hike in the spot price of all Rare Earth Oxides and assuring them that production targets would be maintained.

At this point there had been a deep-background interchange

between Beijing and the State Department, which insisted that Washington had neither knowledge of, nor intent to support, rebellions in Inner Mongolia but–reminding interlocutors of the proximity of the twentieth anniversary of unfortunate events in Beijing – urging leniency in the punishment of any dissent.

By the time Brough watched the Snow Leopards take up their attack position in the desert, using the downstroke of the character "June" as a makeshift trench, the Cancer Village Commune was waking up to its third day. The workers had draped a red banner over the perimeter fence, painted with white letters.

"What's that banner say?" Brough asked.

Miss Lai peered at it for a moment and scowled.

"Some bad Chinese grammar written by gangsters: 'First Winter, then Spring.'"

"What does it mean?"

"Dunno. Maybe some kind of veiled threat to adjust the spot price of Rare Earth for seasonal demand. These people are freakin' illiterates y'know, and gangsters always speak in a kind of code."

5

After Miss Chi had informed them they were surrounded, and sent a ten-minute speech about social order echoing across the desert, the workers brought up their own stereo system, which began blasting out a scratchy medley of communist marching tunes.

"There's no persuading 'em," Chi shrugged, handing the microphone to a subordinate, "we'll have to take that fence first and then…"

"Can I have my Blackberry back?" Brough interrupted.

"Yeah sure, so you can post a video on Youtube showing riots in China the week of the twentieth anniversary!"

Her lip curled with Elvis-like disdain.

"I'll be a witness anyway. If I ever get out of here I can write about it. So why not gimme the mobile back so I can shoot it? Pictures can't lie. I can go away and write any kind of biased crap about China but the shots won't lie."

"That's just it, Mister Brough," Chi sneered. "We don't care about the written word anymore. You write it, we get twenty Chinese netizens denounce you as a fascist, fifty Cantonese emigres in Los Angeles denounce them as fuckin' net cops, the

BBC runs an online poll in which both sides total about nine hundred and ninety-nine each, for and against. The written truth is relative. Write what the fuck you like."

She stamped off.

"Don't be hard on her," Lai grabbed his arm; "we're tooling down for this one and Minimum Use Of Force is not really Chi's forte."

Brough had been wondering about the sudden disappearance of carbines and the sudden appearance of civil unrest hardware.

"That plant looks massive," Brough stared at the smokestacks and the ramshackle network of conveyor belts, concrete sheds, furnace pipes towering above the fenceline. "How many d'you think you're up against?"

"About two thousand if you include the women and kids. The hard core's the problem. Remove the hard core of gangsters and miscreants, and the whole social-order problem goes away?"

Brough looked at her, quizzically.

"These guys are impeding the operation of market forces. Market forces work properly where man behaves as a rational economic being. These guys are just being irrational."

"Are you absolutely sure a bunch of fashion models can…" he began, but she'd stood up, binoculars scanning the skyline of a ridge beyond the plant.

"You heard o' Sun Tzu? Sun Tzu says generally, in battle, use the ordinary force to engage the enemy, the extraordinary force to win?"

He'd heard so much Sun Tzu bullshit thrown around in military drinking joints that he knew large chunks of *The Art of War* by heart.

"Yeah, well," Lai handed him the binoculars, "over there, to the right on that ridge, you see 'em?"

There was a dust-cloud and a swarm of beetle-black motorbikes buzzing and scrambling down the uneven slope. On each bike there was a rider and a passenger, the latter toting what looked like scaffolding bars. There were about a hundred of them, clad in leather, black helmets, goggles and checked bandannas.

"That's the extraordinary force," Lai's voice rose triumphantly.

"You've got Hell's Angels here?"

"China's Sorrow, Baotou Chapter. Now we'll see what happens to people who think they can manipulate the spot price for anti-social aims!"

6

The Snow Leopards took the perimeter fence after about an hour, ripping down the banners and trashing a couple of makeshift barricades as they advanced beneath a testudo of aluminium riot shields and a creeping barrage of baton rounds.

He'd filmed a female unit of the FARC once, in the jungle, and made a documentary about a training course for female ratings in the Royal Navy. But there was none of that "we are women" thing going on here. Their body language became like that of tall, studious boys and–he had to stop himself thinking – robotic.

But the hardcore barricading had been done inside the perimeter of Cancer Village: rubble-filled skips, overturned vehicles, steel billets, smelting slag, iron spikes, broken crockery, empty VHS cases and a large amount of office furniture had been piled up, welded, melted and soldered, barring all ways into the plant and leaving the Snow Leopards in control of only the car park and the basketball court, which now looked like a medieval free-fire zone.

As the Leopards' advance paused, on the other side of the plant Brough could hear the sound of glass smashing and the chirruping of light voices raised in anger – the key signature of a Chinese riot. The Hell's Angels were putting in the main attack.

After a minute's rest the Leopards began forming up to assault the next line of defences but now, behind the barricades, which were devoid of human life, Brough spotted a mobile crane moving jerkily around as if driven by an amateur. Eventually it stopped and began hoisting what looked like a hookful of used bike leathers, except for two limp, pink heads dangling sideways out of the tops of them. The extraordinary force had run into trouble.

The air felt suddenly thick, oppressive. The sight of cadavers had its usual effect: sickness and anxiety plus the quiet elation you feel at not being dead yourself.

Silence fell, disturbed only by the creaking of the crane's rusty jib and the wind blowing sheets of paper across the concrete. The Snow Leopards broke up into small riot squads, Miss Chi barking out commands on the helmet comms to stop them venturing too far into what was now beginning to look like a trap.

A man's voice began ranting, metallic, out of every speaker in the complex, first in Mandarin and then, without explanation, in English.

"Retreat immediately! Look what you have done! Those boys should be alive. Their lives have been lost senselessly. Retreat now beyond the perimeter fence and we will begin negotiations. Be warned, we are dead men on leave."

Brough, crouching behind a coal bunker, watched the Leopards form up into a single defensive shield wall while Miss Chi, her own stereo system brought up now in a Chiang-Jiang sidecar, began to castigate the defenders with shrill Hayekian economics. He saw the Leopards fire gas canisters from hand-held launchers, leaving an arc of what he hoped was only CS gas and not some DIY chemical weapon.

"Cease firing and we will negotiate," the defenders' speaker clanged. "There is no sense…"

But the earth began to judder, and the shark-nosed shovel of a Komatsu super-dozer reared up as it mounted the barricade, yellow and black, obscuring the sky. As its tracks reached the tipping point, it slid, sideways, splintering wood, crushing filing cabinets, dislodging skips, scattering rusty pellets of iron ore and flattening burned-out automobiles.

The wind swept a cloud of debris into the air and the heavy sky forced it back down into people's eyes and lungs. There were about a dozen strikers clinging to the sides of the dozer, half of whom were thrown off by the impact as the front end landed. Brough's stomach tightened as the dozer tracks crushed one striker and severed the arm of another, before busting spectacularly off their drive-wheels and stranding the steel monster there in the open.

Miss Chi, seizing the initiative, pulled a pistol from her jacket and opened fire at the cabin of the dozer, but it had been bulletproofed with inch-thick iron, like Ned Kelly's helmet, and the rounds pinged off.

Suddenly the Leopards' shield line broke and scattered, the women scurrying towards the breach in the fence they'd come through. Brough had seen this moment many times before– where the will of the attacker breaks–and he had to admire the Leopards for their collectedness in retreat. The strikers surged forward, but a small group went too far and the women cornered them, smashing their limbs with expert non-lethality using metal truncheons.

As he cowered in what had become no-man's-land, Brough saw Miss Lai 'crouched by the fence' signalling for him to retreat. There were more workers swarming over the barricade now, catapulting the space with ball bearings and metal bolts, bashing the ground with scaffolding poles.

A group of women strikers in overalls hoisted a new banner into place. It was spattered with hastily painted Chinese symbols Brough could not understand, but carried one symbol that he could: the cloth was divided diagonally into a black triangle and a red one – colours you will never forget if you've had your microphone snatched and your shins kicked by masked demonstrators at a G8 summit. It occurred to Brough that not many Chinese gangsters would go out of their way to implicate themselves as anarcho-syndicalists.

"Come on!" Lai mouthed at him, taking her helmet off for clarity and pushing her shield forward to draw missiles.

A gas canister landed in front of him and his throat began to burn. There was about a cricket-pitch length of space to cross. He could have made it, but instead held his hands out in that gesture of futility habitual among football managers, which tightens everything between the lower lip and the collar-bone.

A stun grenade bounced into the yard and hammered everybody in the chest. Inside his head a ringing silence exploded. Through tear-smeared vision Brough saw Miss Lai coolly replace her helmet, pulling down the visor and pushing her hair behind it. She put a riot-gloved hand to her neck and yanked something from it, tossing it towards him.

Amid the flecks of shattered glass and concrete, discarded shoes, bits of paper, the smoke, the silence and through a burning film of his own snot, Brough saw the eyes of the young men on the barricade. Angry eyes, Lagos slum eyes, Aymara-separatist eyes, Westbank-settler eyes. And he saw his gold chain, missing a few links, spatter onto the ground in front of him. And a little plastic oval slug bearing the logo of the Conn-Selmer Corporation, Elkhart, Indiana.

"Now you know why the Communist Party is obsessed with social order," quipped Big Wu. "When it breaks down it breaks down big-time. Chinese people have this rage inside them…"

He looked at Brough as if waiting for an explanation, but Brough was fiddling with the video camera they had lent him, light as a toy and shaped like a stubby plastic revolver. The picture in the LED was incredibly clear but the autofocus sticky.

"There's an eight-gigabyte SD card in there, enough for a good four hours," Frank Wu interjected.

"Yeah if the cops search you," Big Wu laughed, "you have to take it out and put it…"

"I know," Brough stopped him.

They were in the office of the smelting plant – a prefab hut welded high up next to the roof and reached by metal stairs without a safety rail. Big Wu was tall and beefy, his forehead permanently wrinkled; Frank "Lloyd" Wu smaller and wirier, a smirk playing around his eyes that Brough took to be the product of a lifetime of frustrating circumstances.

"Do you have the Internet here?"

"Up till this morning, but they've cut it off. They've cut the GPRS signal too – but why do we need it when we can get all our information from Chinese state television?" Frank joked.

"Have you ever lived in London?"

Brough was picking up all kinds of Essex tonal flecks in their English, reminding him of dockers he had known at Tilbury. They had that same look, too: gentle, slow, the outrage shining from their eyes, constantly clouded with puzzlement at the fact that nobody else is outraged.

"We're big *East Enders* fans," Frank grinned. "Box set. DVD."

If he ever got these rushes into an edit suite, Brough knew, a professional VT editor was going to have a good laugh at all the thumbs, peering faces, crap sound and shaky vision.

The camera recorded straight to memory, and chunked the action into separate files every time a button was pressed. So they would see three seconds of fingers and fumbling. That whole 2'36" clip where Brough had put the camera down on the floor next to his leg. The bit where the women's commission voted against letting him film and all you could see on the rushes was Brough's joggly, upside-down retreat, to their raucous laughter.

There were his panoramic views of the sintering plant, each shot held just long enough to cause a VT editor to throw a computer keyboard at the wall and shout: "Why don't you hold your fuckin' shots!" There was a pan, way too fast to be useable, up a house-high heap of iron pellets. There was a poignant shot of debris strewn on the baseball court.

Then the bodies: three strikers and the two Hell's Angels, lined up toe-to-toe in the factory yard and covered with a tarpaulin. He had remembered not to dwell on details and took only one good tight shot of a crushed biker-boot, going wide and wider still to avoid gruesome, unusable images.

Then there were the pieces-to-camera:

"Channel Ninety-Nine has gained exclusive access to a Rare Earth processing plant being run autonomously by a group of striking workers…"

Brough's face froze for a moment and he stopped speaking. Ludicrous lines. So he tried it again, camera propped on a wall, with the exterior of the plant as backdrop:

"I've gained exclusive access to a place the authorities didn't want me to see. Cancer Village is home to an illegal processing plant for a substance called Rare Earth. The population here believe it's killing them. And they've had enough."

He followed Frank Wu to a committee meeting, pulled a few "psychological tight" shots on people's faces: Frank, eyes screwed to convey a mixture of ruthlessness and amusement; Leon Wu next to him, bored, distracted by the love-juice smell he can't get off his middle finger; an ancient, chemo-ravaged former Red Guard speaking only in lists; three young production-line women, egg-brown faces scarred by skin disease, urging the immediate planting of dynamite under the main pelletising drum.

Then there was the interview with Big Wu. Frank, though declining to take part, listened in, off camera, by agreement. There was a split developing already between a Jacobin wing around Frank, which wanted to blow the plant sky-high, and the workerists, led by Big, who wanted to negotiate. Every few minutes Big's gaze would be drawn into the camera lens and you could hear Brough remind him "look at me, not the camera":

"We came to Cancer Village when the plant opened, just after eighty-nine. They were closing the factories in Beijing and we're sintering experts, the Wu family. Deng Xiao-ping said then, you remember, 'Saudi has oil, China has Rare Earth' – but who cared about Rare Earth at that time? We worked the iron. Iron is our life. That's what our dad used to say."

"Where did the cancer come from?"

"That's the problem. Multiple causes. There's all kinds of

shit in the river. Plus the whole living compound is riddled with asbestos. By the time they installed the acid line for the REO..."

"Rio?"

"Rare Earth Oxide – by the time they'd installed that, there were already a few kids being born with defects. I think the acid line probably accounts for no more than 25% of all carcinomas. In the cave–"

"Cave?"

"The cave underneath the grinding shed, we think they found traces of metallurgy dating back to the Song Dynasty."

"Who did?"

"The archaeologists, in the 1940s."

"Has anybody done tests? Have you sampled the air and water for cancer-causing agents?"

"We were getting there about five years ago. An investigative journalist came down. But then the government cracked down on the polluting plants and we had to close."

"Close?"

Brough cocked an ear to the racket beyond the door. The pelletising unit was cranking and grinding, spitting out inch-round balls of green iron into a dusty hopper.

"When I say 'close' of course," Big Wu caught his meaning, "I mean 'close' as far as Beijing is concerned. By then the REO had become the main business and the iron just a sideline, so closing down was not an option. Look..."

Big Wu hauled himself up, ignoring the camera, which Brough grabbed shakily, attempting a follow-shot into the light streaming through a dirt-streaked window. Big Wu's fingers, clasping a cigarette, began pointing:

"That building there was the dormitory, when we first came here. That one there, that shit-pile, was the cultural centre. The school roof has fallen in. The houses are built of cinders – I think a little kid could nut those breeze blocks in half after a week's *kung-fu* training, eh, Frank."

"They're like rice cake," said Frank, off camera.

"The clinic's a disgrace. The roads are dirt. The iron rice bowl – you know that term Mister Brough?"

Big Wu stared at Brough and mimicked his head-shaking gesture, wondering at his ignorance.

"The iron rice bowl was Mao's promise to the workers. You will never starve. The factory will look after you from literally," his eyes went limpid with anger, "literally! The cradle to the grave."

Big Wu paused a moment to re-light his cigarette and took a draw.

"Its all gone now. What's the point of mourning? You have to live with the world as it is. The Chinese working class, now, is just a bunch of peasants making toys in Guangdong. It will take them twenty years to organise. In the meantime we work with metal; it's our life."

"What's the deal with the Rare Earth?"

Brough's key skill was drawing people away from their obsessions and to the point in hand.

"Like I said, who knew back in the nineties what Rare Earth could do? Did you know the Neo magnet was only invented in eighty-two?"

"Really?" Brough's voice would betray, to any seasoned video editor, the fact that he did not know what a Neo magnet is.

"D'you know how a Neo magnet is produced, Mister Brough?"

The interview stopped while Big and Frank enthused about the production process, dragged him over to a diagram he didn't understand, poked their iron-calloused fingers at a grimy Periodic Table on the wall. By the end of it, Brough knew that most permanent magnets in the world are made from a mixture of Neodymium, Iron and Boron, and that these magnets – how had he lived forty-four years without knowing this? – actually provide the power in things like hard disc drives and wind turbines and MRI scanners. That the battery in every Toyota Prius needs 15 kilograms of Lanthanum to make it. That the average wind-turbine contains two metric tons of Neodymium. That the whole future of green technology was dependent on Rare Earth.

The next mpeg file showed Big Wu seated, nodding at Brough, who had been coaching him to deliver a comprehensible summary:

"At this plant we turn Rare Earth into a powdered alloy to make magnets. We've been operating illegally since 2005 with the full knowledge of the Inner Mongolian authorities. We're pretty sure most of the blood cancers are linked to the use of acids in the production process."

"And you've taken over the plant to demand better healthcare?"

"Better healthcare," said Frank Lloyd Wu, off camera, "and justice for the victims of Tiananmen Square."

"We've also hiked the spot price for the alloy as a kind of instant tax. This place needs rebuilding if they want social harmony restored," Big Wu continued, struggling to stop his eyes addressing the camera instead of Brough.

After he'd shot some cutaways and got Frank to hold the camera for a setup shot of the two of them looking at the Periodic Table, Brough accepted a cigarette. Something in the atmosphere – maybe the sweet smell of fresh carbon, or the cigarettes, or the diesel fumes from the generator, or the overalls black with iron filings – it was some deep memory anyway, just like Proust with his cup cake – some deep memory made him think of the seventies.

"My dad worked in the steel industry; as a driver, though, not in the mill."

"You are from Sheffield?"

Brough nodded.

"They got smashed as well, I recollect," Big Wu pondered. "*The Full Monty* is a big favourite in our video club. And *Brassed Off*."

"We've been smashed all along the line," Frank piped up; "Huanuni, Bolivia; Allentown, Pennsylvania; Sheffield, England. What is it the world hates about the man who puts his hands to metal, Mister Brough?"

8

Big Wu slid open a steel door, ushered Brough through it and slid it shut, hitting a Bakelite switch to make a few weak buds of light bloom along the stairway, leading down. The clank of the factory was soon dulled and the smell of damp sulphur pricked and probed inside Brough's nostrils.

They were quickly deep and through an airlock, submarine-style, with a wheel to close it behind them. The cave was long and narrow, levelled off at the bottom with concrete and at the top, high above, sealed by the steel beams that formed the factory's foundations.

"It's not really a cave," Big Wu shrugged; "It's a ravine. They built the plant to seal it shut. It would have been open-air when they did this…"

Brough's gaze followed the arc of Big Wu's hand, upwards, to where the sky might have been during the Late Stone Age. The side of the cave was of smooth, cream stone–pitted and streaked with metallic red. About twenty thousand years ago somebody had decided to scrawl the whole of human life across it.

The sun was a dot with two concentric circles, wild lines of energy spreading out from its circumference. The stars were drawn as children draw them. The tribe that had lived here were cavorting in the same shapes as ecstasy-fuelled ravers make when the laser-light freezes them for a nanosecond on a dancefloor. The subtle strokes of stone on stone had created sluts, ice-queens, drunken teenagers, cool dudes, Dad-dancers, crying toddlers, wallflowers, puking boys – each forever captured in the act of making shapes to the music of stone and wood and antlers. Around them tigers prowled, snow leopards slunk, pinto horses galloped. A river curled like a snake through their vertical world.

At the edges things became more conceptual. War masks, spirals, snakes, cunts. Fantasy women with giant hips and breasts. Pictograms depicting only magic, energy and mystery. The scene came to an end, in mid-thought, where the rockface had been sheared off, catching a stick-woman trying to attract the attention of a stick-man, whose reaction we will never know.

"The Red Guards blew it to smithereens in '69," Big Wu sighed. "If you go along another twenty metres it picks up, though it's very scarred at that end."

Brough, his mind stilled by awe and silence, said nothing for several minutes but tried to process the information. He shot a series of grainy stills on the DV camera, its firmware struggling to boost the ISO value against the gloom.

"Where's the furnace?" His voice was trembling in the damp.

Big Wu led him upwards to where the ravine branched off into half-caves and gullies. There were the remains of a stone hearth and, picked out by a fickle lamp, flecks of spelt and sheen amid the ashes.

"If it's metal it can't be Stone Age?"

"Much later. Different culture. We think this was the Scythians. They'd have smelted bronze in there. Look…"

Big Wu played his torch against a painted wooden sign. Large parts of it had been obscured with red daubs. He translated:

"'This cave is thought to contain a Bronze Age hearth. Artifacts of possibly Scythian design discovered and can be viewed in the Beijing History Museum. The Ordos Culture – blank, blank, blank, blank, blank.' Somebody in 1969 did not like the Ordos Culture," Big Wu snorted and shook his head.

Something at the back of Brough's consciousness was clawing to get out; a story about pollution, missing colleagues, the black hair of a Chinese woman strewn over his face in the sticky dark of a tent, his career – but it all seemed irrelevant.

Big Wu pulled him by the elbow into an alcove where, mounted under glass and lit by a 40-watt bulb, a single fragment of metal brooch was displayed, two inches across. It was dull, greenish bronze; a man's figure framed in a partially-missing oval. The man was wearing bell-bottom pants with triangular turn-ups; a belt was visible and he was standing, arms akimbo, clutching the handle of a sword. His chest swelled towards a protective collar: a tiny warrior, maybe in leather armour or chainmail. Above that his face, framed by flowing hair, with round eyes, a bulbous nose and a moustache that made Brough think of Mehmet, the owner of a kebab shop in Shoreditch.

"He's Turkish!"

"Could be Turkish, could be Asterix the Gaul," Big Wu chortled. "Anyway the Red Guards didn't like him. They concreted him three feet down with a load of other things: belt buckles straight out of *Lord of the Rings*; swords shaped like tigers; horses everywhere, prancing, getting eaten by leopards; beautiful filigree things the like of which," Big Wu's mind was straying towards exalted wonder in the cave, "the like of which even we, now, with three thousands years of metallurgy between us and them would struggle to achieve."

The two men looked away from each other.

"When did you find it?"

"We knew the fuckers were hiding something and when we

had the first factory occupation – in '94 – we had a good root around down here. There's other parts we can't even get to."

"So they made it into a museum in the forties and then obliterated it in the sixties? Because these Scythians might have been European, not Chinese?"

Big Wu nodded.

"But why did they blow the wall carvings apart? There's no faces. Can't even see if they have Chinese eyes! These people are hunter-gatherers aren't they? What did it matter to the Red Guards?"

Big Wu sighed white breath into the cold air.

"Take a look at them, Mister Brough. Tell me what they are doing."

Brough gazed upwards.

"Living life."

"And tell me what the artist – or the artists – were doing when they made it."

The figures were so clear and black, the spirals so snaky and voluptuous, the animals so frizzed with energy and menace that even without rationalising it Brough could, in the magic dark, understand.

"Telling the story of the tribe, from one generation to the next?"

"Yes," Big Wu looked bored now. "That's the thing, isn't it. That's the thing you are not allowed to do. What else?"

Brough peered at him.

"What else can you see?"

Brough caught the rhythm of their dancing arms and legs, the leant-over stance they'd called "trucking" in the 1960s, the subtle connection between the stick figures, the angle of their gaze.

"They're happy, for one thing."

"What else?"

"Free."

9

The armed police battalion arrived just as the sun was beginning to slant, turning the smokestacks peach and crimson. They formed a line across the desert like a medieval army: snatch squads interspersed with armoured cars and water-cannon trucks, rubber bullet platoons, small mortars to fire CS gas and an SUV with a sonic laser on the roof.

Brough saw it all through the flip-screen of the DV camera, its "battery-low" icon forcing him to shoot sparingly now. He was squatting atop a rubble barricade about fifty yards inside the main gate, which the strikers had welded shut.

The youths of Cancer Village swarmed around him with their scaffolding poles, but Brough could feel the fight draining out of them as the police commander ranted through a speaker system. A helicopter began playing a powerful light onto Big and Frank Wu, standing shoulder to shoulder and surrounded by their own security team.

Middle Wu shouted a rough translation into Brough's ear as the police commander began megaphone negotiations. The cops pointed out the hopelessness of their situation and urged them to see sense, maintain social order and promote scientific development. Big Wu shouted back, outlining conditions for their surrender. Then Frank Wu launched into a long speech delivered in jerky Chinese phrases that Brough soon realised, through Middle Wu's faltering English, was something more than just a list of demands:

"If I a dead leaf. If I blowing cloud. If I wave in sea. I strong as you. Out of control. When I little boy I fly faster than wind. Wind lift up wave and cloud and sea. I fall into thorn-bush. I bleed."

Brough realised that Frank was reciting Shelley's *Ode to the West Wind* in Chinese. The air seemed electrified as Frank finished speaking, and Middle Wu had to whisper the last line, the Cancer Village Commune's founding slogan:

"After cold winter, spring certainly comes."

The pickets fell silent, some shedding tears.

The police commander ordered them to put down their weapons. Big Wu, his shoulders hunched, gave the order to comply.

They threw away their poles and catapults and swarmed toward the main gate, where the front rank linked arms. Soon the spark and screech of an acetylene torch ripped into the metal and it swung open to reveal a couple of hundred riot cops formed into a flying wedge.

Big and Frank walked forward, Frank acknowledging a desultory cheer from the pickets with a grin, and an upward toss of the eyes. He turned to his smelting buddies, pointing at his watch and miming a fishing reel: don't be late for fishing next weekend. Big Wu gave the crowd a last, sorrowful, angry look.

"Is that it?" Brough's voice was rigid with anger.

"It's a negotiated settlement," Big Wu said gently.

"Us two will be charged with desert calligraphy. The workforce will get re-educated for a few weeks. The spot price will come down. The managers will get sent on a course about the Important Theory of Three Represents. It's a typical Chinese strike. It's chemotherapy day tomorrow, in any case, and they were threatening to withhold the drugs."

"Why bother to fight in the first place, if that's all?"

Brough had, in these past few minutes, noticed something about the crowd of workers pressing together to block the gate: they were the first large group of people he'd seen in China where everybody looked different.

In the Muslim village on day one all the blokes wore wispy beards, robes, white hats and puzzled smiles. The Snow Leopards were all girls of a similar age and hairstyle. The officials he'd had to meet had all beamed with the same slickness from beneath the same hairstyle.

But every face in this mournful crowd was different: the middle aged woman, belligerently fat with tousled hair; the grey-haired, cherubic man with liver spots across his face; the gangly boy, the spotty girl; the mean girl and pallid boy – each with the other's spindly elbow wrapped around the next. There was a gawky kid with a mullet hairstyle and a Metallica T-shirt. Next to him a heroin addict with sunken cheeks. An old man weeping sentimentally and hiding it with his cap. The three egg-brown, face-scarred girls still whispering to each other about dynamite.

Everyone's face wore the same look of bitterness and defiance; the slapped look of those who've suffered not just defeat but begun to comprehend that everything they want is pointless to be asking for.

"What will happen to you?"

Big Wu's shoulders shook with forced laughter.

"Either they'll put us on trial or they'll beat us to pulp in the cells or they'll put us to breaking rocks or steal our kidneys. And then, later, they'll give us money and tell us to fuck off somewhere else. But we won't. We'll come back here. We always do and they always let us. I think it was the Paris Commune reference that got them wound up this time."

"What's happened to the biker gang?"

"Cops got them corralled in a ravine. It's the nature of Bonapartism: it has to create chaos and then crack down on chaos. Who cares?"

Brough watched the crowd part silently. Big Wu's wife ran out to scold him for allowing the surrender but, after pummelling him with her fists, she collapsed onto her knees in the dirt, wailing. Big Wu stroked her greying head unsentimentally and turned away. They both seemed to have gone through this before.

There was silence apart from the thwok and throb of the helicopter blades. The police shields shimmered and glinted. In the sky the deep-grey thunderheads, lit by the setting sun, turned the colour of molten lead.

The crowd was gripped with a kind of guilt; an urgent impulse to look away from Big and Frank; to avoid eye contact; to avoid having to watch as they offered their upturned wrists to the handcuffs. Then they were seized with the urge to throw things away: not just incriminating things like weapons and printouts of illegal websites but trivial things – small coins, cigarette stubs, paper towels saved from lunchtime, sachets of plum sauce, wax picked out of their ears.

They would all be processed soon. Lined up, shouted at, interrogated, shoved. Ideological work would be done. Leon Wu, his face grey like the ash they were standing on, squinted at his mobile phone.

"I'm getting bars. Bastards have switched the signal on again."

Music began, tinny and monaural, from the police command vehicle's speakers. A sickly, exhilarating melody designed to invoke calm. Smoke billowed and black-edged scraps of paper blew across the yard as the helicopter made a low turn around the chimney stacks.

Brough slipped the flash memory card out if its socket and handed the dead camera to Leon Wu. He stuffed the card into his pocket, where the USB stick lay too. Then he froze as the helicopter search-beam bathed his shoulders and eyelashes in a blinding silver light.

PART FIVE

*"Practice the action of non-action,
and everything will fall into place."*
Lao Tzu

1

"Tell me again," Brough was fighting to speak through a mouthful of cocopops and chili-noodles, "how filming a theme park fits in with my story?"

Georgina flashed a pair of spite-chilled eyes at him across the table, cool as iced melon.

"*Our* story," she said. "The one *we* came here to do. It fits with *our* story."

Chun-li slurped her breakfast soup and texted, both actions being a great excuse to stay out of eye contact with the others. Carstairs did that cameraman thing of ignoring them, like a minicab driver ignores a drunken couple arguing in the back seat.

They were at breakfast in the restaurant of the Ordos Summer Palace Hotel, a revolving glass platform populated with waitresses in medieval silk, perfumed by fountains and cooled by nuclear-strength air-conditioning. Brough was fighting back one of those hangovers that feel more like an acid trip than alcohol poisoning because you are simultaneously a) still drunk, b) remorseful, c) possessed of spine-tingling clarity of thought.

"Georgina when you see these rushes..." he began.

"S' gonna be hard, matey," Carstairs chipped in, "that little flash drive you gave me doesn't work with my laptop. Sure it was formatted right?"

"USB stick's OK?"

Carstairs nodded:

"Fumigated it. Copied it. Fed it to London on broadband."

Georgina gave one of her sighs. She was wearing her bruises and lacerations well: since coming round from sedation, she'd scraped her hair into a vertical ponytail and gone for a lip-gloss-only look. This was a clear signal that she was about to pull some kind of Nietzschean stunt to sabotage Brough's story.

"So we're sitting on a story about, what? Pollution? Or is it corruption? They try to kill us? They've got a whole underground production process for this Rare Earth stuff and I get, on tape, *in English*, a Tiananmen Square survivor telling me the whole thing? And we're not interested?"

Georgina gave him that silent look of dismay the English upper-class reserves for total losers.

"Look David," she was keeping it gentle given the unassailability of her position; "it's Tuesday. The program goes out tomorrow. We have to fly tonight and the edit's going to be a bastard. I've just spent twenty four hours," she glanced bitterly at Chun-li, still texting, "unconscious; followed by a day on the phone to London, the British Embassy and the *wai-ban* trying to organise a search-and-rescue mission in the desert and then half the night getting it all called off, simultaneously with getting you out of jail, and my ear irradiated," she held up her new, Chinese-issue cellphone, "all because of your," she paused, "your little mishap."

She let the silence ring with irony.

"I've had Twyla on the phone this morning threatening to cancel the VT and let Shireen do it as an extended voiceover; I've had the Embassy trying to send us somebody who sounds very much like a member of MI6–and we've only just persuaded the Kubuqi Desert *wai-ban* not to impose a minder."

"Actually," Chun-li's voice was weak and exhausted, "*wai-ban* just text me. Insist on having minder for rest of trip. Say otherwise David's visa be revoked."

Brough, like all TV journalists, was adept at doing one thing while planning the next, so had been mentally preparing for a fight with Channel Ninety-Nine from the moment he'd worked it all out: that the battery plant, the illegal mining and the sintering plant in Cancer Village were all part of the same illicit operation.

But he had not expected to be having that fight with Georgina.

After arresting him, the riot cops had put him into an armoured car and driven him to a detention centre. They'd neither body-searched him nor heavied him. They'd left him in a cell with a lightbulb and a surveillance camera and he–still getting his brain ready for some kind of sadistic mind-fuck, which is usually what they're planning if they don't hit you – had lain on a bare plank for an hour in silence, staring at a point on the ceiling, reciting the only poems he knew by heart: the mist-filled doggerel of Matthew Arnold, full of dead leaves and corpse-cold chapels.

Mentally he'd prepared himself for everything except the arrival of Georgina, fuming, Jimmy Carstairs trailing behind her with a wry smile, and Chun-li in tears.

"I thought they'd killed you," he'd blurted out, fighting back tears himself.

"I'll fucking kill *you*," Georgina had hissed.

He had filled them in on the Cancer Village Commune and had been getting round to a heavily censored account of his journey with the Snow Leopards when the effects of beer, Mongolian barbecue and an adrenaline slump had kicked in.

He had put his arm around Carstairs, hugged Chun-li – who had been officially sacked for four hours until the moment she'd

located Brough at the riot-police barracks – and even touched
Georgina affectionately on the arm with the back of his hand.

He had heard the story of their helicopter ride; of some weird
kid trying to shoot them (how had he missed that detail?); of the
clinical efficiency of Chinese medics. Chun-li had not bothered
telling any of them about her encounter with Khünbish.

Brough had explained – he thought lucidly – the black
economy in Rare Earth, drawn the relevant part of the Periodic
Table on a napkin, and proposed they ring up Channel Ninety-
Nine's newsroom immediately to offer a ten-minute exclusive,
with a quick, secret filming trip back to Cancer Village to complete
the story. They would need to commission a pie chart to show
how China was sitting on 90% of the world's Rare Earth output
and how it planned to tighten that grip using export quotas.

"Did you know that?" he'd queried Chun-li mistily as they'd
bundled him into the van.

"Everybody knows Rare Earth a Chinese monopoly," she'd
butted in. "Also everybody knows about illegal mining. Illegal
mining has been covered in Ordos local paper, also *China
Daily*, also long documentary on *Radio Free Asia* quoting many
anonymous Chinese sources but never visiting illegal mine."

Brough had stared at her as if in love.

"However if David has found illegal production system, that
means involvement by local officials. Hence very sensitive."

"Yeah, very sensitive," Brough remembered saying, but not
much else, because after that he'd gone to sleep on Chun-li's
shoulder.

Waking up, finding a pile of smart-casual clothing purchased
by Chun-li, plus a brand new Chinese mobile, he'd cursed the
fact that his Blackberry was gone. To tell the story of his passage
through the desert they would have to go back and shoot some
landscapes. Maybe, he daydreamed, they would do a few "think
to camera" shots of the kind they reserve for the silverback

males of TV reporting when the words they want to say are too pretentious to be seen actually coming out of a human mouth.

Then his *Lichfield Guardian* training had kicked in: they would need to fact-check. Put the allegations to the management at Cancer Village and Tang Lu. Locate Big and Frank Wu in the criminal justice system. Get the Chinese ministry of–who-gives-a-fuck?–but anyway somebody Chinese and official, to respond on camera.

Okay, forget the car crash, the gunshots at the crash scene, the kid they'd tasered. It puts the reporter too far into the centre of the story and it's incidental to the narrative. Big-up getting pulled in by the cops in Tang Lu; tell the full story of the fighting at Cancer Village – the brutality of the strikers; the bodies of the biker-boys. The relative restraint of the riot cops. Spectacular pictures. Impartial storytelling.

By the time he'd come out of the shower – he'd let the hot jets play on his bruises until his skin zinged – Brough had already won a Rory Peck Award, a Royal Television Society trophy and been shortlisted for both a Pulitzer and an Emmy. The jeans Chun-li had selected for him were too long and the checked cowboy shirt a little bit too close to the Village People look, but he'd felt refreshed, vigorous, pleased with himself and ready for an argument.

But now, at breakfast, he was already losing it.

"*Wai-ban* chief at reception imminently," Chun-li announced, scurrying off towards the elevators.

"There is no way we are going off chasing this Commune story," said Georgina.

"No need to chase. Just fact-check and get some shots, love," Brough protested.

It was the word "love" that seemed to make Georgina snap. She stood up, hair flying in the air-conditioned breeze. And the sight of her mouth–contorted into the spite-fuelled deadly weapon with which she had fought her way up through the indy production sector – made Carstairs cower.

"Get this fuckin' Walt out of my sight!" she shouted at Carstairs: her voice was laden with menace.

Brough went into the innocent act, shrugging his shoulders: what's the fuss? She screamed at Carstairs:

"He's a fuckin' Walt, you know that? That's what they call them, don't they? Walter, fucking, Mitty. My brother's in the Army. They call them 'Walts'. Wannabes. Menopausal, wannabe, fat middle-aged fucking fantasists."

Brough tried to deflect her anger by going into a Travis Bickle "you talkin' to me, cos I ain't talkin' to you" impression, with a chopstick, but it fell flat.

"He panics. He legs it into the desert. He miraculously acquires a DV camera and shoots ama-a-a-zing stuff," she laid the sarcasm on, full-English. "He comes back with a story. An uncheckable story with no pictures, no corroboration. Meanwhile the Tiananmen Anniversary Special has a teeny-weeny gap in the timeline – minute fifteen to minute twenty two. No VT about pollution. And you know what it's all about, Jimmy?"

Carstairs' gaze seemed captivated by the remains of a bowl of cornflakes. Brough had given up trying to do anything other than stare into space.

"The tiny, frustrated penis of the foreign correspondent."

"Let's cool it," Brough said, gesturing to the stunned and static audience of waitresses behind her.

"No, fuck it, you have to hear the truth," Georgina had braced herself by folding her arms tight across her chest.

"Here's the truth," said Brough; "I'm in the news business; you're in the entertainment business."

"You are a cunt. A morally inadequate sexist cunt," she yelled.

"In fact you are in the propaganda business," Brough yelled back. "Just like him."

Georgina's gaze followed the direction of Brough's chopstick, which pointed to a small Chinese man in a tweed jacket who'd been edging towards Georgina's elbow for the last minute.

"This is Mister Bo," said Chun-li, beside him.

Mr Bo blinked and nodded helpfully.

"Mister Bo is Deputy Chief of Kubuqi Desert *wai-ban*. Mister Bo has personally cancelled several important engagements to ensure our shooting day becomes a success."

2

Superintendent Xiao was already sick of Ordos. Last night he'd checked into a crummy hotel, phoned his wife, resisted numerous calls to the bedside phone from ding-dong girls, filled the room with smoke, finished off every bottle of peach yogurt in the mini-bar, wandered the streets and bought *Zhongnahais* from a local store, together with a pot noodle.

He hated eating alone; he found it offensive. Xiao loved comradeship and banter. In this town there were too many prostitutes prowling the corridors, too many doormen on the take; too few finished buildings. Too few actual citizens.

And too much tension. That nameless tension of the kind that grips a town if, maybe in the next town, there is some inexplicable breakdown of social order; or somebody has been raped by members of an unpopular ethnic minority but no-one is allowed to report it.

He'd spotted numerous teams of district management goons in uniforms he'd never seen before, stationed in golf-buggies or on motor-scooters at strategic points. Xiao knew what they were there to do: intimidate small knots of workless migrants off the streets, prevent something that was happening somewhere else from happening here.

He'd phoned Hard Man Han, phoned a couple of minor officials in Ordos, worked the networks of face and favour. His *guanxi* was surprisingly good in Ordos, once he was on the phone and being Superintendent Xiao again and not a bum.

He'd tracked the news crew down to the Summer Palace; located a man of Brough's description in the riot police HQ; got Han to send Chun-li an anonymous text to tip her off about Brough's whereabouts; gleaned as much as he needed to know about the conflict at Cancer Village.

The dusk had been blue, nuclear, riven by the lightning from the desert. There'd been helicopter rotors in the distance. He'd drifted off to sleep with the lights and his shoes still on...

Now it was morning. He had done 20 press-ups, changed his dirty underpants for clean ones as the text message from his wife instructed, checked out of his hotel almost without shouting at anybody on the reception desk.

Most important, he had received two more texts from his Ordos contacts: one informing him of Brough's release, another outlining the filming schedule of the news crew and the time of their flight out of Baotou, which was midnight. He had less than 18 hours to put his plan into operation.

The harsh light of the morning sun found Xiao stumbling along the unpaved edge of a road to the howl of traffic and the creak of locked tower cranes. He would hail a taxi, head for the Ordos Desert Beautiful Genghis Khan Theme Park and complete his mission there.

He was mentally rehearsing the action-on-contact he would take when he heard a terrifying noise: thud-splat! Thud like when you punch somebody in a stomach full of beer; splat like when you snap the claw off a roasted chicken.

Xiao had seen a parachute jump go wrong during his time in

the PLA and had a subconscious memory of what that thud-splat sound might mean. He looked up.

In the top corner of his vision, where you don't expect to see a falling object, he saw a falling object. It was a man. Why had the thud-splat sound already happened if the man was still falling? Well now he spotted another man's body on the pavement in front of him, freshly shattered and already leaking brain fluid onto the neat concrete paving slabs.

Thud-splat, again. Now there were two bodies, right on the pavement, and somebody's guts had spilled out.

Xiao's response to stress was to think in words and phrases, not concepts. To say sentences to himself, often hackneyed and cliché, like:

"Oh-ho, what's this then?"

That's what he said to himself now as he saw the two bodies lying on the concrete:

"Oh-ho. Something fishy going on here!"

He went into cop mode, listening and looking. What he heard was the moan of air-conditioning vents in the wall beside him. And heavenly chatter: as if a football team was having an argument about who should take a penalty, eight floors above his head. He looked up: little faces were peering over the lip of a roof.

"Oh-ho! Maybe this is some kind of mass suicide attempt!" he heard himself think.

That triggered a survival reflex: with shoulders hunched like a cartoon villain, he tiptoed away from the base of the building and into the middle of the road to avoid being killed by another falling body. The faces on the roof had vanished.

Xiao was sweating: getting old – fool!–sweating in the presence of death. He lit a *Zhongnanhai* and stared at the bodies. Two middle-aged men. Han ethnicity. Certainly not rich. One, a big guy, was lying on his front as if dead for centuries; what

was left of his face wore an expression of resigned disgust. The
smaller guy, the one Xiao had seen falling, was lying face up, his
leg bent comically behind his back. This one wore a frozen look
of irony. Actually, now he noticed it, the stuff that looked like
guts splattered on the pavement was actually the contents of a
colostomy bag.

The fire escape of the building slammed open and a group
of men spilled out. They looked excited, dejected and guilty–as
if they'd just been in a combat zone and now they had to go
back to everyday life, drink tea, admire their parents' calligraphy.
They were all dressed in casual clothing: jeans, T-shirts, no-name
training shoes. They looked fit and alive: the opposite of mopes.

"Ah-ha!" Xiao thought. "So maybe it's not suicide. Maybe
these guys are up to no good."

And he shouted.

"Hey you! You there! Leaving the building. Can't you see
there's been an accident? You might be witnesses! Wait there
until the police arrive!"

Xiao is big, has a mug on him that would stop a T-72. His
presence commands respect. So naturally the men did stop, did
look him in the eye, did gaze at the dead bodies silently for a
moment. And one of them, wearing a grey hoodie, maybe the
leader, did peel off and saunter across the road, pulling a cigarette
from inside his sleeve and lighting it.

"Who are you?" the man mumbled, blowing smoke over
his fists.

"Just a citizen trying to be vigilant," Xiao's eyes probed
the other man's. He flicked his gaze across the group of men
beyond. They were not sweating in the presence of death. They
look elated.

"Well citizen, best be on your way," the man in the hoodie
drawled. "These suicides are a nuisance; the cops will be round

in no time taking statements, and they might class this as some kind of threat to public order. Double suicide? Could be seen as some kind of *political* statement, given the time of year. I'd be moving along…"

Xiao now admitted to himself that these were plainclothes police. That plodding delivery and querulous, penetrating way of stating every word as if it's a proffered bargain, the subtext being: do this and we'll leave you alone. It had to be the "opposition".

"You guys are State Security, am I right?" Xiao gave the man in the hoodie an avuncular, scolding frown.

The man in the hoodie cracked a weak smile, dropped his cigarette and crushed it with the toe of his training shoe. Then, from out of the hoodie, he calmly pulled a taser and fired it straight at Xiao's chest.

Xiao screamed and dropped, twitching, to the floor.

The man in the hoodie squeezed the trigger of the taser again, pumping 50,000 volts into Xiao as he lay there shouting words that should have come out "Stop! I am police too!" but came out as muffled yodelling instead.

The man in the hoodie turned to his friends, who stood there a mixture of amused and exhilarated in their smart-casual gear. And he enunciated clearly, as if reading from a manual:

"Armed police. Taser, taser, taser."

And with each word "taser", he pumped more juice into Xiao, whose urine was pissing vertically out through the cloth of his trousers with each surge of electricity.

Bystanders scurried away, bowing their heads. Wizened bird-sellers; foot-bound women who'd lost their parents in Shanghai when the Japanese came; chartered surveyors cycling to work; all-night video game addicts wandering home penniless; shop-girls stumbling through the curtain of life that begins at their eyelashes; migrant builders on a smoking break. They all managed to ignore Xiao's twitching limbs and to find routes away from the scene quicker than drops of mercury on sand. So too did the plainclothes cops.

Now came the sound of an ambulance siren; the LED-lights of motorcycle outriders turned the daylight silver and a police speaker began announcing calmly, "Disperse, disperse!"

The sun was glinting off thousands of mirror-glass windows in Ordos. The sky was cornflower blue with a twist of desert sand turning it pink in zonal bands. Xiao, horizontal, could see all this through the fish-eye vantage point of his half-paralysed eyes, so at least he knew he was still alive.

3

"Hel-lo Twyla!" Georgina let her eyes smile persuasively, "How was your flight? Wow! From business to first? No way! What do you think of Shanghai? No-ooo! What time did you get in? Hey, great. Had your first taste of Chinese breakfast yet? Wow! Phillipe Starck? Yeah, they've got those robes in the Beverly Hills one too!"

They were all wedged into the van: Mr. Bo up front instructing the driver; next Georgina, trilling into her mobile phone; Chun-li sitting as far away as possible on the same bench, trying to upgrade their airline tickets and at the same time get a discount by switching between calls to two different travel agents; behind Chun-li, Carstairs–his stitched and iodined knuckles clenched around his camera, silently computing overtime payments. Next to Carstairs, Brough, scribbling script-lines onto sheets of hotel notepaper and crumpling them onto the floor in violent bursts of frustration.

Taking up the back row were Rupert Wong, a cameraman, and Hyacinth Deng, a reporter, both from Kubuqi Desert TV. Hyacinth had a face made-up in the bright colours and shapes of a manga character and was already competing with Georgina and the CD player for the van's soundscape by having her own trilled phone conversation with her own boss. Mr. Bo had – as Chun-li explained – "kindly invited local TV crew to film our filming for news feature on foreign media interest in rapidly-booming GDP of Kubuqi Desert".

Brough had made a profane remark about this arrangement.

"Better not make too many comments about Mister Bo," Chun-li had whispered. "He pretends not to speak English but actually has degree in media studies from University of Bedfordshire."

"Yes he's here," Georgina sang, pulling a face of hate at Brough, "he's fine. Just let his ... imagination get the better of him I think – d'you want to speak to David?"

Brough made a masturbating sign with right hand and stared out of the window, mouthing the words "fuck you".

"Well anyway he's fine now and the rushes from the polluted factory are all fine too – yes, *allegedly* polluted factory–and all we need to do now is – yes, Twyla, he does know – all we need to do is make sure we get the balancing interview..."

Brough checked his mobile. It was brand new and had no stored numbers, but there was a text there from Allegro Harp, his regular video editor, sent from a Chinese mobile number: "Beijing. God. Nightmare. Call me. Allegro."

Allegro Harp is black, gay and lives in New York's East Village, where the all-night noodle scene and the proximity of rent boys from the housing projects in nearby Loisaida suit his lifestyle. An industry legend, Allegro can edit anything into a masterpiece using only an Apple Mac, a hard drive and his fingertips, provided he is supplied with cocaine at the start of the process and bareback Latino sex at the end. Chun-li had been asked to put both these things on her to-do list for Beijing but was not hopeful.

"Howya doin' good buddy," Brough always talked like this to Allegro Harp.

"Ohmygod is Beijing a fuckin' nightmare? Bodysearched me at the airport; reception guys at this hotel treatin' me like I'm a disease."

"Maybe they're not used to, er…"

"You gotta be kidding. This place is queer Shangri-la! I even had some already!" Allegro dropped his voice. "Problem is the other thing, y'know, the toothpowder…"

"So, yes, situation is," Georgina's voice tart as lemon juice; "we're on our way now to finish off the filming. We've got the foreign affairs department with us and a *lovely* news crew from the local television filming us as we film…"

"Thing is," Brough whispered to Allegro, "I've got these amazing rushes on a flash drive, but Jimmy's laptop can't read it. It's a bog-standard SD card far as I can tell so I just want you to work your funky magic on it."

"Yeah right," Allegro chimed, "but it's a tight edit. That stuff you shot in the village is er, well, draggin' it down off the server right now, but Jimmy needs to have a look at his camera – white balance is totally fucked."

"Hey Jimmy," Brough nudged Carstairs, "Allegro says your white balance is shit."

Carstairs grabbed Brough's mobile phone.

"What's the problem, dickbrain?"

Chun-li nudged Brough's arm: "Miss Deng say she very impressed with your calmness and focusing, working already through twenty sheets of scripting paper."

Brough turned to smile at Miss Deng, who was still in mid-chatter on the phone, and noticed the Chinese cameraman pulling a sneaky shot of the whole van full of cacophony.

"Yes we have the name of the factory: Tang Lu Nickel Metal Hydride." As Georgina started to spell it out over the phone,

Chun-li, breaking off from her own tirade of abuse at the airline agent, grabbed Georgina's arm:

"Better not to give name of company to boss-lady in Shanghai!"

"Why not? Excuse me one second, can you ask the driver to turn this effing music off because I can't hear myself – thank you." Georgina cupped her hand over her phone to prevent Twyla hearing, "Why not? We have to put the allegations to the Central Committee guy when he comes on the program; they need to be able to…"

"Oh my God," Chun-li said quietly, her face falling.

Hyacinth Deng broke off her conversation to ask Chun-li what the problem was. When Chun-li explained it, both Hyacinth and Rupert let out a simultaneous sigh of dismay.

"Going into a tunnel," Georgina lied. "Call you ba-ack! *What's the problem now?*"

"Chinese media never put allegations to authorities in live interviews."

"What do you mean?" Georgina pinned Chun-li with a cryogenic stare. "Listen. Chun-li. Just let me explain. I've got seven minutes of airtime to fill and I've got half a story about – will you just tell that man to stop filming me for a minute – half a story about air pollution and the Channel's extremely jumpy about upsetting the authorities over one small incident that might not be representative – so we have to check it out. We have to say to them: what's going on at so-and-so factory in Tang Lu? In fact didn't I ask you to make that call yesterday?"

"Yes. I make that call to the propaganda department in Tang Lu. Confirmed by email official response: No Comment." Chun-li tapped her phone and held the email, in Chinese, in front of Georgina's face.

"But our program goes out internationally. What we've got to do is give the Chinese government right of reply."

"Problem is, if Channel Ninety-Nine boss-lady tells Central Committee liaison person about Tang Lu pollution, probably two outcomes: first outcome, maybe the Central Committee guy withdraws from interview. Second outcome, Central Committee uses party apparatus to make Tang Lu pollution problem go away before program goes on air."

Something suddenly seemed to lay heavy on Chun-li, like a bereavement.

"You mean a cover-up?" Georgina frowned.

"More like…" Chun-li's nails clacked against her translating machine for a moment; "Make-over."

4

While Xiao lay paralysed in the street, his urine drying in the morning sun, a crew of paramedics encased the two corpses in body bags of pastel blue, placed them in the ambulance and sped away. Next, two street cleaners arrived in a hi-tech electric float, which steam-cleaned the pavement and sprayed the air with peach-blossom scent, its loudspeaker tweeting and bleeping with a synthesised Shanbei folk song. A solitary motorcycle cop stayed to observe it all through his Raybans; glancing now and then at Xiao.

Eventually Xiao managed to crawl into the gutter and sit there, his palms quivering like raw pork-belly. He watched the street-cleaning team finish up, leap into their van, kill the music and drive off. He saw the cop kick his stabiliser back and rev the motorcycle, executing a text-book clean, slow, fascist glide away from the scene, flicking a visor down over his sunglasses without a further look at Xiao.

"Hey old fella."

It was a man and a stupid youth. The man – one of those chubby, effeminate guys with a smile so gleeful that his eyes disappeared into his cheeks – held a bottle of mineral water in front of Xiao's face. Xiao took it, wiped the rim and drank.

"Bit particular this one," the gormless youth sang, "don't like to drink from the common ladle."

"Hey Grandad, what you doing here on the ground? You got nowhere else to go?" said the smiling fat man.

Xiao's hands checked things: his wallet, the money taped to his lower back in a security pouch; the handle of the holdall still wrapped around his hand; one hard, vital object still in there among the dirty clothing. Nothing missing. His breathing slowed.

"Hotel…"

Xiao's brain was on tape-loop, as if every time he tried to focus his thoughts something hit him in the face and jolted him back to pain and panic. He needed to find somewhere to wash his face, dry his trousers and drink green tea.

"We know a hotel nearby. Come over there and get cleaned up," Smiling Fat Man offered.

"Yeah, very cozy," Stupid Boy giggled.

Xiao ignored them, struggling to his feet, but immediately lost his balance and retched the water straight back up. He heard the handbrake of a taxi and soon his shaking legs and arms were being helped into the back seat. The taxi smelled of rancid sweat, tobacco, unwashed hair – but most of all it smelled of the fresh urine on Xiao's pants. The man and boy jumped into the taxi, either side of him, and it jolted off.

Xiao's muscles, which had clenched hard as a rifle-butt during the taser attack, were now flaccid. He let his head loll onto the seat and concentrated on getting his mind back into order.

"One more asshole in Ordos is going to wish he'd never lived," Xiao managed to think.

But the effort of getting angry tired him. He watched the streets of slanting light go past; raised flower beds full of fake foliage, the soil on the roadsides painted green to resemble grass; knots of migrant workers smoking, sullen; their crushed and embittered faces.

He needed a hire-car and a driver. He couldn't tail the news crew now–too late. He could meet them "accidentally" out at the theme park. Plenty of time.

The cab pulled up to an iron gate. They were at the edge of the city now: a compound with high walls, dust-black windows and rusty razor-wire that made Xiao homesick for Tang Lu. Inside there were dogs barking: two mangy ridgebacks, a metre high, who'd developed the habit of trying to snap their own necks off against the iron chains that bound them to the wall. Xiao watched them lunge and snarl at the cab, the white-eyed shock on their faces every time the chain halted their momentum.

An eight-year old kid with a dirty face and florid cheeks ran up to the dogs with an iron bar, slamming it into the floor right in front of their noses until they cowered back, whimpering into their metal hut. The gate swung shut behind the cab and another, in front, swung open.

He pushed himself out of the taxi. It was a courtyard with uneven brickwork for a floor. There were a few tin buckets with withered geranium plants. The courtyard was edged with single-story hovels: they could have been built in the 1960s or the 1860s. There were the pink remnants of Spring Festival banners around their doorways, some chalked messages.

A few of the inhabitants came out into the sunlight, squinting. Xiao noticed they were mostly old, wearing the washed-out colour-scheme of poverty. Those who were not old were cripples. One young lad with stumps for legs, pushing himself on a skateboard, shouted:

"Hey, mate, run for it. This is a black jail."

"Shut-up you legless turnip!" It was a plump girl, her hair in a towel and her breasts dangling half out of her kimono. She wobbled gracefully up to Xiao:

"Ignore him, mister. This is a good place. They give you cheap food and they look after you. The rent's decent too."

"Your rent is your cunt!" the legless youth shouted.

The plump girl tried to burn him with her cigarette, but he scooted away.

"That girl was raped three weeks ago by one of the security guards," an old woman muttered at Xiao's elbow. "We all saw it. Raped, in the night. Never said a thing and then the next minute he's bringing her dumplings of a morning. Now she's part of the bloody management as far as I'm concerned," and the old woman scurried away on bowed legs, patting her filthy grey hair.

Xiao turned to the Smiling Fat Man and the Stupid Boy.

"Black jails do not exist in China," Xiao presented it as half a statement, half a question.

"Of course not."

"Then I am free to go once I've cleaned up?"

"Actually, the district management office did ask us to look after you for a bit. You may need to stay here for an hour just while we check you are OK. Have you got your ID?"

Xiao sighed, warily, and fished the false ID card from his wallet.

"We just need to make a photocopy. I'll give it you back in a minute," Smiling Fat Man chuckled.

Xiao handed the card over but refused the offer of having his trousers taken away to be dry-cleaned.

"I'll bring you some green tea," said Stupid Boy.

"Hey fuckwit. Say goodbye to that ID card and get used to cabbage soup!" The legless cripple hissed at him from somewhere in a dark pool of shade.

Xiao marched over and kicked the skateboard out from under him, venting the frustration of the last hour:

"There is no such thing as a black jail in China!"

"Okay, okay!" the cripple was wincing and laughing at the same time, rolling around on his stumps to pull the skateboard back beneath him. There were flies buzzing around an open toilet in the corner of the yard. Xiao felt the hot breath of the sun on the back of his neck. A few pallid faces peered at the commotion out of the doors of shacks.

"Call it a grey hotel if you want," said the cripple, scooting out of Xiao's way; "Grey hotel!"

5

"I am an undercover cop, Superintendent rank, from Ningxia Province," Xiao was seated on an upturned bucket in the dark of an empty hovel. His audience was three ancient men, two old ladies, the skateboard cripple and a mentally ill tramp. He was using the slow, didactic speech the Party had taught him, long ago, not just as a means of communication, but as a kind of unwritten guarantee of authenticity:

"When I get out of this black jail I will report it to the authorities immediately," Xiao continued. "It is an outrage that you are being held here without charge."

"Yes brother Xiao," said one old man, eyes rheumy in the dim light. "What's the penalty of Administrative Detention for, if not to lock people up without a trial? Why do they need to go and do it outside the law as well?"

"Tell me what you have done to be sent here?" Xiao's face was a study in sympathy. He'd pulled a small notebook out of his suitcase and licked his pencil, ready to make notes. He was in his underpants, his trousers still drying on the stones outside.

One old man had seen his son killed in a car accident by a rich kid in a Mercedes, doing handbrake turns in the parking lot at Ikea. He had travelled to Beijing to seek justice; drifted from one department to another; and finally taken to intercepting people with a placard outside the Mercedes showroom on Wangfujing Street.

Another old man's daughter had been asphyxiated due to faulty gas pipes in an apartment block, together with her children; he had made an emotional outburst at the acquittal of the gas contractor.

The third, Xiao was a little daunted to discover, was a rightist from 1956 who'd been petitioning for rehabilitation. The old man's shaky fingers presented him with a tiny photograph full of white cracks: a young sergeant with an ecstatic smile, in a PLA uniform from donkey's years ago. "After that", said the old rightist, "nobody took my picture for 15 years".

The two women had formed a kind of petitioning tag-team; both had lost sons to industrial accidents and wanted compensation. They would rush up to dignitaries in the City Hall car park shouting: "There is no justice in China!" When they had done it to the wrong dignitary they had ended up here.

The cripple had lost both legs in a skateboard factory in Shenzhen, made his way to Beijing for the Olympic Games to seek legal redress and, well, now he was for some unknown reason in Ordos. The mentally ill tramp was, as far as Xiao could make out, just mentally ill.

Until the Olympics they'd all lived the enervating lifestyle of the urban ghost, on the pavement edges of big cities. Now they'd been swept up.

"The courtyard is clean but the outside toilet smells and attracts flies," said the car-crash oldster. "That's my biggest complaint."

"That and the fact that you are imprisoned, fool!" the skateboard cripple yelled.

"You make me laugh," said the rightist, his voice as fragile as calligraphy paper. "This jail is not bad. In my camp we starved and had to work. People were shot for insolence. Here there is food and idleness. You don't know you are born, son…"

But the cripple was retreating from the door, breathless, in a clatter of skateboard wheels:

"Plump Girl, Plump Girl – and the boss is with her!"

Xiao spotted Smiling Fat Man and the plump girl marching towards the hovel, both armed with that sense of routine outrage and annoyance that comes with having to run an institution whose inmates do not want to be there.

"Where's Xiao?" the jail boss made a shabby silhouette in the doorway and the plump girl pushed her head around the doorframe blocking the light some more.

"Here," Xiao stood up, embarrassed that the legs protruding out of his boxer shorts were hairless.

"You are in big trouble. Your dotcom empire has ruined thousands of investors. Now you've been caught red handed!"

"Ha!" said the rightist, "I knew he was never a cop!"

"What's he been telling you?" the plump girl entered the room and poked the two women with her finger. "And what have you been telling him?"

"Everybody out into the courtyard now," Smiling Fat Man commanded; he spoke as if somebody was ordering him–as if somebody else's rules demanded it. They all shuffled out, blinking, and stood in a line. Xiao joined it.

"Congratulations comrades, we have apprehended a master crook," Smiling Fat Man chuckled; "Xiao Yi-ming, dotcom millionaire, where are your riches now? You were disgraced and fled to Taiwan. Maybe you should have stayed there instead of returning to the People's Republic of China."

"My name is Xiao Lushan!" Xiao bellowed, leaning like a falling building into the face of the prison boss. "That ID is a fake!"

"Oh so you are an ID faker as well!" the plump girl looked pleased with herself.

"Comes in with wee on his trousers! What a stupid disguise. Spotted this one a mile off, I did."

"Is this some kind of reality TV show?" the old Mercedes petitioner muttered to Xiao; "Is there a hidden camera? Will we get a prize?"

"Why don't you bribe them to keep quiet and let you go, if you really are a millionaire?" one of the old ladies muttered.

"I have another question," the rightist's parchment voice interjected. Everyone fell silent out of veneration:

"What I want to know is, now that we've denounced him, do we get extra rations? Do we get anything extra or not," his voice quavered indignantly, "is what I want to know!"

6

"Okay, in a minute, we're coming up to the best place to shoot panoramic shots," Chun-li announced. She had been sleeping a second ago and it was a mystery to everybody how she knew.

Brough was already seething. Even though the route to the Beautiful Genghis Khan Theme Park was apparently straight, and Mr. Bo's only mission was to get them there, he had managed to get them lost. Then he had insisted on a mid-morning tea-break at a camel farm belonging to a coalminer who had become a millionaire thanks to judicious stock market investments, and then there'd been a further delay while Rupert and Hyacinth got out of the van to film a colossal concrete statue of Genghis Khan. When Carstairs, out of boredom, had got his camera out to shoot the statue, Rupert Wong had switched to filming Carstairs filming the statue.

"Is it always like this, or are they just doing it for us?" Brough had whispered to Chun-li.

She answered without looking at him, her face mesmerised by her text-message list: "Chinese propaganda departments have whole playbook for wasting time of Western journalists. This just Chapter One."

Now, as they piled out of the van again to take some landscape shots, Brough was on the point of rebellion. He could see the impossibility of standing everything up into an investigative blockbuster, given the time available; but since the Channel had already started the ball rolling over the Tang Lu pollution incident he would cling to that.

He would script everything around Tang Lu: they arrive at Tang Lu, it looks like shit; they interview the people in the chlorine cloud; piece to camera – backplot. Could they get a Chinese academic to talk about the general problems of pollution? Could they, even better, get some Western tree-hugger based in Beijing maybe to slip in the point that much of the pollution is down to illegal activities? In the edit that would be the moment at which the rushes shot in Cancer Village come into play, if Allegro could sort the pictures out. Brough had it all worked out. No big deal about the Rare Earth story, just the human story of a community struggling with diseased land, air and water. Big Wu onscreen in English, bemoaning the state of the facilities and delivering that one coached and perfect line about the illegal operations and the multiple causes of cancer. Finish the piece with the standoff with the riot cops. Need some kind of piece on camera to draw the links together.

Brough was aware, guiltily, that–amid swigs of breakfast milk and warm Coke and snide text messages to Allegro and even to Carstairs sitting right next to him–he was altering the story to fit what Channel Ninety-Nine would broadcast. He was selecting facts not just to suit Georgina's scowling imperatives but also the needs of storytelling.

Television can only tell one story at a time and the Rare Earth story, which was still pre-occupying him, was messy; it lacked proof and pictures. Outside Gorazde with the Royal Welch Fusiliers in 1995 he'd had both; in New Orleans there had been clear villains and victims. China? Shit, he'd not been here a week and the complications were overwhelming the story. Even in Northern Ireland it had been easier to rationalise…

But now, the stunning white light of the Kubuqi Desert, shimmering over the brow of the hill, paralysed his train of thought. This was a real desert, not the metallic dust and scrub he had stumbled through before. Hourglass sand, pristine, scooped into waves one hundred metres high from peak to trough. The light wind was pushing veils of sand into the air off the lip of each dune; it seemed to twist like translucent fingers towards the sky, which was deep, cloudless.

"It's a rubbish shot, of course," Carstairs chipped in, as they all stood there awestruck.

"Yes the light is flat," said Georgina. "Can we wait for the sunset?"

"Baotou airport requiring early check-in due to heavy discount negotiated on tickets," said Chun-li.

"Just a couple of hours so I can get some shadow on that sand," Carstairs pleaded.

Mr. Bo sidled up to Chun-li and said something in Chinese. Chun-li had a rapid-fire interchange with him and reported back.

"Mr. Bo suggests that as sky not suitable for landscape shots maybe we save for later and progress to next location…"

"Which is, let me guess?" Georgina was striding around with her hands on her hips, excited by the vast, stupendous ripples of desert.

"Lunch," said Chun-li.

7

The walls of the fortress were white. On the battlements were banners of pale pink and yellow. The silhouettes of two men in medieval armour seemed to be dodging around playfully between the turrets–but as he got closer Brough realised these were just crude dummies and their movements must have been a trick of the desert light. It was a substantial battlement: thick clay walls twelve metres high, angled backwards and pitted like a sponge with swallows' nesting holes.

"This fortress is classic Qing Dynasty design," said Mr. Bo. Chun-li translated.

"What year was it built?" Brough was making small talk to kill the pain of having to speak to Mr. Bo at all.

"Nineteen eighty-seven," said Chun-li.

"You mean seventeen eighty-nine?"

"No, 1987. This whole complex was rebuilt from scratch on the foundations of a Qing Dynasty fort in 1987."

She added, under her voice: "Mister Bo doesn't want to mention it but the real fort was destroyed during the Cultural Revolution."

Brough nodded. They were in the inner courtyard now. There

was a pre-fab hut, a gift shop selling plastic swords and helmets, an artex replica of the Great Wall for having your photograph taken against. A few Chinese tourists pottered among stalls that sold barbecued corn, mobile phone fascias, fake designer sunglasses. There were two or three lone, middle-aged men loitering in their nondescript windbreakers and comb-over hair, arms folded, always looking into the mid-distance to pass the time. Brough clocked them for plainclothes cops and so did Chun-li.

At the centre of the fort was an octagonal tower, twice the height of the outer walls and built of charcoal brick, with lacquered red woodwork at the eaves. It reminded Brough of the Golden Gate at Kiev: that, too, had been fucked up in the 1980s by communist archaeologists. Mister Bo beckoned them all inside; Rupert Wong took shots as they trooped in. Georgina and Hyacinth filled the cavernous stairway with oohs and ahhs.

They came out onto a balcony: below the fort, the ground fell away to an escarpment. The valley below marked the point where the vast, rippling seascape of the Kubuqi Desert came to an abrupt stop and the normal, scrub-strewn grit of the Ordos Desert resumed. There were a few camels jogging along the floor of the valley with Chinese tourists wobbling along on top; a decrepit fun-fair, a go-kart track, a supermarket-sized trinket shop and beyond that a ski-lift. A few tiny figures were sliding down the near-vertical slope of a massive sand dune on toboggans. In the far distance, some Communist officials on an away-day were chasing each other across the dunes on quad bikes.

"What's that?" Brough pointed to another fort about a kilometre away along the cliff top.

"Ming Dynasty fortress, rebuilt 1994", Mr Bo announced. "Now a conference centre and living museum of Mongolian culture. Re-enactments daily."

"Let me guess what our next filming location is going to be," Brough muttered as they entered the restaurant.

"Actually," Chun-li grabbed his arm and put her face close to his, "Ming Dynasty complex is off limits today because a *quite sensitive* event is taking place."

They parted so Brough could join in the wowing and neck-craning. The interior of the tower was an exercise in geometry and quiet power: four tiers of mahogany balustrades and pillars ranged around a hexagonal atrium, cream-plastered walls, light from the midday sun glinting off the buttery bronze of an ancient bell suspended from the roof-beams. A staircase connected each balcony with the next, and around the balconies were private dining rooms, quiet for now, attended by chalk-white waitresses who looked like they had been recently worked on by a makeup artist.

Fresh orchids in the wall sconces, antique scrolls hanging from the pillars: to Brough, seeing Chinese opulence for the first time, it solved part of the mystery; it explained the viscerality of the violence, the randomness of the cruelty. You would do a lot of things to defend a lifestyle like this.

They filed into a dining room with a circular glass table at the centre, resting on a large stone sculpture of a leaping fish; the scroll-armed chairs were rosewood. Carstairs, who's been running a dodgy antique dealership on eBay as a sideline, queried the authenticity of the furniture. Mr. Bo laughed and attempted English:

"In China, all antiques doubtful. However, this restaurant formerly museum owned by state, so probably real, or if fakes, quite old!"

Rupert and Hyacinth pealed with laughter and applauded politely. Hot towels came in, followed by cooled waitresses, frozen glasses and lukewarm beer; then julienned eel, smoked bacon and seared green beans; a medley of chicken beaks and claws; pork sliced so thinly that it melted on their chopsticks like cheese. Finally a two-foot long steamed carp, arranged on the plate with its head and tail in the attitude of leaping out of a bed of golden lily flowers.

By now Brough, in a series of sub-tabular text exchanges with Chun-li, had established that the nearby Ming Dynasty fortress was to be the venue for an emergency meeting of the Rare Earth cartel and that, if her intelligence was right, key members of it would come to the Qing Dynasty restaurant for lunch to commemorate a landmark day in the history of Rare Earth metallurgy.

"Why landmark?" Brough had texted.

"GM finished." Chun-li had replied.

"Crops?"

"Cars. Gone bust. Obama make speech."

"Apparently General Motors has gone bust," Brough chipped in to the conversation.

"Inevitable matey, wasn't it?" Carstairs wiping his mouth on a linen cloth.

"Bit of a surprise to me – not many Bloomberg terminals out in the desert."

"Been on the wires since Friday."

"Maybe China's sovereign wealth fund will chip in to buy it," Georgina joked.

Everybody laughed nervously.

For Georgina, each minute that passed without Brough doing something unpredictable or exploding into a childish rage was a bonus.

"Will it have much impact here, d'you think, Chun-li?" said Brough, insouciant.

She stared at him blankly across the table and replied:

"Maybe the light is good enough now to move to shooting?"

"What was that bronze bell for, at the top?" said Brough.

"Telling the time," said Chun-li.

Mr. Bo launched into a long-winded explanation, complete

with demonstrative hand movements, miming a waterfall, bronze casting, peasants digging in the fields.

"Short version is," said Chun-li, "in Qing dynasty landowners used water vessels, filled from a tank in the roof to measure the hours and then a mechanism made a hammer strike the bell."

"Can we film it? Can we film the bronze bell?"

Georgina looked at him, confused. Brough was legendary for refusing to "waste tape" on the landscapes, details and covering shots producers need in order to make a TV package complete. A bar-stool legend tells of Brough refusing to stop and film graves outside Monrovia back in 1999, confident that they would find fresh bodies further up the road, then refusing to stop and film the bodies because his instinct told him there would be "something better" a mile further on. That footage, of Brough crouching in a ditch, whispering a piece to camera and then pausing as the microphone records the sound of a firing squad, is still shown on the hostile environment course run by Armageddon Solutions in the session entitled "Some Risks Are Unacceptable".

"Why do you want to film an antique bell?" Georgina's tone was that of a mother with a disappointing child.

"Because," Brough improvised, mixing insolence and whimsy, "I might be able to write to it. I might," he waved his hands in slow circles, "make the scene symbolise order amid chaos; tradition amid modernity. Fabulous wealth…"

Carstairs threw his napkin to the table and reached for his camera:

"Maybe Rupert would like to come and film us filming a bell."

Rupert beamed and grabbed his camera. Hyacinth, sensing the tension of the day draining off, to be replaced by fun and charm, moved places to engage Georgina in a pidgin-English discussion centring on the topic of Yves Saint Laurent. Mr. Bo lit a cigarette. The driver, who had smoked throughout the meal, scraped his plate for leftovers and belched.

"In the cool, palatial ruins of this nineteen-eighties era, Disneyland repro of a Qing Dynasty bell tower," Brough began under his breath, imitating the television-delivery style of 1970s legend Alan Whicker, "the power-brokers of Inner Mongolia gather to fix the price of what few yet realise is to become the world's most precious," pause for breath, "metal."

He slipped through the door, followed by Carstairs and Rupert Wong, Chun-li clutching her arms around her chest to stem a rising panic. They climbed a flight of wooden stairs and then another. A waitress asked if they needed help. Chun-li said no, but the waitress insisted on making a slow hand-gesture and a beatific bow as they struggled up to the platform next to the bell.

By now there was clattering, slurping and male hubbub coming from behind the doors of other private rooms, all closed. At the foot of the tower Brough spotted a flurry of coat-taking and bowing by the waitresses, who had lined up like modern slaves and begun chanting a melodious greeting to their guests.

"Just get me faces," Brough snapped at Carstairs. "Don't care how, just faces."

Carstairs scrambled to a position above the bell, plausible enough to be filming it if he'd had a wide-angle lens on, which he did not, and ideal for the telephoto lens to pick up detail as the men came up the stairs. From the sound of them, there were maybe four or five: the rustle of linen suits and the creak of nicotine-ravaged lungs echoed into the atrium.

"Can't see faces," Carstairs whispered. There were only hands visible, sliding and gripping the banister; "Wrong angle."

An old wooden mallet from the Qing Dynasty was fixed to the wall with brass hooks. Brough wrenched it, pulling the hooks out of the plaster, and hammered it into the side of the bell.

A shimmering deafness overtook them. Chun-li wailed and covered her ears. Rupert Wong lost his footing and tumbled backwards. Brough was already stumbling down the stairs, wearing a fake smile to intercept the restaurant manager, who was running up towards them with a deranged face. Meanwhile Carstairs was pulling tight, methodical, four-second shots on the peering faces of the businessmen whose heads had moved, like curious turtles, out into the stairwell at the moment the bell clanged.

They were well-kept faces. A jowly, earnest guy like a Chinese Vito Corleone pulled a grimace and was gone. A fat slob in the middle of a conversation on his Bluetooth earpiece peered upwards under a wrinkled brow. Two Jiang Zemin look-alikes scowled in unison. A venerable oldster and his foxy secretary glanced up together, the camera pulling a two-shot that if it had been a still photo would have scooped first prize in any competition on the theme of "innocence and corruption".

Now a bald security guard, his face flattened by the telephoto zoom, began barking at the camera. His leather-clad finger pointed at Carstairs and the camera magnified the fingertip to the same size as his angry face.

"Oh my god!" Chun-li had been saying this under her breath, over and over, but now as the sound of the bell subsided she tugged Carstairs' arm and pointed, and jumped up and down as if she'd spotted a shark.

"There, there!"

Peering from directly below them, so that their faces were upside down in the viewfinder, were the flat-top hair, roof-tile eyebrows and charming smile of Oktyabr Khünbish. And a gum chewing kid wearing Oakleys.

8

"What's going on?" Georgina walked straight into the shoving match that had begun at the top of the stairs, with a spoonful of grapefruit segments poised elegantly between bowl and mouth. Brough, Carstairs and Chun-li had formed a tight human ball around the camera while the manager, the cartel bodyguard and Oktyabr Khünbish were trying to prise the camera away–in Khünbish's case from a position on the outside of the balustrade which he had leapt to in order to grab Chun-li's hair.

"You whore!" Khünbish yelled. "Why do you refuse to answer my text messages?"

"Tell these foreign assholes that if they don't hand over the tape in ten seconds they are dead," the cartel bodyguard jabbed Chun-li in the chest.

Georgina shouted:

"Hey leave her alone!"

The bodyguard felt affronted by Georgina's attempt to tug the sleeve of his coat, so he pushed the rest of her grapefruit into her face. Khünbish, clambering over the balustrade, twisted Chun-li's arm.

"I had my blood tested, and urine! Guess what? Nothing!

But the CCTV footage shows me going under like a truth-serum victim after you fed me that champagne! Who are you working for, witch?"

"Channel Ninety-Nine! We have permission to film!" Chun-li squealed, drawing on deep resources of *wu-wei* now to still the urge to put three straight fingers into Khünbish's carotid artery at high velocity.

Georgina, stunned and splattered with grapefruit, saw Hyacinth Deng step to the edge of the melee, face to the natural light, and begin speaking into a stick microphone. Shit! Rupert Wong was filming the chaos and now Hyacinth was doing an on-location piece to camera explaining, presumably, how Western news crews cause mayhem.

"Don't give them the tape!" Brough shouted.

Despite the hair-pulling and shouting, the camera and its adherents had made decent progress down the stairs, but now the cartel bodyguard grabbed Carstairs between the legs, causing him to shriek. And the Oakleys Kid, having sprinted up the stairs, wedged his shoulder into the melee and got a hand on the camera.

"Stop!" Georgina shouted.

There was immediate silence.

"Give them the tape!"

"Fuck off," Brough said.

"Jimmy, give them the tape!"

There was so much menace in Georgina's voice that Hyancinth Deng, who had stopped her piece to camera in mid-sentence, now used the balls of her feet and the tips of her high heels to shuffle silently away from her.

"You, let go of this lady's arm," Georgina pointed to Khünbish.

He did. The cartel bodyguard released his grasp on Carstairs' balls without being asked. This, Brough thought, is what you pay for when you send your daughter to Cheltenham Ladies College.

"Now give them the tape. We are very sorry," she moved into staccato English-for-dummies, "that we have caused upset to the guests. We did not know that filming was forbidden. We are English journalists."

And she smiled like Margaret Thatcher.

Carstairs flipped the door on the tape deck, slid the tape out with finger and thumb and slapped it into the gloved palm of the bodyguard. Brough noticed, in the silence, that all the mobsters had retreated into the dining rooms, whose mahogany doors stood shut.

"Clear fucking cowardice," Carstairs' voice had gone blank and fatalistic.

Only once had Brough ever seen Jimmy Carstairs give up a tape, and that was after they'd inadvertently filmed a Lebanese militia boss at a gay disco on the outskirts of Beirut. Then it had been the threat of a one-way ride to the olive groves that had clinched it. Anyway, they'd joked later, who cares if gays can join Hezbollah. *Yallah Habibi!*

This felt different.

9

"Twyla's given me the authority to terminate your contract if you do anything else," Georgina announced.

The three of them were pacing unsteadily on the slope of a sand dune. They had ditched Mr. Bo, together with Rupert and Hyacinth and driven out here, leaving Chun-li and the van in the next valley, out of sight:

"All I was doing…" Brough began.

"How did you know those men were part of this so-called Rare Earth cartel?"

Brough made an insolent face. It dawned on him that Chun-li had probably known about the cartel's meeting and steered the filming plans to put them near it. It dawned on Georgina a split second later.

"Right, I will sack her on arrival in Beijing," Georgina struggled to control her voice: "In fact I will sack her now."

"Can I be threatened with the sack as well?" Carstairs was sweating with the heat and anger, swigging water from a bottle.

"Why, what have you done?" Georgina jeered.

"Bought a Firestore."

"What do you mean?"

"After you gave that tape up in Tang Lu, I decided to install a Firestore. It's a little box that backs up the tape to hard disc: just clips to the back of the camera. Chun-li got it for me in Ordos. They're quite common in professional TV outfits…"

He lifted the camera to show the device. Georgina had assumed it was an extra battery.

"So we've still got shots of their faces?" She looked pained.

"Correct, d'you want to delete them now?"

"What do you mean?"

"Do you want to wipe the disc the same as you wiped that little flash card?"

Brough, who'd been revelling in Georgina's discomfort, exploded.

"What?"

"After you collapsed in a heap last night she wanted a look at your rushes from that Cancer Village place. Took them to her room; she came down ten minutes later, said the card wouldn't read."

"What are you implying?" Georgina took a swig of her own water and pulled her sunglasses over her eyes.

There was a sharp blast from the horn of the van, the other side of the dune.

"It wouldn't read on mine, either," Carstairs went on. "So, waking up at four in the morning, as you do, I got my little loup out and my tweezers and scraped off the blob of nail varnish that had somehow got onto the contacts. Then it read."

There is a special level of despair journalists experience over lost pictures, akin to bereavement, and Brough began to feel it now.

"It's blank. Sorry. Formatted. Actually Georgina, with SD cards, they record the time and date of last formatting."

Brough grabbed his own hair and pulled it.

"You knew about this and never said anything?"

Carstairs shrugged, but Brough knew why. He'd seen cameramen take decks to pieces, re-thread hundreds of metres of tape by hand, ship special gadgets from LA to Jakarta by overnight courier using their own credit cards–even fake coronary thrombosis–rather than admit their pictures had been lost.

There was more urgent honking from the van.

"This is totally shit," Brough shouted. "You have destroyed evidence – probably of a major global story. What's the excuse – I was only obeying orders?"

He tried to spin on his heel and march away but lurched across the sand instead. He needed to get out of the sun and think. If Chun-li had set up the entire encounter with these cartel sleazebags then she knew a lot more than he did.

In fact you had to put it down as one cool piece of media manipulation. With shots of the cartel together, in a way, you could ditch the interview with Big Wu: put names to faces and you have a bigger story. They can't bury the sintering plant in the desert like they hide the illegal mines, so you can always go back there and film it. The cancer rates will be documented somewhere. The pollution cloud in Tang Lu will still come rolling, bang on the dot of seven each night. You could reconstruct it all with some good research. What's missing is the big picture: what's the cartel trying to do? What's General Motors got to do with it?

Brough realised he had to put it down on paper now, draw lines and arrows between people and places. The story was clearing, like a pint of cloudy bitter, but taking time. Probably stop filming and get out of Inner Mongolia...

He crested the lip of the dune. Below him was the van, with the driver for some reason wriggling in the sand with his hands tied behind his back and duct tape over his mouth. He could not see Chun-li. She was gone.

10

Chun-li wished she was not wearing a skirt because it was allowing the Oakleys Kid to put his hand up there, requiring her to kick him.

They were in the back of an Audi Q4, identical to the one they'd totalled, with Khünbish driving. The Oakleys Kid had taken the Beretta out of her bag and was maintaining a wobbly aim with it, at her head. Her mouth was sealed with duct tape and her hands bound with it.

She was sure Khünbish's plan was to have her gang-raped and killed, because his conversation had been revolving around these two subjects for the whole ten minutes they'd been bumping and swerving along the desert road:

"Why didn't you answer my text messages? I will take you out to the desert now and watch while camel herders make you choke! Then the sand will strip you to a skeleton. Huh? Wish you'd answered my text messages now?"

Khünbish was sweating and his face was frozen into the perma-scowl of the betrayed lover, the man who's lost his wages at poker, the sent-off footballer.

He yanked the steering wheel and switched to four-wheel drive, pushing the Audi off the narrow service road and onto the sand: it seemed simultaneously to slow down and begin flying sideways–up towards the lip of the dune, tens of metres above them.

At the top Khünbish revved the engine crazily and spun the car backwards, near vertically, over the hard edge of sand and onto the crest, where he made another sharp yank of the wheel to bring it to a standstill.

"Oh no! Your foreign friends are coming after us!" Khünbish mimicked a woman's voice. He had spotted the Ruifeng van bumping along the road a couple of miles away, like a small boat on a choppy sea. He revved the engine.

"Wave goodbye!"

They sped off into a long, looping curve down the hump of the next dune, the Audi's chromework glinting in the afternoon shadows. Chun-li, whose kicking defence together with the pitch and whine of the 4x4 had driven the Oakleys Kid into a grim passivity, considered her options.

Racking her brain, she could not find any obvious explanation for how she'd ended up here, at the edge of death. Her life seemed to divide into a short period of positive choices in her teens and a long period of *wu-wei* after that. She'd chosen to study genetic medicine; she couldn't remember choosing to give it up. She had chosen to learn English and *tai-chi*, but she could not remember ever choosing to study the ancient game of *wei-qi* with General Guo, nor how it came to happen that she drifted into this weird, informal intelligence-gathering role. She had always meant to ask whether there was an insurance scheme or some kind of certificate she could present if she got into trouble, but she'd sensed Guo steering her away from the issue on all occasions.

Swiftly computing the data, Chun-li explored the question: why, given so much contact with Western business delegations and journalist teams, had she never been in this kind of situation before.

She let her eyes try to understand the curve of the dunes, her nose to find traces of the hot, clean desert on the air that was blasting from the a/c system.

Maybe it was a western China thing? Maybe out here the rules are different and she'd just missed that? Maybe the spirits that protected her on the East Coast, the restless ancestors she'd sometimes glimpsed through the purple slant of a Powerpoint projector beam–maybe they just didn't operate out here.

But she'd seen something at the site of the car crash – and not the driver's spirit leaving his body. Something else – just at the corner of her eye – slinking away from the propaganda boy's Honda. So if there really are, as the saying goes, deities a few feet above our heads, they needed to get cracking and do something.

"Why are you doing this?" she shouted, though the duct-tape made it sound like a series of squeals.

Khünbish reached back and ripped the tape off her mouth.

"Why are you doing this?"

"Why didn't you answer my text messages?"

In the 36 hours since waking from his Rohypnol coma he had sent her 108 text messages. Scrolling through them, she'd spotted a pattern. It was simply "Call me" for the first twenty, escalating to "Call me, need to speak" once he'd become fully reoriented and then, around cocktail hour last night, it had gone into a medley of threats, love haikus, cryptic quotations from Danzan Ravjaa, stopping around midnight, resuming around 3am, conking out at 4am, and resuming again over breakfast with the plaintive, two-character, "call me" plea.

She'd been wondering how to deal with it, but the battle with Georgina and the search for Brough had been front-of-mind and she'd assumed her usual strategy, the action of non-action, would sort things out.

"Why do you want to kill me? Don't you realise there are witnesses? There are three Western journalists in that van! Think you're immune to international criticism? They don't care about your horses and your sex slaves. Don't even care about the cartel. That filming was a total accident…"

"Save your energy for screaming. You will need it soon enough. Those camel boys think it's a red-letter day if they even get to have sex with a camel!"

Khünbish had become melodramatic, harsh. He lit a cigarette and ignored her in a way that, if she'd seen any Chinese *film noir*, she would have read as calculated to convey menace. But Chun-li would only watch movies that depicted magic and large battle scenes.

"What happens now GM's gone bust?"

"You know too much already!" Khünbish sneered. "You think I didn't get that security camera footage lip-read? Yeah, the lip-reading expert nearly had to go and masturbate after watching you writhing around all over my little man!"

"The CCP will never let control of Rare Earth pass to organised crime," she shouted.

"Ha! Rare Earth will be around longer than the CCP!"

Khünbish for a moment replaced his frown with a genuine chuckle:

"Anyway, nobody's trying to take Rare Earth out of government control. It's just a play. You understand what a play is?"

She shrugged and gave him her goofy look through the rear-view mirror.

"Here's the play. Like I explained to you while under the influence of that truth serum – and let me tell you that I really do not care who you are working for, even if it's Chinese State Security or the FSB, because you are going to disappear. Repeat, disappear. Like I involuntarily explained to you: the CCP strategy is to put the burn on the rest of the world by reducing Rare Earth production on environmental grounds. And by the way, check the share ownership status of various Western-located mining companies, when you reach the afterlife, on your supernatural Bloomberg terminal…"

He paused so that he and the Oakleys Kid could both cackle at this.

"… yeah check the shareholdings of the Canadian and Australian mining companies who own the other 5% of the market; but that's a side play. The Chinese government's going to screw the world's balls to the floor with Rare Earth once the resource crunch gets going and good luck to them. But now GM is fucked it means that Li-Ion's fucked, at least for a decade, so the cartel…"

"You are not a member of this evil society?"

"Ha, ha. You are gonna die anyway and we are gonna fuck you stupid. You should have answered my text messages!"

Suddenly she knew what had happened; understood what disrupted the flow of compromise, appeasement, backscratching and acquiesence. It was Brough.

Brough, she realised, was the first person she had ever met who gave a shit about the outcome of his actions. Why did he give a shit? She made up her mind to ask him if she ever laid eyes on him again.

What would Brough do right now? Not *wu-wei*, for certain.

"Khünbish," she tried not to hate the name as she said it, "I think you're an unfortunate man."

He stared out of the window like a teenager damaged by love.

"You have good looks and appreciate High Art. Why do you need to be involved in this hoodlum lifestyle? Why don't you go legit, like Michael Corleone in *Godfather II*, become some kind of horse connoisseur and live in Macao?"

"Baby, you are annoying me." He refused to meet her gaze in the rear-view mirror.

"Maybe I could come to Macao with you and be your lover." Part of Chun-li's brain wanted her to go, cartoon style, "tee-hee-hee", acknowledging the naivete of this strategem, but another part just kept telling her to continue. She had never realised it before, but the opposite of *wu-wei* was hopeless, heroic, random action, with no prospect of success.

"Like I said, you should have answered my text messages."

"We could go through the whole *Tao* of Danzan Ravjaa. I found that stuff we did a little weird but I've been, you know, thinking about it. A lot."

She put her head back and opened her mouth, trying to do the kind of dirty smile she'd seen romantic actresses do.

"Gimme that pistol!" Khünbish yanked the steering wheel and shoved the Audi into a low growl that made them churn the sand and slide as if surfing down the face of the dune.

The Oakleys Kid, who'd been leering at her while she tried this two-bit seduction strategy, slowly transferred the Beretta into Khünbish's outstretched hand.

He slammed the brakes and the Audi swung 180 degrees, its wheels half buried in the sand-slide he'd set off. As they drifted sideways Khünbish seemed for a moment fascinated by the gun, which he lifted close to his face, like a kid with a toy.

"Beretta. You ever see a James Bond movie called *Doctor No?*"

She shook her head. Khünbish pointed the pistol at her face:

"This gun's basically useless. Low velocity, tiny hole. In *Doctor No* James Bond has to swap the Beretta for a Walther PPK."

He jerked his arm back, pointing the gun upwards, next to his temple, to make the James Bond pose.

An instant later he jerked his body down into the seat-well, left hand gripping the wheel, and shot the Oakleys Kid under the chin, splattering his cheekbone against the sunroof of the car, never losing eye-contact with Chun-li.

"With a Walther PPK you get a one-shot kill whereas with this," he ignored her screams and fired the Beretta casually into the Kid's twitching body, "you always need two."

11

Khünbish dragged the Kid's body to the edge of a dune, the wind whipping sand into his face, and dropped it onto the near-vertical slope below. Chun-li peered after it. As the body slid, so did the sand it had disturbed, gradually overtaking the Kid's splayed limbs and soaking up the blood. By the time it reached the bottom, sixty metres below, the corpse had been engulfed by sand. Khünbish said:

"Cool, hey? Have to know the right kind of dune. That could have been you."

He skimmed the Beretta over the edge so that it, too, would disappear beneath the desert.

"Now we go to the car and have anal sex. If you don't obey me I will take you to the camel farm and leave you with those guys all night."

As he took a step towards her, Chun-li wondered what Brough would do in her situation. Something unpredictable, probably. Needlessly confrontational.

She hopped backwards and threw herself over the edge of the dune.

As she hurtled downwards the sand burned her leg and began

to fly up her nose. She let herself go limp, like a kid on a water-slide. Her heel dug into the slope and flipped her over, tumbling sideways now with the sand clawing at her hair as it whiplashed around, her shoes flying away. She saw Khünbish leap over the edge, attempting to slalom his way down in pursuit, but losing his balance and going headfirst–now managing to arch his body and lift his hands to fly towards her like a parachutist in freefall. Behind him the lip of the dune collapsed and set off an avalanche of sand.

She slid to a halt at the bottom of the slope, her arms and legs splayed. Khünbish, his eyes white with desire, slid towards her like a guided missile but then the avalanche picked him up and shot him past, half burying Chun-li.

There was silence. She tried to stare up at the harsh, sizzling, lazuline sky but the sand made her eyes blink and sting. She pulled one arm out of the sand and used it to lever the rest of her into a crouch. The palms of her hands and her knees were burning against the hot powder.

She watched a black beetle scurry away beneath her nose. Then, like a bigger beetle, elbow first, then knee, then buzz-cut head, Khünbish crawled out of his own sand-trap, maybe twenty metres below her. In the space between them was the Beretta, glinting carbon black against the sand.

The sight of it set Khünbish into motion, making powerful but laboured strides through the sand that was still pouring off the dune's steep face, swamping him above the ankles at each step. She made to move, but cried out in pain as the desert seared the soles of her feet. She curled into a protective ball and watched Khünbish inch his way towards the pistol.

He tried to shout something at her but was too hoarse for sound to come out. Every step made the sand hiss like brush strokes on a cymbal. There was a buzzing in her ears. She cleared the sand out with her fingers but it got louder.

Khünbish picked up the gun. The metal parts were already hot enough to burn his skin. He shook sand out of the barrel and blew it off the recoil, wiping sweat off his face with his shirtsleeve.

Chun-li's world seemed to close around her; her vision narrowed into a dark blue cone. At the end of the cone was Khünbish, staggering forward with the gun aimed at her head. Weirdly, at the edge of the cone and only half visible, there was a mischievous looking old man flying along in the lotus position, smirking, pointing at the sky as if to say: welcome to the afterlife.

The buzzing sound turned into a roar above her head. A black machine with four wheels flew over the edge of the dune and plummeted, like a ski-jumper who has misjudged, all the way to the bottom where it bounced, somersaulted onto its roll-cage, spun and then righted itself. It was some kind of quad bike. The rider, face hidden behind a helmet, revved the engine and sped towards Khünbish, still up to his knees in sand.

Khünbish raised the Beretta with a two-handed grip and braced himself to fire. But the quad bike braked sharply, sending a sandcloud billowing thicker than a smoke grenade. When it cleared Chun-li could hear the quad bike rider screaming at Khünbish to lay the weapon on the ground. He replied by pulling the trigger.

There was only a click. And then another.

The man in the blackmarket store had already told to Chun-li this James Bond folklore about a Beretta needing two bullets to kill, so she had chambered one round and left one more in the clip, tipping the rest into her makeup bag.

The rider, recognising the snap of the empty pistol, slammed the quad bike into reverse, skidded away and, standing up in the saddle, executed a slow glide across the trough of the dune, a lazy arc up the slope at the other side, and then opened the throttle. Khünbish continued to pull the trigger of the gun and shout obscenities at Chun-li until the bike, an aluminium-framed

Quadzilla 500 with a top speed of 80 mph, severed his legs just below the knee and spun the rest of him into the air.

"That man was an anti-social element," Superintendent Xiao smiled bashfully at Chun-li a minute later, as he helped her crawl onto the quad bike seat behind him, "but you are not much better. Why are you helping foreign journalists disturb our social order?"

12

The theme park had closed. The sunset was turning the edges of the dunes molten. The camels had begun to herd together into the long shadows. The chair-lift had stopped, leaving its chains and wires to clank in the evening breeze.

Deep in the desert, Hyacinth Deng was delivering a piece to camera next to a line of tape slung between two police SUVs. Mr. Bo, off camera, was checking the draft he had prepared for her against delivery:

"Fast action by an off-duty member of the Public Security Police, taking a hard-earned recreational break here in the acclaimed Kubuqi Desert natural beauty spot, has prevented an abduction attempt by a man Inner Mongolia's police department describe as 'driven mad by passion'…"

Inside the gift-shop five sizes of laughing camel toys smiled plastic smiles as the sun's last rays turned the synthetic fur on their humps from beige to russet red. Among the low-grade cashmere shawls, leather cowboy hats, Ghengis Khan masks, plastic swords and fake Chanel sunglasses, there were a few formica tables designated for the use of tour groups.

Xiao sat with his back to the sun, a surly hulk reeking of sweat and gasoline. Next to him sat Chun-li, still prone to shivering now and then but rehydrated and composed, despite her burns and scars. Opposite, blinking into the orange light, sat Brough and Georgina.

"Superintendent Xiao says we have to be very quick since the Inner Mongolia police department will soon question him," Chun-li began.

Brough and Georgina were still too stunned to be reacting much, but nodded and swigged bottled water. Xiao spoke, Chun-li translated.

"First, Superintendent Xiao admits he is out of his jurisdiction. However, since there is now at least one fatality, his role as an expert witness could be crucial and he urges you to listen to his proposal."

"What do you mean at least one fatality?" Georgina's voice was a hoarse whisper.

"Since the boy with the Oakley sunglasses is buried beneath a sand-dune, Superintendent Xiao thinks the police here will not bother recording this as a fatality," Chun-li paused the translation and blushed.

"Continue," said Xiao.

"Also Superintendent Xiao is willing to forget the illegal purchase of a handgun by our team."

Georgina's hair cascaded over her fingers as her head slumped into her hands.

"So it was your gun?"

Brough did not give Chun-li the look of admiration she had hoped for.

"Superintendent Xiao has already wiped the gun for prints, re-printing the handle from the body of," she faltered, "attempted Mongolian rape perpetrator, and then re-printing over that with his own fingerprints."

"Let me guess whether Superintendent Xiao has gone to all

this trouble out of a sudden surge of gratitude or wants something in return?" said Brough.

Xiao cut him off.

"Superintendent Xiao says he does not want to confiscate our rushes," Chun-li explained. "Instead he would first like to return something."

They watched as Xiao extracted Brough's battered laptop, retrieved at the car crash site, from a bundle of underclothes in his holdall. He slid it across the table.

"Thank you very much, does that mean we can go?" Brough's deadpan face was caked with the salt from perspiration.

Xiao barked something at Chun-li.

"Superintendent Xiao," she struggled to maintain control of her voice, "asks whether you have ever heard the Chinese saying: journalists go to the coal mine by taxi and return by Mercedes-Benz?"

Brough snorted.

"It means," Chun-li began.

"It means," Brough cut across her, "that journalists who uncover safety violations at coal mines where there've been fatalities are often confronted with the option of binning their discoveries in return for a reward, correct?"

Chun-li and Xiao conversed briefly and Xiao smiled, an avuncular smile, and made the thumbs up signal. Then he reached into his holdall again and produced a small brick of pristine 500-euro banknotes.

"This is one hundred thousand Euros. Superintendent Xiao invites you to choose any note and check its digital watermark. The checksum 13 and serial number N indicate they were issued by the Austrian central bank in 2007."

"What does Superintendent Xiao want us to do in return for that?"

Georgina glared at him while Chun-li translated:

"Simply to downplay Tang Lu elements of the story. One reason the Superintendent decided to come himself, in person, and in plain clothes, is to speak man-to-man to senior correspondent Brough," – it was Georgina who snorted now – "and not to attempt crude, Chinese police tactics such as the seizure of pictures, which the Superintendent now realises to be futile."

"What are you trying to do?" Brough looked straight into Xiao's eyes, which did not flinch.

Xiao leaned back and lit a *Zhongnanhai*; he offered Brough one, which he refused–and looked surprised as Georgina grabbed the packet and, with jittery fingers, accepted a light. Now there was smoke in the air, and fresh banknotes on the table, Xiao's voice mellowed a notch.

"Tang Lu has a bad name for pollution but a good name for social order. To my regret, I've turned a blind eye to something that was undermining social order. When I get back, I expect the production process at Tang Lu Nickel Metal Hydride will be altered, maybe relocated. Some money will stop flowing into the bank accounts of certain high officials. The Tang Lu Police Department will get on with its job of rooting out minor crime and preventing drunkenness. The Western TV channel will show its report. The bosses in Beijing will get angry at the bosses in Ningxia; they will get angry with me; they will probably retire me anyway for getting involved in an incident with," Chun-li paused the translation, "with a criminally obsessed sex pervert. But you have found bigger things than pollution, right here in Inner Mongolia."

"Why don't you just keep the money yourself?" Brough asked.

"Because I am not corrupt. This is the official corruption fund we keep at the Police HQ and I had to sign it out. I see from your defiant response that you do not believe you are corrupt either," Xiao chuckled.

"Shall we terminate this?" Georgina snapped at Chun-li.

"Superintendent one more thing has to say," Chun-li's translation skills were fading with fatigue. "Please check laptop."

Brough opened the computer, which had been left on standby. Xiao watched with satisfaction as the faces of the two Westerners shrivelled with disgust.

"Sixteen hundred such images have been detected on this hard drive," Xiao's voice became businesslike. There was a special CD full of child pornography on hand at police HQ to deal with threats to social order like David Brough.

"What the?" Georgina began.

"What chapter is this Chun-li?" Brough sniggered.

"Huh?"

"What chapter in the manual for wasting the time of foreign journalists?"

"Oh," she laughed wearily, against a pain-seared ribcage, "probably chapter seventeen."

"The bribe will not be necessary," Georgina pushed the money back across the table. "Nor will the attempt to frame Mister Brough. David, I will accept your word that these images are not there because of any of your sexual deviations. Chun-li, say thank-you to Superintendent Xiao for rescuing you, and also for agreeing to forget the matter of the gun. Tell him we don't care how many bodies the police find, since we were not responsible for killing anybody."

She stood up and offered her hand to Xiao, who shook it rhythmically, making her voice undulate.

"Please convey to the Superintendent that Channel Ninety-Nine is a responsible broadcaster and was never going to call into question the conduct of the police department at Tang Lu, which was always courteous. And that our primary interest in this case was always in presenting a balanced story about pollution, of which Tang Lu is just one of a number of elements. We have no interest in any wider story about rare metals, or alleged market manipulation, and certainly do not want to draw attention to any of the unfortunate events that have befallen us, since these are part of the job of being an international news crew."

Chun-li gabbled fast in Mandarin and Georgina maintained a saccharine smile. Carstairs, sitting outside as lookout, gave a whistle as the headlights of a small convoy of police vehicles bumped towards them.

"What the fuck are you agreeing to do?" Brough hissed at Georgina as Xiao exchanged pleasantries with Chun-li, burying the cash back into his holdall.

"I don't give a shit about you and effing Rare Earth obsession – but this little cow and her gun could have got us into serious trouble."

Xiao had become magnanimous now, playing the gentle giant with the one-pip Mongolian Superintendent in charge of the incident. He'd followed the Audi in a hired taxi, he explained to the awestruck local cops, simply because he'd noticed the occupants, two criminal-types, observing the Ruifeng van through binoculars.

They all trooped outside, the lights from the police vehicles casting everybody's shadow, harsh and black, onto the walls of the ravine. Brough and Georgina were hissing threats to each other; Chun-li was squirming as Xiao patted her on the head.

Then, in the dark of the gift shop, a pair of red, electric camel eyes lit up and they heard the park's Mongolian theme tune echoing at them, from a tinny speaker inside its hump.

Now a second pair of eyes lit up and a second electric camel began singing, setting up a discordant Bactrian fugue; now a third and a fourth. A dark figure was moving along the whole row of camel gifts, pressing each of them on the head to start them singing. Soon there was a trashy camel symphony echoing out of the gift-shop's open door and into the ravine.

The cops and journalists fell silent. Rupert Wong raised his camera to catch the moment but Mr. Bo's hand halted it halfway. Against the last sliver of dusk they saw the silhouette of a man move over to the formica tables, reach beneath one, and pull away something small that had been taped there.

"What's this?" Xiao glared at Chun-li, who could only reply with a panicked look.

"Who's that?" shouted the Mongolian police chief, flipping the press-stud on his holster.

A skinny youth with a bruised and peevish face emerged into the headlamps. It was Li Qi-han.

"This man is an impostor!" Li Qi-han pronounced, in a refined and vintage Beijing Party School accent, pointing a stiff finger at Xiao.

"He is Xiao Yi-ming, failed dotcom entrepreneur and swindler. Only this morning he incited the residents of an old-people's hostel into senseless anti-social acts, aided and abetted by a known rightist element.

"He has re-entered the country from Taiwan and intends to speculate on the market for Rare Earth minerals with an illegal hoard of foreign cash, in order to fund his online child porn empire. If you don't believe me," Li's voice cooled to a steely stacatto, "check the holdall."

13

Brough burst into his hotel room, grabbed the TV zapper, marched straight to the bathroom, hit the shower tap with his knuckles and switched the television on, to a loud quiz show. Carstairs, in the next room, was frantically piling his kit into a holdall while Georgina, one door along, was doing the same but into a fake Vuitton Daimler bag.

Chun-li, who never unpacked, stood at the door of Brough's room, warbling nervously into her phone. They'd left the theme park minus Mr. Bo, Hyacinth and Rupert, leaving room in the van for Li Qi-han and his long-legged ladyfriend. These two had now collapsed, giggling, onto Brough's bed and were having a nose-touching competition.

"Mr. Bo is approaching the hotel and demanding an urgent meeting with our team. Superintendent Xiao still held by local police but allegations of Deputy Propaganda Chief Li not really standing up." Chun-li summarised, one hand over the phone.

"We need to get out of here in the next fifteen minutes," Brough's voice was stoked with adrenaline.

"Five minutes," Chun-li snapped.

Long Tall Daisy slipped her shoes off and tiptoed into

the bathroom, from which the scent of luxury bodywash soon floated.

"I will not go on tape," Li Qi-han began. "I will not hand over my recording of Xiao's bribery attempt but I will allow you to make a copy. I will give an off-camera briefing in the presence of witnesses. Also documentary evidence."

"Can I not persuade you just to…"

"Five minutes," Li cut Brough's sentence in half. "I hope your shorthand skills are good."

Carstairs and Georgina bustled into the room while Chun-li delivered their luggage to the bellboy, together with high-speed instructions and a handful of cash. The door slammed shut and Li Qi-han began to speak, Brough scribbling on a hotel envelope while Georgina tutted at him and paced around.

"I am Li Qi-han, deputy propaganda secretary, Tang Lu Industrial Suburb, Ningxia Province. This briefing is strictly unattributable. The source may be described as a senior local official."

Brough nodded.

"Tang Lu Nickel Metal Hydride is an unlisted private company formed from the assets of a previously state-owned battery factory. Official turnover is about 20 million US. Official output last year was 120,000 NiMH batteries – that's N, small-I, M.H: rechargeable versions of the normal AA battery–plus maybe a million of the usual, alkaline ones you buy from a cigarette store. You will not find this out from any public source since all industrial production in Tang Lu is regarded as a state secret. However, the official figures are bullshit. In reality the plant produces almost no NiMH batteries…"

He paused for dramatic effect.

"The issue is what happens to the raw materials it does not use."

"Does this really matter?" Georgina was only voicing what the others were thinking.

"It matters," said Li. "Do you remember the EV1?"

"Who doesn't!" said Carstairs, mystifying the others. Li pressed on:

"After General Motors crushed all the EV1s – that's their self-destructed electrical car based on NiMH technology – they sold the patent for the NiMH battery. And why not in your wonderful freemarket non-corrupt capitalist system? Why not sell it to an oil company that just sits on the patent and refuses to develop the electric car?"

"Chevron took Toyota to court to stop them using these nickel batteries in an experimental version of the RAV4," said Carstairs.

"How do you know this?" Brough was irate.

Carstairs shrugged: "Common knowledge in the East End of London, mate…"

"Hold on," Georgina frowned. "I am not liking the sound of the word Chevron. Is that *the* Chevron, the one that names its oil tankers after Condoleeza Rice and hires scientists who deny global warming and *sues your fuckin' pants off* at the drop of a hat?"

"Chevron is a marginal issue," Li Qi-han continued; "Everything I'm telling you is checkable fact."

"Mr. Bo has arrived at hotel reception," Chun-li chipped in.

"So Toyota can't make these nickel batteries?" Brough's eyes probed Li's, but Li's gaze was focused into the distance, as if following some invisible moth fluttering around the room.

"Toyota?" Brough insisted.

"So nobody can make a NiMH battery without paying Chevron a fee, until 2014. However, in the meantime Toyota does two things. It becomes the world's biggest customer for Lanthanum – that's a kind of Rare Earth you need to make

NiMH – and the world's dominant supplier – to everybody else – of NiMH batteries.

"Except General Motors," said Chun-li, stunning everybody except Carstairs. She continued:

"General Motors ditches the patent for this kind of battery and instead decides to go for making a pure electrical car based on Lithium-Ion batteries. Not escaping from Rare Earth problem because Li-Ion electrical motors also need Rare Earth for magnets, but not Lanthanum element – a different element."

"Neodymium," said Brough, surprising everybody.

"Yes, but what does the Tang Lu plant do? Why is there so much pollution?" said Georgina.

"The pollution is just incidental", said Li. "It's what all battery plants produce. Chlorine gas, all kinds of other stuff." Li Qi-han leant forward like a conspirator:

"What the Tang Lu plant does is underproduce on purpose. It processes the Lanthanum to battery grade but uses maybe a tenth of its order. The rest is sold on the black market."

"Who buys it?" Brough interjected.

"One fifth of all Japanese-imported Lanthanum is black market. And that's what they admit to. There is only one global source for Lanthanum," said Li.

"So this plant is a strategic piece of trade piracy organised by the Chinese government?" said Brough.

Li's face folded into an angry scowl.

"No way! The Chinese government knows nothing about it. It's just a play: a scam by corrupt local officials. D'you think I'd be telling you this if it was part of our national strategy?"

"How can we prove it if..." But hammering on the door drowned out the end of Georgina's question.

"Urgently require interview with correspondent Brough!" shouted Mister Bo.

"Ignore that guy," Li sneered, standing up to kiss Long

Tall Daisy, who'd breezed out of the shower wearing one of the hotel's Ming-style bathrobes; "I can tell you for a fact he has come merely to offer you one hundred thousand US dollars in brand new fifties, and to threaten you with some bad Photoshop forgeries of a man with this guy's face," jerking his chin playfully at Brough, "getting ready to eat something really unhygienic out of the asshole of a naked lady."

The hammering persisted. Li produced a handwritten sheet of paper full of numbers and Chinese script.

"All I can give you are serial numbers of the batches they sent out this week. And the names of the Imp-Ex companies they deal with: destinations, quantities and types. Seems to be routed via Lebanon and Venezuela but the destination is Japan. Nobody can get documents out of the plant but these were copied by a reliable informant."

"It's not enough," said Georgina. Everybody in the room knew Georgina was right. "For one thing it does nothing to connect the Tang Lu plant with the cartel."

"There is no connection," said Li. "This is China. The cartel's the cartel, the battery plant is the battery plant. Cartel operates in Inner Mongolia; battery plant operates in Ningxia. Cartel screws the battery plant the same as it screws the legit customers, by manipulating the spot price and taking massive leveraged speculative positions. The cartel's production is supposed to go strictly into the Chinese market – in fact, if it leaks out it screws with their position. Two completely separate scams. I thought you guys knew that?"

The doleful look on their faces confirmed they did not.

"Why are you helping us?" said Georgina. "What happened to trying to kill us?"

"It's the whales," said Li, wistfully. "They've just got to be saved." And he gave Daisy a weak, earnest smile, which she returned–with spiteful eyes and a sudden loquacity:

"Those whale-killing little dwarfs with their bottle-thick spectacles, their war-crimes, their god-stealing activities and perverted manga cartoons make me sick. Their Rare Earth piracy efforts are aiding their crimes against humanity!"

PART SIX

"Imagine an iron house without windows, absolutely indestructible, with many people fast asleep inside."
Lu Xun, 1922

1

As Brough slept, the 747 left a silver trail across the lacquered sky. Below, the city of Baotou snatched a brief, shift-worker's sleep. Wide expressways, drawn pale and orange with a wet brush of streetlight, curved past vacant building lots.

The Yellow River squirmed like a fevered patient in sodden bedsheets, making its escarpments jink and twist. On its banks, the relentless pumps and sluices of Baotou vomited up acids and dyes, untreated sewage, toxins, oestrogen, dead dogs: a cruel, industrial diarrhoea.

In the heat and dark, an old woman hurried to the public toilet in a *hutong* yard behind a faceless building. Smoke the colour of dead leaves belched out of a factory chimney. A conveyor belt spat coal onto a heap the size of a town.

Behind windows latched tight against the acid air, the Internet flickered into the bright blue faces of teenage netizens typing furious insults at the world: at CNN, at the Japanese, at the International Olympic Committee, Barack Obama and Uighur separatism; or mousing through multiplayer fantasies of death and mutilation; or slipping acronymic mischief onto bulletin boards–KB, come in your mouth; LJ, gang rape; ZF, government; ZW, masturbate.

In a brothel dormitory the drunken owner hit the girls, pointlessly, through their duvets, with a leather belt. In a tin shack an exhausted peasant rolled up his bed, tied a torch to his head with string and staggered outside to root around in the soil for *pak-choi*.

The air was not cooled by the river's flow. It was baked by blast furnaces and hung heavy with the odour of coal and gasoline; the odour of 9.9% GDP growth.

And thousands of pairs of eyes peered beyond grimy windowpanes into the moonless sky, looking for something better.

2

In Brough's dream, the ghosts of Big and Frank "Lloyd" Wu appeared, right beside him in First Class. For one terrifying moment a wave of cold death passed down his spine: maybe he really *was* awake, and these were really ghosts? But then he remembered he had hit the gin and tonic hard just after takeoff and popped a Valium, so it was just a hallucination, and he chilled out.

"You guys look well," he said.

"Yeah," Frank joked. "Can't believe how much better it feels to be rid of the whole white blood-cell issue."

"You feel a sudden lightness." Big Wu's jokes were always grim and deadpan.

Brough was too embarrassed to ask why they were dead, but Frank saved him the trouble.

"Think the cops had an order from higher up: make it all go away."

"That could have been my fault," Brough said.

"No mate," Big Wu clapped an immaterial hand on his shoulder, "not your problem. Tell you the truth it's a bit of a result. Me and him had, between us, a couple of years left, maximum. This way we go down as martyrs, not cancer victims, as long as somebody remembers to tell our story."

"That interview I did with you...the SD card...it's lost..." Brough's voice faltered.

"Yeah we know!" Frank laughed the resigned laugh of the perpetually betrayed. There was a long silence.

"Can you see into the future?" Brough said finally.

"No. We only see what's around us. We can zip about a bit though – we're actually travelling at 600 kilometres an hour just to keep up with you. And the information flow on this side is much better than on yours."

"You planning to haunt me forever?"

"No," Frank said sternly: "We'll be haunting some poor bugger in the State Security Police once we trace the chain of command."

"Are you in purgatory?

"Nah," said Big Wu; "What it is – here in China at any rate – is that it's the *unquiet* spirits who have to float around for a bit, avenging themselves and causing mayhem. After 20 years or so you can try and pass to the underworld: some have to hang around a lot longer, depending on what happened to them, and what they did. All that spirit money and incense people burn to speed things up makes no difference. It's all bollocks as far as we can make out – mind you, nobody tells you anything: there's no induction course, no St. Peter with his trumpet – and no God, of course."

"Can you help me out with my story?"

"Already did, didn't we?" said Big Wu.

"I mean," Frank butted in, "what exactly is your story? Our story is about social justice. Rare Earth's just a side issue. So, China has a monopoly on Rare Earth? It's not our fault. We didn't invent Rare Earth – we just sat and watched while the rest of the world decided to become dependent on the stuff."

"But the cartel. How high up does it go; how do I put names to faces?"

"We can certainly do that. We were haunting those guys all the way through lunch."

"You were there?"

"They don't care whether your cameraman got their faces on tape. They've paid enough bribes, got too many officials paying peppercorn rents on penthouses, plus whole hard drives full of snapshots of Party leaders having illicit sex – nobody's going to bust the cartel."

"I still need the names," Brough insisted.

Frank reeled off a list of names and descriptions. Brough, reasoning he was in a dream anyway, decided to memorise it all instead of struggling with pencil and paper.

"Does the name Khünbish mean anything to you?"

"Does Vladimir Putin have a personal trainer?" Frank chuckled. "Where does he fit in?"

There was a metallic bong and the fasten-seatbelts sign went on, together with the cabin lights. Big and Frank vanished.

Brough awoke–though the transition from dreaming to waking seemed suspiciously slight–gripped with a feeling of cold grief.

3

Allegro Harp had personalised his hotel room, eight floors up from Wangfujing Street, by replacing the shades on his bedside lamps with red, Chinese paper ones. He had created a shrine in his bathroom out of ornamental pebbles stolen from a fountain in the hotel lobby and scented candles purchased from the Wangfujing branch of Chanel. He had installed his MacBook, a pair of speakers and a connection box for the card readers and hard drives that cluttered his dressing table. He was now sitting in his gym shorts and a South Park T-shirt, hair nappy with sleeplessness, fingers flying over the Mac's keyboard, sipping vodka and Red Bull.

It was 11:45 Beijing time, 3:45 in London, and still last night in Times Square. There were six hours to go until deadline. They would finish Brough's report by early evening and FTP the file to Shanghai to be played into the studio recording of *Live At Nine*.

Brough was perched on the edge of Allegro's bed, Georgina had commandeered the armchair to look over their shoulders, Chun-li sat crosslegged against the bed headboard. Carstairs, in his own room, slept.

"Just a few more minutes," Allegro was pulling and pushing

blocks of video around in the timeline of FinalCutPro, trance-like, as he had been since they'd dumped the rushes on him three hours ago. He had a look on his face that seemed to blame the rest of the room's occupants for existing.

Allegro's method was to do a "rough assemble" of the pictures and make the reporter write the script to that. Other people did it different – some starting from script, others edging their way through, scene by scene, as in the days of tape. But it didn't matter. If you used Allegro, and wanted to get three days' work done in a single afternoon, you worked Allegro's way.

The land line rang. Allegro's middle finger zapped out from the Mac and hit the speakerphone button. It was Twyla in Shanghai.

"Hiya guys! Hear you got some great material for me there!"

"Hi-ii," Georgina sang, letting her eyes go bright. She had, on arrival in Beijing, procured the power-wardrobe of a female exec: black, flared pinstripe trousers, pointy shoes, boxy jacket. Twyla's voice announced:

"Now we're gonna be joined on conference call in a moment by Jacob Zacarelli of our legal advisory firm, Klein, Burgerlich & Kunz LLP. Jake is in New York. Hi Jake!"

"Hey you guys, it's a lovely spring evening here and the Mets just lost three-one to the Pirates!"

This jovial exchanged confirmed that Jake Zacarelli's purpose was to destroy Brough's report.

"Whaddya have for us, David?" Brough could feel Twyla manipulating the situation even over speakerphone.

"Just wait one minute and I'll play it to ya," Allegro yelled. "There'll be no track of course, only an Allegro Harp director's commentary."

Allegro's method, legendary in the business, was to lay his own commentary, suggesting scriptlines for the reporter over the pictures he had chosen.

"I think it best if I just make notes at this point rather than stopping the tape or raising problems as we go." Zaccarelli's voice was laden with helpfulness.

"Jake's a wizard at Chinese media law," Twyla's tinny voice enthused. "There's apparently a defamation law we've gotta be aware of? Local officials have been known to sue people who file complaints against them?"

"Chinese media just ignore this law," said Chun-li into her notebook.

"Ready to go," Allegro sang, pulled the phone speaker over to his Mac and hit the spacebar. On a two-inch window, a miniature version of the rough-cut began to roll.

It opened with shots of smokestacks belching steam and pollution above the skyline of Shizuishan.

"We're seeing a rustbelt skyline," Georgina shouted.

From the Mac's speaker came Allegro's voice:

"So here's where you put your doom-laden track about the pollution threat in China."

Everyone except Chun-li jiggled with mirth.

The scene switched to tracking shots they'd taken as they'd crossed the Yellow River.

"And here's where you explain the Yellow River is fuckin' doomed!"

Shots of Old Mister Jin poking at the soil with his hoe:

"So save the planet or this peasant gets it!"

Now a Chinese bureaucrat with hair the consistency of a slug's flesh was speaking. They'd filmed him on the first day.

"Ay-and," Allegro pointed a finger at Chun-li: "Cue translation!" And he hit pause.

Flustered, she flipped through her notebook:

"Chinese official, Yinchuan farm bureau: We are doing everything we can to conserve water, and develop the economy scientifically in harmony with nature."

With the timeline paused Georgina leant toward the phone: "Anything so far?"

"Have to see the actual smokestacks at the start of the piece," Jake replied. "Make sure we're not suggesting those particular factories might be emitting pollution."

"Carry on," said Twyla.

The dusk-lit shots of Tang Lu Nickel Metal Hydride's chimneys came into view.

"Now meet the victims," Allegro's commentary resumed. The editing style became urgent: it was the scene in Tang Lu East Village: the woman in a silk coat complaining, the old man gagging for breath, Busybody Guo turning up with her hatchet face. Then Brough's piece to camera with the cloud of white gas rolling in behind him.

Brough looked at the man speaking from the screen. He seemed to understand so much less then than he did now.

"That's the bit I told you about," Georgina bawled at the speakerphone.

"Okay we need to go in detail through the translation and…"

"Ay-and here's the bit where you put all your pathetic little corporate, ass-kissing caveats so's the sequence is fair and balanced," crooned Allegro's voiceover, against the wide shots of Tang Lu. They heard both Twyla and Jake make an effort to produce laughter.

"Now this stuff here," it was a sequence Carstairs had snatched in the theme park, with quad bike action on a long lens against the rippling desert, "I think is freakin' awesome. Basically you could write all kinds of stuff here about China: you got these rich mo-fos," Allegro was speaking live now, not from the machine, "and this gorgeous landscape. This weird, dead, merry-go-round. I mean wow. Poetic. I've left it loose for now – there's shitloads…"

They watched as the quad bikes zipped, camels chewed, and the wind whipped the synthetic manes of carousel horses.

"We're looking at really nice pictures here," Georgina told the speakerphone. "Great landscapes of desert, sky, lots to write about desertification. I think it allows us to put the other stuff into context and present...hold on a minute, what's this?"

Brough had put his hands together, as if praying, right in front of his mouth, which had dropped open.

"Oh my god," said Chun-li.

Flickering, grainy, and with timecode burned into the bottom right-hand corner, there was Big Wu pointing out of a soot-blackened window.

"Man points at factory he does not like," Allegro's commentary continued. A shaky setup shot of Brough and Big Wu peering at a poster of the Periodic Table.

"Man spills da beanz on ba-ad factory."

Big Wu's pixellated face began to speak:

"We've been operating illegally since 2005 with the full knowledge of the Inner Mongolian authorities. We're pretty sure most of the blood cancers are linked to the use of acids in the production process."

"Stop!" Georgina shouted.

"Er, what is the name of that, er, interviewee?" Jake queried.

"You know what, man, your camera technique sucks," Allegro told Brough, hitting the pause.

"We'll call you back," said Georgina.

After a glare from Georgina, which Brough met with a series of shrugs, Allegro explained:

"It just came back. I did what you tol' me. I stuck the flash card into the reader. Zilch. I ran my diagnostics on it. Zilch. I leave it there with this de-scrambling programme running in background and about an hour into the edit, it comes back to life. Bing! A whole bunch o' files. Take a look!"

He hit the enter button and Brough saw the Cancer Village footage tile, sequence by sequence, across the computer screen.

"Something else very strange also happened," said Chun-li. "Last night I deleted 108 text messages from my cellphone emanating from that deceased crazy person. Now every one's been restored."

"And now you mention it," Allegro grinned, "all the porn I deleted before I brought the Mac through customs has re-appeared as well!"

4

"Okay you've seen that footage: is it a story or is it not?"

Brough and Georgina were striding side by side along a hotel corridor too long to see the end of, orange microfibres flying off the carpet and sticking to their legs.

"Yes," said Georgina finally.

"So I'm pleading with you: help me get it on screen."

She stopped and stared at her trousers.

"What the fuck is it with this carpet!" She started brushing the static-charged fibres with her hands, staggering backwards against the wall for balance. The fresh paint on the dado rail left a vermilion stripe across her jacket.

"What's wrong with this place?"

"You've got to stand up to them. Those pictures–you ever seen anything like that come out of China?"

"It's not me," she replied, through her teeth, jabbing at the paint stain with a rolled-up Kleenex. He went on:

"All they want is a manufactured, fake, secondary, useless, pre-scripted, tiny …thing! … to confront the Chinese government with. That's right isn't it?"

"But this Rare Earth cartel story? Shit like that doesn't work in VT. You old newspaper guys never get it: television tells one story at a time."

He fantasised about strangling her. Then he said:

"I think those two guys are dead, you know: the ones that get led away by the riot cops at the end."

"You don't know that for sure."

"Alright, let's track them down. Let's get Chun-li on the case..."

"Did he sign an affidavit?"

Brough stopped walking and stared at her blankly.

"Did this Big Wu guy, the interviewee, did he sign anything? And is there any documentary evidence that what he says is true? We're not talking about the *News of the World* here, we're not allowed to just make stuff up: we've got a public duty..."

"This could be really good. You could be the news queen of lower fucking Manhattan in no time with this on your CV."

"Listen, David, don't worry about my career..." she let the thought trail off into the hostile silence.

It lasted a long time. Eventually Brough realised something:

"What? They're going to sack me? Fuckin-A, that's what I say to that. This is this, Stanley," and he used the USB stick to do an impression of Robert De Niro holding up a bullet in *The Deer Hunter*. "This ain't something else, this is this."

"I hope you've never said anything detrimental about Mahmoud Ahmadinejad!" she was shouting now, arms folded tight around her chest. "Because if Channel Ninety-Nine lets you go, the only network that's going to touch you with a bargepole is Iranian state TV."

He stuck his hands into his pockets and began striding along the corridor, she half a step behind him.

"What if..." he began. But his mind had already begun computing the consequences of being sacked. He'd bought his apartment at the peak of the property bubble and was already in negative equity. Before that he'd lost tens of thousands in the dotcom crash, and his retirement income was dependent on four or five scraps of private pension plan, each with its own minor, value-destroying defect. Only his deftness at expenses scams left him in the black at the end of each month, and he lived in dread of the January tax deadline.

On top of that, there was the issue of television. The Channel's global audience was close to half a million at 9pm; they'd grown it from nothing in a straight fight with AJ and CNN. Shireen may have been discovered on a talent show, and need all foreign names spelled out phonetically on the autocue, but she was a natural. Twyla, serially sacked by every American network, had a world-class talent for manipulating stories and people.

Brough's elbows had rubbed all too often, at the bar of the Basra Lounge, with those of print journalists whose column inches had been shrunk to the point where the story was impossible to tell; or documentary filmmakers whose masterpieces would only be viewed at an anarchist cinema on Tyneside. Television, to Brough, was a drug and – as with all addicts – not being on it sounded a lot worse than being on it just a little bit.

"What if," he began again, "we just show the Cancer Village factory, play the clip from Big Wu, put a massive balancing statement over a Leni Riefenstahl-job depicting clean, unpolluted Beijing. Jimmy could nip out now and shoot it. Qualify the whole thing by saying nothing is corroborated but it leaves the government with questions to answer. Pre-warn the bastards by playing them the clip…"

"I'm not liking the flippant reference to Leni Riefenstahl but go on," Georgina struggled to suppress the triumph in her voice.

They rounded the angle of the corridor. Their path was blocked by a team of carpet layers and painters, one lot painting the walls as the others unrolled fresh carpet. Beyond them, electricians were powerdriving cables into bare concrete as the shell of a new hotel wing took shape.

"Okay," Brough took a long breath. "No riot cops, no arrests. No piece to camera on a barricade. Just a factory and an allegation, the clear Beijing sky, peach blossoms. 'Can China's government manage the vast challenge of cleaning up its industry in the midst of economic downturn?'," he imitated himself: "Only time will tell."

5

By late afternoon they had whittled it down to the essentials. The Tang Lu pollution episode would stay in, but all reference to, and identifiable shots of, the Nickel Metal Hydride plant would be removed. The complainants never named it, Zaccarelli argued; that's to our advantage. There would be a long sequence on desertification, using a montage of the Kubuqi sand dunes and some library footage of the Gobi desert, which would be dropped in at the Shanghai end.

Finally a generic reference to the many villages suffering pollution problems, plus a setup of Big Wu and his 20-second clip. Then, over freshly shot footage of Brough and Chun-li in the hotel room trying to call the Cancer Village management office, and the clear sound of the answering machine, the words: "Channel Ninety-Nine attempted to put these allegations to the management at the factory, but they did not return our calls."

Finally shots of Beijing in springtime, the soft blue of the sky, student lovers riding their bikes side by side, holding hands. Peach blossom. Only time will tell.

"Okay, now everybody gettoutahere and let me work my magic," Allegro ordered.

"I feel like I need to take a shower," said Brough.

6

He headed for the hotel bar, a subterranean cave with indigo lights whose predominant textures were black Artex and fur. The fur was white and bristled against his ears as two tall Chinese waitresses dressed in rabbit-skin bikinis steered him, coercively, towards a bar-stool.

"What I can't work out," said Carstairs, who was already sitting there fingering the rim of a $50 gin and tonic, "is how The Carpenters became such a global phenomenon."

On a cramped stage, a bikini-clad chanteuse, backed by a tawdry duo on Roland FP-7 and electric bass, was chugging through *I Won't Last A Day Without You*. Brough ordered a $25 beer and spotted Chun-li threading her way, eyes to the floor, between tables of shaven-headed British engineers, fat Americans in shorts and some sleazeballs resembling John Cazale. He ordered her a glass of date juice and an ice cube.

Chun-li, who had changed into a don't-mess-with-me outfit of white blouse/tan skirt, drew stares of derision from the barmaid, which turned into outright hostility when she ordered the television to be switched from basketball to news and haggled the price of the juice down to a few Chinese yuan.

"Well here's to you, Chun-li."

Brough felt raw. Once a report was in the can the adrenaline always drained away, leaving only the emotions he'd gone through to produce it.

"Hey and here's to you mate!" Carstairs grinned at him. "Nearly died laughing when I realised you'd legged it into the desert. And you, young Beretta lady, we should probably get you an honorary membership at the Basra Lounge!"

"And here is to great journalistic team of Brough and Carstairs," she mocked her own accent; "greatly sabotaged by Georgina, aided by mysterious forces, completing mission to expose corruption in Western China! Oh no…"

Something on the TV screen had made her face go sickly. The newscaster was speaking: behind her the back-projection pictured a familiar industrial skyline. Next, the bulletin switched to a live outside broadcast: aerial shots of a large industrial complex and a female reporter trilling like a songbird.

"That's whatshername!" said Carstairs.

Hyacinth Deng, dressed in a smart red chemise with matching lipstick, now leant into a brisk walking shot: she was making her way into a dusty *hutong*, camera following her on the shoulder. The place looked familiar.

"What's she saying?" Brough whispered. Chun-li gabbled a translation:

"Here in Tang Lu East Village pollution been a problem many years. Now residents win campaign for less pollution and movement of entire community to new homes."

In the street there was a crowd, fronted by Busybody Guo, who began lecturing Hyacinth. Chun-li translated:

"For years, says boss-lady Guo, we had to live next to this pollution coming from factory but thanks to tireless efforts by editor of *Tang Lu Daily* (founded 1958), local government have finally agreed to move residents."

Now it panned to a two-shot of Editor Sheng flanked by

Commerce Secretary Zhou, both smiling expansively. Sheng made a bland statement, acknowledging the factory's world-class safety record but pointing to the poor standard of the housing and explaining how concerned the residents have become.

Chun-li's phone was buzzing. It was a text from Georgina. Had she seen what was on the TV news?

Now Commerce Secretary Zhou explained that the factory has already cleaned up 56.9% of its pollution, consistently beating the targets set by central government, and was now in transition to carbon-neutral production through an offsetting scheme to plant saplings in the middle of the Kubuqi Desert. He was pleased to announce that the first two families had been moved out already. There was no sign of the grey-faced man or the silk-jacket woman.

Now Hyacinth Deng spun around, with her back to the Tang Lu Nickel Metal Hydride chimneys, standing just where Brough had stood for his piece to camera.

She checked her watch. It was five past seven – "the time when a cloud of steam is emitted every night", she confided chattily to the camera.

"The local people know it is harmless, because chlorine gas is scientifically proven to dissolve within 440 seconds of emission. But they will be very happy to move to a more salubrious neighbourhood, to live a healthier life."

She cracked a joke with the presenter in the studio, which struck Brough as very slick.

The white cloud approached over her shoulder and Hyacinth, giggling, gave a wink to the crowd, who could not resist her fizzy smile and give an equally effervescent cheer as the cloud engulfed her.

"Text message from Georgina. May have to re-edit our piece," Chun-li's voice had become lifeless. "That's why never pre-warn Chinese officials about story."

"Is this out of the textbook too?" The beer had made Brough lightheaded.

"Chapter 19," Chun-li said flatly.

"Is there a Chapter 20?"

She let her face go blank and sighed, coming as close as Brough had ever seen her to despair.

7

The heat on Wangfujing Street was fierce despite the dark, like somebody holding a hair dryer to the small of his back. Brough strode quickly – past sixty-foot LED screens flickering with dreams of social harmony and mobile telephony; past the tourist choo-choo train with a cartoon face and robotic jingle; past the street girls who stood beneath the silver birch trees launching smiles, sighs and hip-swings at him with an intensity he had only experienced before on the Malecon, in Havana.

He had gone to the men's toilet in the hotel bar and decided to not come back. No reporter equals no re-edit.

He needed to kill time. He saw golden arches and an arrow indicating a 24-hour McDonald's somewhere inside a shopping mall. He sprinted up the steps, but not fast enough to evade a girl in Adidas shorts who tagged behind him.

"Sir do you speak English, what country are you from–is it maybe Sweden?"

He carried on upwards, striding two steps at a time, which she mimicked with her own scrawny legs, catching up with him.

"Sir..."

"Why are you asking me that question?"

She shrugged and strode past him, legs first, into the McDonald's strip-light, looking for somebody else to hit on, but finally settling into the corner with her friend, similarly dressed, both flashing him regular sideways glances.

He approached the counter and pointed to a quarterpounder-with-cheese on the picture menu they held up. Within a few seconds it was on a tray under his nose, smelling Western, greasy, assembled hours ago.

He picked a two-seat table put there for sad parties of exactly half that number. The Coke tasted like shit, as it always does. He picked the gherkins out of the burger: they were hard and fresh, not soft and pickled like at home. He ate a stone-cold salt-sodden french-fry. He bit a semicircular chunk out of the burger. There was some kind of chili sauce in there, which dripped down onto the table.

There was a text on his phone from Georgina:

"R U there?"

And an earlier one.

"Come back 2 room. Need 2 re-track."

He switched the phone to divert-all-calls. They would need to re-track if they wanted to acknowledge the massive counter-claim implied in Hyacinth Deng's propaganda piece.

In a rare departure from his usual chaotic mode of operation, Brough had persuaded Allegro to download everything: the whole of Carstairs' rushes, his own Cancer Village shots, Li Qi-han's recording of Xiao's bribery attempt plus – an added bonus – Chun-li's secret recording of Li Qi-han's confession in the hotel bedroom, done sneakily on her mobile phone and only revealed that afternoon, and only to Brough. He had on the USB stick now enough material for a 15-minute film on the whole story, plus a feature article in the *New Yorker* or some such upmarket outlet.

He would start pitching first thing tomorrow. Right now there were only three ways of dealing with that Hyacinth Deng report.

You stick to your guns and expose the Chinese TV report for what it is: a whitewash job. Or you bottle out and acknowledge it as a valid counter-claim. The third way is you get Zaccarelli to rule your whole report legally indefensible, remove any reference to chlorine and tacitly accept the Chinese version of the story. By the time he was halfway through the quarterpounder, Brough was pretty sure which one of these options Georgina would take.

But if Brough was gone and could not be found that only left a fourth option: run the piece as made. Failing that, bin it, leaving a seven-minute hole in the programme and the channel looking "like cunts" – as the industry parlance puts it – for failing to cover the environmental issue.

A woman rustled past his table in tracksuit bottoms, a petrol-blue silk jacket, large diamond crucifixes hanging from each ear and clumpy heels: she paid no attention to Brough, McDonald's, nor any one of the Chinese nighthawks slumped over the greasy tabletops. She sat down at the table next to Brough's, pushing her hair off an oversized pair of sunglasses, and began to poke at a McFlurry with a pink spoon. She did this with such delicacy and intelligence that Brough was mesmerised. He began, in his mind, to construct a life for this lonely and beleaguered woman.

After a minute she turned to Brough and peered at him through the narrow gap between her fringe and spectacles:

"S'matter? We all look the same to you now or sumpin'?"

It was Miss Lai.

"Is this a coincidence?"

"Oh sure – frickin' MBAs from NYU, yep, we come here all the time weeknights jus'ter study the micro-economic synergy between the sex industry and fast food."

Her voice had become sharper, angrier than he'd remembered it.

"What happened to you?"

"Huh!" She slid onto the seat facing his. "Impounded the

Chiang-Jiangs. It's gonna take us weeks to get that stuff back. Cartel's lying low right now in any case. Once the mothership flies in, the lights go off – just like the end scene in *Close Encounters*. You get your story?"

"I've got a bad feeling about what happened to the leaders of that strike."

"Yup. This is China. Jumping off buildings is like the new Olympic sport. You finished?"

He tried to catch her gaze through the iridium sheen of her sunglasses.

"Your report? Did it go out yet?"

Brough explained that Chinese TV had just put out a blatant propaganda job conflicting with his report on key details and that the text messages alerts pinging and buzzing out of his shirt pocket were the sound of his managers panicking.

"So what? Just ignore Chinese TV. They put out one version of the truth, you put out another. Nobody cares. You're Western: no Chinese people gonna believe your story; no Westerners gonna believe Chinese TV. You mention Rare Earth much?"

"Tried to."

"The report mentions Rare Earth, right?" She flipped her sunglasses onto her head.

"What are you doing tonight?"

"Ha!" she shouted "You askin' me for a date, Mister date-o-birth Nineteen Sixty Four?"

The two street girls in the corner stopped guzzling the dregs of milkshakes and laughed out loud.

"No!" he whispered. "I am asking if you know anywhere I can go to stop these guys tracking me down."

He held up his cellphone, which now had anxious texts from Georgina, Chun-Yi, Allegro, Twyla and even one from a U.S. number saying: "Mr Brough we need urgently to communicate. J. Zaccarelli."

Miss Lai snatched the phone from his hand and flipped it through the air to the girls in the corner, who shouted something in Chinese that made her laugh.

"You're a dog-fuckin' cheapskate, according to them." Lai sniggered and in a mock Chinese accent: "Why you no have iPhone? Oh I forgot," she rummaged in her bag and pulled out his Blackberry, which she slid across the table with a midnight-blue fingernail.

"Your cellphone got stolen. You got mugged in Mai-Dong-Lau. You got took to Nancy Kiang…"

"What?"

"That's your story – they can't fire you on account-a getting rolled by two purty girls in short-shorts…" She swished out of her seat and let her glasses slide down, precariously, to the tip of her nose.

"Rolled?" said Brough, puzzled.

"Oh yeah, sorry, I forgot!"

And she aimed a back-hand strike at Brough's forehead, too light for brain damage but whippy enough so that the diamonds in the skull ring she was wearing drew blood, which Brough had to stare at for a few seconds, smeared across his fingers, before working out that he should probably say next:

"And who exactly is Nancy Kiang?"

8

The bouncers at the Nancy Kiang Club are legendary: *wing-chun* trained, obviously, but banned from pumping iron or developing that hard-staring eye that thugs at the wiry end of body morphology use to compensate for lack of bulk. In their Nehru shirts and Marc Jacobs sandals they reminded Brough of the busboys at some boutique hotel in Tribeca.

This being Wednesday, and before midnight, there was a mixed gay-straight Chinese crowd downstairs taking a Lindy Hop class, sipping blue martinis in a Deco ballroom salvaged more or less whole from Canadian Pacific's ill-fated cruise liner *RMS Empress of China*.

"Hiya chica!" The maitre de, a guy wearing skin products and dressed head to foot in Armani black, caught Lai's waist as they crossed on the sweeping staircase.

"Longtaaaaym. You wanna booth or you goin' alfresco? And," stylus poised over a handheld electronic guest list, "your friend's name is?"

Lai whispered something to him and he made a face at her signifying the word "ghastly".

They reached a roof garden themed like a 1930s brothel

in Shanghai: dotted with palms, strewn with opium couches, lit by lampstands of polished steel. On the low sofas Western women lounged who were a shade too blonde and tanned; and taut-skinned Western guys flashing twenty-thousand-dollar chronographs from beneath their Lanvin cuffs.

Lai pointed out the global finance director of a major bank, the entire corporate social responsibility team of a luxury car marque, three Italian soccer players of declining skill and their Malaysian girlfriends, a famous Parisian dee-jay, a minor Eurocrat and his two boyfriends, the Russian military attaché, plus three undercover Venezuelan ladies getting ready for their mid-week group-sex encounter with some Colombian anti-aircraft guys.

Subtly interspersed with the Westerners were svelte Chinese women, lithe young Chinese men and – rare, hardly participating in the glamour, almost fading into the gloom–the avuncular faces of middle-aged Chinese businessmen: agents and fixers for Western firms, discreet go-betweens for the CCP and Western capitalism.

Oh, and an ill-dressed, wan-faced table full of lost-looking expat Western journalists.

"Well I never, Davey Brough! My word! What have you done to your head? And who's your friend?"

In the alabaster glow Brough could only just make out Terence Stansgate's face, but his strangulated English accent was unmistakeable.

"I *heard* you were in Beijing!" said Stansgate. "Heard you scooped the whole Beijing press corps with a story about some *preposterous* substance called Rare Earth! Come and sit down, matey, with your charming companion…"

Stansgate introduced a mousy English girl who was the Beijing correspondent for an American newspaper, a South African bruiser and his Aussie buddy who were camera crew for a news agency and already leering-drunk, a Swedish shoot-producer working for an Arab TV network; and–as politely as possible–their various

Chinese companions, gay and straight, male and female. Miss Lai drawled politely at them in Mandaringlish, stressing crucial terms like "web-two-zero" and "seedcapital", picking the flesh off a langoustine that the maitre de had personally delivered, sizzling, together with a slipper of Krug in a diamante ice bucket, compliments of the house.

"They like *you* here," said Stansgate.

"My dad commands, like, a whole division in the PLA?" said Miss Lai, gaily.

"In the north?" Stansgate let the outside of one eyebrow rise a millimetre, indicating a subtextual question only a true Beijinger should understand.

"In the south," said Miss Lai, letting her own perfectly plucked eyebrow arch to indicate a subtextual answer. At least Brough would not have to waste time playing the perpetual foreign correspondent's guessing game about the local press corps, known as Which One Is The Spy?

Brough's Blackberry, its email clogged with messages he would read when he cared about the world again, had been bleeping to signal the arrival of new texts ever since he'd fired it up: jokes from his mates in England about football and politics; "welcome to the network" junk. He glanced at it now to check the time. It was 20:30 local, half an hour until they would have to record the show. There was a message from Chun-li.

"David. Please reply. Major problems. Help."

"Why am I here?" he mumbled to Miss Lai's ear, pouring himself a second flute of champagne.

"Gotta introduce you to some people. Maybe have to take you down to the Toi-kish Bath later and, y'know, have another try at, y'know, getting the trigger sequence right on, well, y'know…"

His Blackberry rang. It was Chun-li.

"How did you know to ring me on this?" He spoke sotto voce.

"Georgina leave the hotel one hour ago to meet you in McDonald's but instead her credit cards get stolen by two young girls. Also punched in nose and clothing ripped." There was a quiet laugh in Chun-li's voice. "So logical conclusion is that motorbike lady has returned into your life and restored possession of your Blackberry."

"Hey honey my guests are arriving we gotta go join 'em," Miss Lai squirmed next to him.

"Be very careful with motorbike lady," said Chun-li.

"I will."

9

Miss Chi had arranged her hair into a 1940s-style French braid and wore a vintage polka-dot dress that ended not far below her waist, with nothing but legs between that and a pair of orange Puma trainers. Miss Lai, losing the silk tunic on a visit to the bathroom and at the same time acquiring a persistent sniffle, was showing a bare midriff, sapphire navel stud and white leather brassiere. All this amounted to a clear semiological statement that, once the business part of the evening was over, they would be going to some place even cooler than Nancy Kiang for drugs and Dubstep, and minus Brough.

Brough sat wedged between them, in an alcove, feeling like a character from a time-travel comedy: wearing the wrong clothes for the era and being the human vehicle for somebody else's joke.

Four young Chinese men had joined them, also clad for clubbing. They had that muscle-bound sullen confidence Brough recognised from rich-kid rowing types in England: square jaws, sprawled limbs, eyes dazed in wonder at the world and in ignorance of their own naivete. They explained to Brough in languid American English their various unique and promising attributes; their degree specialties, dance-music tastes, favourite holiday destinations, love of Ayn Rand and Spotify; hatred of France, CNN and Amnesty International.

Kid One broached the subject of Rare Earth with Brough, hearing on the grapevine that he had run into trouble out West and hoping that everything was going to be OK. Kid Two detailed his father's stock-brokering business in Macao. Kid Three ventured the opinion that "not enough was known" in the West about the sheer scale of the Chinese "position" in the global Rare Earth supply chain. Kid Four offered Brough the use of his father's villa up by the Great Wall, architect-designed and with a heated open-air lap pool, should he ever stray up that way.

Brough told them the story of Tang Lu and explained how Chinese TV had just simultaneously scooped and sabotaged his story. They, in response, tended to nod and gaze in an eye-dulled awe at Lai and Chi, and at Brough, and at the clientele of Nancy Kiang, swapping the occasional homophobic sneer with each other in Mandarin.

At 20:58 he glanced at his Blackberry to find a warning from Chun-li, followed by messages from both Twyla and Georgina and a note of commiseration from Allegro Harp.

Georgina's read: "You are officially sacked. Dickhead."

Twyla's said: "Pls read ur email. V disappointed in U."

Allegro's said: "Sorry they made me do it, love ya!"

Chun-li, in a comprehensive email, explained the situation:

"David, Urgent problems here. Twyla insisted that report goes into programme so Georgina forcing Allegro to find individual words from outtakes of your tracking lines to make new script. Sounds like a robot speaking but is Allegro, expert at sound editing and has forced Georgina to grant him a major cash bonus to make track sound natural. Script now very cowardly. Piece to camera in Tang Lu removed. Also Mr. Wu no longer featured. Take care. Chun-li."

The champagne was making Brough's eyes swim already so

when he burst out laughing he was not surprised also to feel tears run down his cheeks.

"What?" said Miss Lai.

"I've been sacked by text message."

There was immediate consternation among Kids One-Through-Four and an instant six-way Mandarin shouting competition.

"OK Mister Brough you are so not helping us here," Miss Chi pinned him with a haughty stare. "Are you, like, saying here that the Rare Earth report will not go out? They nixed the report?"

Brough shook his head.

"They've doctored the report but it will go out. They've sacked me for refusing to play a part in my own self-censorship. Why do you care?"

There was another cacophony with the rich kids, at the end of which everyone fell silent and stared at Brough, as if expecting him to pronounce on something massive.

"What?"

Lai grabbed his arm. Chi, beneath the table, laid a languid hand on his crotch and let her curls drape onto his shoulder.

"Ha," giggled Miss Chi, "the boys here just got a little jumpy on account of the high stakes involved, but you can assure them, right, that the profile of the Rare Earth issue will rise dramatically in the West once your report goes out?"

"Oh yes," Brough gasped as Chi jabbed a finger into his testicles; "dramatically".

10

Once, in a futile attempt to teach him transcendental meditation, a girlfriend had introduced Brough to the concept of "awake without thinking". Later, on a balcony ledge in Kirkuk, pissed out of his brain in the moonlight and trying to teach the Elephant & Castle Style of *tai-chi* to a video-journalist called Narciso Pirandello, they had together reinvented the concept as "drunk without slurring".

The idea was to be so drunk, preferably on a single type of alcohol, that your senses became wide open, alert to the world—including its manifold subtexts, secret pheromonal messages, fleeting refusals of eye contact and the trajectory of incoming artillery shells.

It was in this state that Brough excused himself and staggered to the bathroom, not without a smile in honour of Narciso, shot in the head in Baghdad a few weeks later. In his drunk-without-slurring mode Brough had managed to figure out that Chi and Lai were working some kind of scam – on, or with, Kids-One-Through-Four—and that it involved his report. The sound-system in the club was playing that kind of pointlessly hip, French

Cocktail Disco that made him long to sit down with a pint of bitter and a Pogues CD.

The bathroom was heavily populated with Chinese sex-workers, male and female, being simultaneously both a toilet and the male changing room for the Turkish bath. Brough placed an obstinate palm in the way of advancing male helpers, shrugged his shoulders to dislodge the hands of a woman who was trying to give him a muscle rub, and lurched towards a urinal.

Seconds later, Terence Stansgate arrived at the adjoining stall.

"We can't go on meeting like this, matey," Stansgate began.

"Got any jobs going at your place?" Brough snorted.

"Ah. Has there been unpleasantness at Channel Ninety-Nine?"

"You could say that. They've fucked me over with my story."

"Your big mistake," Stansgate sighed, they were both staring straight ahead into the wall; "was trying to do an actual story. Everybody tries. I did, once."

He paused.

"What you've got to understand is that there is only one story in China and that's the China story. It's like a Mandelbrot thingy: deeper you go, crank up the microscope, you just get the same pattern, over and over again. And the terrifying thing is: to really understand it you have to think like them. And once you do that it suddenly dawns on you…"

"What dawns on you," Brough zipped his fly and struggled to clear his brain.

"That they are right. That human rights *should* come second to economic development. That our democracy *is* just as corrupt as theirs only they, naive little souls, don't bother disguising it – No thank you!" he snapped at an attendant sidling toward them with an eau-de-cologne spray as they began to leave.

Brough looked despondent. Stansgate placed a hearty heterosexual arm across his shoulders and shook him.

"Theory is, though, you'll be minted after tonight. Minted, isn't that the word?"

"What do you mean?"

Brough's drunk-without-slurring powers were allowing him to pick up all kinds of innuendoes in Stansgate's voice, which made what he said next only half surprising:

"Large trading volumes today on certain small-cap markets. Interesting patterns. Every Rare Earth mining company outside China's seen significant trading: the duff one in Australia that can't produce because of radioactive waste, the one in California that can't get finance because it's in a National Park, the Canadian one blockaded by Inuit protesters. You name it. I might put a few bob on myself, tomorrow."

"I thought," said Brough, "Rare Earth production outside China was insignificant."

"Ha ha, very good. Poker face." Stansgate tapped the side of his nose with a finger. "Insignificant until the West realises the Middle Kingdom's got them by the short and curlies and then, well, just watch the Kaiser Bottom-Fish Index move!"

"What's the Kaiser Bottom-Fish Index," said Brough, staggering backwards from the urinal towards the door.

"Ha, ha," Stansgate was swaying now as he struggled to button his fly: "Good man. Geneva Convention. I will give only name, rank and number."

11

"You!"

It was Georgina striding up the staircase, her eye-anger all the more violent for being surrounded by a mask of purple flesh.

"You did this!" she thrust her face into Brough's face, pointing at the bruises with a cracked fingernail: "I suppose those two girls got hold of your mobile phone by accident? And by the way don't think I've come here to plead with you to retrack the piece. The programme's in the can. It's finished and so are you."

Brough's reaction to female verbal abuse was always to stare into a space exactly one metre behind the complainant's eyes, and two inches above their head, and say nothing, which he did now.

"Shit, honey, what happen'd to her?" It was Miss Lai, a possessive hand gripping his arm.

"Who are you?" Georgina seethed.

"David's a good friend o' mine, this good ol' guy really kicks ass, journalistically speakin,' dontya think?"

"Yes, well." Georgina folded her arms, looked at her shoes, rocked on her heels, considering a response.

"You get my message?"

He nodded.

"Well here's another one," and Georgina hit Brough in the nose with the heel of her palm, knocking him backwards into the chest of Terence Stansgate.

"Hello Terence," Georgina's face assumed for one second a gymkhana smile and then melted back into a scowl, at Brough, who was wiping nose-blood onto his sleeve.

"What I've come for is Channel Ninety-Nine's intellectual property."

"Excuse me?" said Miss Lai, lifting her sunglasses onto her head to squint at Georgina.

"I'm sorry, this is a private matter between myself and my colleague!" and Georgina put out such strong negative vibes that it made Miss Lai, just for a second, take a step away.

"I hear you retracked my piece with bits of outtakes," Brough summoned the energy to say, but she fixed him with an unsympathetic gaze.

"Your words are the intellectual property of the Channel, as is the footage you shot while on our payroll. Likewise all the other material Allegro tells me you have copied onto your USB stick. I would like it back, and you are obligated to destroy any copies. And please don't tell me it is up your fat, melodramatic backside or I will have to ask this gentleman here to personally oversee its removal."

Brough noticed for the first time that she had brought muscle with her: a skinny Chinese guy in a black Harrington jacket standing discreetly, hands crossed over his belt buckle, two steps down the stairway. Typical TV-company cheapskate muscle.

"Ah, Georgina, may I have a word?" said Terence Stansgate and moved to put a hand on her arm, which she brushed aside, screaming into his face: "Fuck off, Terry!"

The noise on the stairway dropped like someone had punched the middle out of a graphic equaliser; only the swish of expensive clothing and the deep bass of the Lindy Hop below bracketed the silence. An Austrian banker with a transgender Sichuan hooker, two male models just in from the launch party of a major label's autumn collection, sundry waiters with trays of cocktails poised above their heads, plainclothes security men for various high-value individuals who'd been loitering invisibly, just like Georgina's low-value guy: everyone froze and stared at her.

It was Miss Lai who unfroze first, stepping into Georgina's space and gazing at her aggressively.

"Okay lemme get this clear, you claiming intellectual property rights over content originated by Mister Brough here? And would the jurisdiction for any such claim be the People's Republic of China – or maybe the registered home territory of Channel Ninety-Nine Incorporated which is, oh yeah, lemme see if my memory serves me correct, the Bahamas?"

"It's our property. Give it back."

Georgina's minder took this as a cue to step forward to just behind her, while Terry Stansgate took it as a cue to go back into the toilet and start texting his contact at the British Embassy.

Brough rummaged in his pocket for the USB stick and held it vertically between finger and thumb in the space between them.

Georgina's thug made a grab for it, which Miss Lai deftly intercepted with a block, a hold and a shove which made him spiral around his own arm through space, with a splitting sound as his acromio-clavicular joint popped.

At this everybody else scurried off the staircase, in anticipation of the arrival of Nancy Kiang's *wing-chun* guys.

"Hey honey don't ruin my evening!" called the maitre de, shimmying down the stairs in a sideways dance step.

"'s over anyways", Miss Lai flipped her shades back down and blew her fringe off her face with an upward puff of breath. "Brough, you comin' back to the party?"

But Brough and Georgina were staring each other out, like two kids in a playground.

"What did you make me say?"

"Don't worry," she laughed, with a worried glance at her writhing sidekick, "nothing disgraceful. Just took stuff out. You still see the gas cloud and the complaints. And you know what? The Chinese spokesman in the studio just said: 'we'll look into it'. We understand the problem, our own people are onto it, the re-housing should have happened months ago. Do these things happen in the West, Miss Berkowitz? That was it."

"What about Rare Earth?"

"She tried that line but nothing doing. We keep all strategic resource exports under constant review and are constantly cracking down on illegal mining as part of our Strike Hard campaign against corruption. To be honest the whole sequence was not scintillating but it ticked a box. You going to give me that thing or not?"

"You know what Georgina…" he held the USB stick just out of her reach.

"This is the truth. It's not the whole truth but it's a substantial evidential base. A cop arrests us, he tries to bribe us; a minor bureaucrat tries to kill us, we get him on tape – OK secretly but useful in any legal action – spilling the beans. It's complex: one factory is supplying contraband Rare Earth to the Japanese, another makes magnets for an illegal cartel. Then there's the nut-job in the Audi – smuggling the magnets into Russia, according to Chun-li. We're dealing with two or three different mafia groups here, and a whole load of low-level fascist coercion. Poverty, pollution, injustice. People on camera one day and the next day involuntarily committing suicide…"

Miss Lai placed her hand, gently, on his elbow as he ranted:

"When this goes out, the whole world will get a case study of how China works. The Chinese won't see it; they won't give a shit if they do see it, probably. But the whole world will know what a bunch of inhuman fuckin' thugs it is that we have to rely on to keep Walmart stacked with cheap toys and the wind-turbines turning."

He closed his fist around the USB stick, wiped his nose, and took a few weary steps up the stairway. Miss Lai, on his arm, flashed Georgina an evil glance. There were too many heavies around now for anybody to try and settle things by force.

Then he stopped, his chest heaving with outrage and turned to Georgina.

"You say this is your intellectual property?" He held the USB stick up to the light as if to taunt Georgina.

"Well, it's my story. So here…"

And he flipped it into the air, where it made a few turns through the disco-light and landed in her outstretched palms.

He would ask himself later why he'd done it, but at the time it just felt like a cool thing to do, and he let himself revel in it.

"What the fuck?" screamed Miss Lai. "You got copies, right?"

"David is trained journalist – can keep copy of information inside his head." It was Chun-li, who had slipped into the scene un-noticed, from the ladies'.

"Give me that!" Miss Lai launched herself down the stairs towards Georgina who was still clutching the USB stick in her outstretched hands, trembling. But Chun-li stepped between them, emitting a *tai-chi* forcefield that made Miss Lai stagger backwards and eventually sit down, defeated, on the velvet stair-carpet.

In the silence Chun-li pulled her phone out and read:

"Kaiser Bottom-Fish Index up 50 per cent. The KBFI, a composite share price of Rare Earth mining companies closed tonight at 1,512, up fifty per cent on the day from the thousand mark where it has hovered since the financial crisis began. Analysts note this remains significantly short of the 6,000 peak registered during the commodity price spike of 2007. Source: Metal Index Outlook 1600 GMT."

"Bingo!" said Brough to Miss Lai, thrusting his hands into his pockets and slouching down the stairs without a glance at anyone–and with only a shrug to acknowledge the presence of Chun-li beside him, her hand in the crook of his arm.

12

They took a taxi to Houhai. The moon shimmered across the lake, turning the posters on the flaking walls silver. The calligraphy, announcing the *hutong's* imminent demolition, had long since faded. Chun-li led him down a white lane criss-crossed by the moonshadows of bicycle spokes, telegraph wires, half-dead osmanthus shrubs, washing lines, old birdcages. The air was heavy, silent except for the slap of water against a stone bridge.

They turned into an alley, clambering over a pile of Qing-era roof tiles, half a rusty pram, some bags of coal. Even the masonry became crumbly, merging with the dust and dirt. At the corner of a grime-caked courtyard, Chun-li paused and drummed her nails on a window whose glass had been made grey by a century of rain.

General Guo's door creaked open. He was totally bald, a liver spot on his cheek, white stubble on his chin. He was dressed in the unofficial uniform of every old man in the world: nondescript brown trousers, checked shirt buttoned to the neck, filthy v-neck sweater and a pair of decaying slippers. He smiled with fossilised stumps of teeth and engaged Brough with an eye rich in irony.

"Do come in," he said, in the English of fifty years ago. "I shall put the kettle on. I am Guo Jie. Guo as in the Chinese word for Kingdom, Jie as in 'outstanding'. Guo Jie," he made signs with his hands for the Chinese tones.

"General Guo now aged eighty-four. Swam with Chairman Mao in Yangtse River," Chun-li's voice had become awed and breathy.

"*Is* aged eighty four, *is*, I keep telling you," Guo scolded. "Her vocabulary is excellent but she is lazy."

He brushed crumbs from an antique wooden chair and made Brough sit on it, offering Chun-li a stool to wobble on while he took his own place in a mangy armchair next to an unlit stove.

The walls were covered in paper from an era in which minor luxuries had been allowed and printing done by hand. Brough's eyes were drawn to brown photographs, cracked calligraphy scrolls, old books, a bust of Lenin, a film poster from the 1940s, a framed medal, the framed front cover of *Time* magazine featuring Zhou En-lai.

"That screen is Qing dynasty," Guo gestured with a yellow hand. A wooden screen carved with birds and dragons was all that separated the kitchen from what Brough presumed was a bedroom on the other side.

"These *hutongs* are about six hundred years old. Of course, when they were built they were open courtyards. We've filled them in over the years with these little hovels. Now they're trying to knock them down. We resist."

"Your English is remarkable, have you lived in Britain?"

"We learned it from gramophone records. In the Korean War I had the chance to confer with some officers from the Royal Marines."

"You're a general."

"I was a general in Chinese military intelligence. They retired me on the day of Hu Yao-bang's funeral. Hu was a good man…"

"Hu Yao-bang has state funeral during Tiananmen protest in eighty-nine," Chun-li interjected.

"*Had, a,* state funeral," Guo tutted.

"*Had, a,* state funeral. At which General Guo *had, a* major argument with line of soldiers attempting to keep students apart from party leadership," Chun-li chipped back.

"I have made a move since last we met," Guo interrupted her.

His eyes directed hers to the *wei-qi* board on the kitchen table where a collection of small black and white objects – pieces of tarmac, human teeth, tiny dice, nail-heads, tic-tac mints, crockery shards, washers and what seemed like a whole packet of codeine pills – were arranged across the 19x19 grid where the smooth playing stones should have been. White and black seemed to have followed each other up the left hand side of the board but were now each scattering stones at random in the top right. Chun-li's shoulders drooped as she saw he had launched an audacious raid into the heart of her corner group.

"You know about Rare Earth?" Brough said.

"Arabia has oil, China has Rare Earth – so said Deng Xiao-ping in 1992. But nobody took him seriously. Guided missiles were in their infancy and electrically powered cars a fantasy. Wind turbines…" he trailed off.

"Is it China's strategy to monopolise Rare Earth?"

"We already do."

"Is that wise? Won't it enrage the West?"

"Let me play you something," Guo reached into the drawer of a dilapidated kitchenette and pulled out a compact disc. "Maybe, Miss Cai, you can load it for me?"

Chun-li slid the disk into a grease-spattered ghetto-blaster next to the stove. She pressed play and a crackly telephone conversation began:

"Look, old fellow, I don't mean to sound like some bloody chink-basher but I seriously think they're up to something with this stuff. Shouldn't we at least do a feature on it?"

"Sorry James, everything's South Atlantic focused at the

moment; no space. Appalling downturn in ad revenue. All I can do to keep them from deploying *you* to Buenos Aires..."

Guo hit the pause button:

"*Sunday Chronicle* stringer, 1982. Very nice chap. Worked it all out. Nobody interested."

"That's a wire-tap?"

"I still have good contacts. When I heard about your exploits I ordered up the file. It's entitled: 'Rare Earth/Beijing Correspondents/1977-2002; there's a fair bit in French and German. Lots in Russian of course." He jabbed the track selector. "This one's in English, 1996:"

"But *jeez*, Bill, I mean the story sounds so hard ta tell," said a rough-edged Chicago voice.

"It couldn't be simpler," said a late-night, drunken South Carolina voice; "The slants are building a world monopoly of this stuff – cay-nt we even get a camera crew out here to film the Tianjin plant? I mean those are American jobs we're losin'?"

"Sorry Bud, the boss lost interest soon's you faxed that Periodic Table stuff – science scares 'em shitless and anyways Bill Clinton's dick is the only story in town right now, gotta go, sorry..."

"There is more," Guo chuckled. "Man from the *Times* gets a whiff of the illegal mining; woman from the *Washington Post* gets a guided tour of the Bayan Obo mine and has cataleptic vision of the future. The editors always have other priorities. I don't think yours' are being especially venal. There is thirty years worth of it on this CD – and of course, all the product gathered under the Hu administration, which is current and therefore unavailable."

"You swam with Mao?"

"He swam a lot. I never got close to him – the Yangtse's a bit unpredictable. A lot of people actually drowned in those swims you know. Mao was excellent at frog stroke."

"Do you regret what's happened to this country?" This was Brough's standard question to oldsters in post-Communist states.

"What do you regret Mr. Brough?"

"The declining quality of bitter and Sheffield Wednesday, the rise of feral youth, casual genocide, Twitter, the push-up bra, Islam getting hijacked by nutters... the list is endless."

"You want to know what I regret?" Guo let the question hang in the moist air:

"Nothing, Mr. Brough. At least three thousand lost their lives after Tiananmen, yet I regret nothing. What we've built, since, is a more or less exact re-creation of the late Qing dynasty. Do you know what I am talking about?"

"I've seen *The Last Emperor*."

"We've got a giant army that can never go to war because the officers' commissions are bought and sold by the sons of businessmen and lumpenproletarian hoodlums *pay* to join as privates. Pay! Consider that. Whole swathes of China are ungoverned: ruled by mobsters and corrupt officials just like under the Qing. At the centre is a walled palace, only it's not the Forbidden City, it's the *Zhongnanhai*, Communist Party HQ. Did you know that yesterday, in central China, three students were killed trying to save a child from drowning, because local fishermen refused to pull them out of the river? They said: there is no established price for pulling a live body out of the river, only a dead one. We have rebuilt the Qing in its entirety."

"It seems fragile."

"It is fragile, but it will not fall like the Qing for two reasons. First, the Qing were foreigners–Manchurians; the peasants hated them. Our rulers are Han Chinese – only their money is foreign. Secondly, the Qing allowed freedom of speech, and what speech! Did you know we had anarchism here in 1911, we had feminism, homosexuality? We had a literary movement inspired by Ibsen and Mallarmé."

"So now you're ruled by a bunch of people who probably think Ibsen is a Swedish sports car. What is it you don't regret?"

"In 1949 I was twenty four years old. For the next forty years

I saw irrational purges, babies eaten by dogs in village streets, starvation; floods killed millions of people. After 1989 things calmed down."

"At the price of what?"

"You know the famous Zhou En-lai quote about the French revolution? 'Too soon to tell'? An excellent quotation, don't you think? I met Zhou. I am inclined to think we may have to reserve judgement on the year 1989, and for some time."

"Everywhere else but here it's been a liberation," said Brough.

"Yes, but, if you step back from it you may discern another pattern." Guo glanced at the clock. He motioned to Chun-li to re-boil the kettle and make tea.

"What kind of people have come to the fore in the Eastern Europe since 1989? And the West for that matter?"

General Guo put the question like a Zen *koan*, the trick implicit in the question.

"The English vernacular is 'arseholes'," said Brough.

"Now this is exactly what happened also in China, despite the non-disintegration of Communist rule. I would imagine that you, with your experience in Russia, Africa, Latin America, are seeing sociological types in China that are completely recognisable."

Brough nodded.

"So maybe there is very little difference between here and there," Guo shrugged, pouring the tea 'almost clear' into miniature bowls.

"And you don't regret it?"

"It goes beyond this. Can you admit that it may be possible that we have entered an era the exact opposite of that which began in 1789? With the storming of the Bastille humanity enters a long swing to the left, during which the masses become the ideal human type; self-sacrifice and freedom become ideals. And maybe what has happened now is not just some 20-year reactionary period. Are you prepared to consider the possibility that 1989 began the era of the, as you put it, 'arsehole': the individualist, the egotist, the businessman, the sexual predator, the human being perpetually separated from society by the self-selected soundtrack on their iPod?"

"Lasting 200 years?"

"It would certainly balance historical *yin* with *yang*..."

"You're winding me up!" Brough shuddered.

Chun-li slurped her tea and Brough copied her. It smelled of freesias but with overtones of antique wood and junk shops.

"Whole stories will go untold!" Brough leaned toward Guo: "You have probably had your equivalent of the British miners' strike, Hurricane Katrina, Watergate, the Watts Riots – you know, epoch-defining stories – just in the last ten years, but they go unreported. The story of the Chinese industrial revolution will never be told; people will never know."

It seemed like a new thought to both Guo and Chun-li. He continued:

"If you can buy army commissions you can probably buy degrees?"

Guo nodded.

"So you can never win a Nobel Prize. You can never produce a Mozart. Your culture will just stagnate!"

"CCP will trade Mozart for 9.9% GDP growth," muttered Chun-li.

Guo sat silently, staring into historical time, his eyes for a moment glazed.

"You and I, Mr. Brough, are maybe forty years different in age, yet we both feel out of place in this modern world. You have seen the collapse of British industrial power, the labour movement, the death of deference..."

"You know a lot about Britain!"

"I have Wikipedia," Guo gestured to a battered laptop wedged next to a pile of books.

"I have seen rationality, dialectical thinking, historical materialism replaced by this pap: Three Represents, Scientific

Development. Anybody who has studied the *Analects* can identify Chinese Marxism simply as re-hashed Confucianism. Inconsequential truths frozen in time, immured to intellectual challenge, a whole new philosophy handed down from the brains of men whose only training was to be civil engineers and secret policemen."

"Brough knows nothing about China," Chun-li's sleepy brain was almost on automatic. "*Analects* are a major work by Confucius."

"So why don't you regret? What's the upside–cellphones for the masses?"

"First, the rise of the individual. In China, after 1919 we had enough Marxists but not enough human beings with a sense of individual worth. Marxism works where individual life is possible– where cause and effect operate, where there is history and logic."

"I have never seen it work," Brough felt tiredness begin falling on him like snow.

"Also," Guo ploughed on, "it is impossible to regret the rise of your own country. For all the dirt at the top this is a clean country, don't you think Mr. Brough? It has a glitter and haze to it, like Florence under the Medici. Its people peer into the future and see only brightness. Have you ever seen the sunrise in Tiananmen Square?"

"I've never even seen Tiananmen Square. I've only been here half a day. I'll probably have to ship out tomorrow – I mean today." Brough glanced at the clock. It was 4am, June fourth.

"Brough recently been sacked by text message," Chun-li muttered.

"Then you must see Tiananmen," said Guo. "You must see the dawn."

13

They glided along the empty streets in a black-window Mercedes: General Guo up front with his chauffeur, Chun-li and Brough slumped together amid plush leather in the back. There were groups of uniformed cops at each intersection, who peered reverentially at the car's number plate and at the access passes glued to the windscreen.

"Whole of Tiananmen in lockdown. Shoot on sight for Western journalists," Chun-li was only half joking. She grabbed the chauffeur's cap and crammed it down on Brough's head.

"Where are we actually going?" Brough pulled the peak down over his eyes and sank lower in the seat. She ignored him.

At Chang'An Avenue, after a flurry of saluting and the dragging of barriers aside, the Merc edged across ten deserted lanes of tarmac. The Avenue's visual signature – clusters of globular street-lights interspersed with trees–was already burned into Brough's memory from the iconic footage of 1989. There were even still the same kind of hooped, white metal fences that the students in 1989 had pulled across the roads for barricades. He'd seen it all in the grainy orange tape-light from twenty years ago. It was all still there in the hissing halogen of today.

Soon they reached the entrance to a building site. An enormous neo-classical portico was having a postmodernist concrete slab built onto the back of it.

The night watchman stumbled toward them, T-shirt rolled to his nipples. He beamed as he saw General Guo, raised his eyebrows at Chun-li and frowned at Brough. Guo bantered with him for a few seconds and made him snigger. Chun-li said:

"Guo telling nightwatchman you are film director Oliver Stone, about to make hagiographical biopic about Hu Jin-tao following cinematic triumph with Fidel."

The air became chilly. The leaves on the trees rustled. Guo led them into the gutted shell of a building and up concrete stairs that reminded Brough of Moscow: clean and sparse, built with 1,000-year confidence and designed to withstand the blast of hydrogen bombs. Four floors up they turned onto a long hall whose roof had been removed and replaced by scaffolding, open to the sky.

"What is this place?" Brough's whisper echoed along the raw concrete.

"National Museum of China," said Chun-li, picking her way across the fire-hoses and power cables. "Closed for refit during major re-appraisal of Chinese history."

"I play an advisory role in curating the *wei-qi* collection. We have a board here from the third century AD," the General purred.

He stopped at a ladder and began pulling himself up it, one rung at a time, with Chun-li nattering precautions behind him.

Now they were on a concrete parapet. Below was Tiananmen Square: unlit, knots of armed police collected at every angle of the concrete vastness. The yellow light filtering into the sky behind them began to give shape to the sculptures; to outline the size and emptiness of everything.

Brough stared at it all. He had run out of things to think about China, run out of snap judgements to make.

"It's a monument to inhumanity," Guo chuckled, "but Chinese people have convinced themselves it's beautiful."

Chun-li wrapped her arms tight around herself and shivered.

"I was only nine," she said.

They heard the sound of a platoon marching. It was soldiers coming to start the flag-raising ceremony in the dark. Brough spotted a news crew setting up to film it.

June Fourth, twenty years on, everything quiet. In London it would still be night time. Brough's report would be about to go on air.

He glanced at Chun-li. But she was peering, rapt and serene, into the square. General Guo stood at attention, gazing into the morning twilight.

"Hey mate, welcome to Tiananmen!"

It was Big Wu, fresh as life, hovering right there next to him in mid-air.

"Where's Frank?" Brough whispered, with a glance to see if the General and Chun-li had noticed anything. In fact Chun-li was giving Big Wu a nervous wave with just her fingers while the General moved his head in a half-inch bow.

"Frank's down there with the rest," Big Wu gestured with his chin.

"The rest of what?"

"The unquiet dead of course!" A tremor of mirth shook Big Wu's shoulders.

"You didn't think we'd let the twentieth anniversary go past without a demonstration did you? They've got the place locked down for the living but they can't keep the restless spirits out. Look!"

Brough squinted over the edge. He could see the metallic

green silhouettes of the platoon in the distance and the pale blue background of the Mao portrait above them, but nothing else.

"Oh my god," Chun-li whispered, and grabbed Brough's hand.

"What?"

"Look!" she cried.

"At what?"

"The problem is," said Big Wu's voice – Brough had lost sight of him now–"you're not going with the flow. Try a bit of *wu-wei*, the action of non-action."

"Just let your mind relax and breathe quietly," Chun-li whispered, unable to pull her eyes away from the square. He could feel his mind obstinately flailing and his heart pounding in his throat.

"I don't get it…" Brough heard himself say, but in the middle of the sentence he caught a movement at the edge of his eye.

Down in the square, right next to the obelisk in the middle, he spotted a clump of people who were not alive having an earnest discussion. One gave him a wave.

"See–that's Frank and the architecture students from '89. They've been having a right old reunion," said Big Wu.

As Brough let his brainwaves go long and deep, the undead crowd came into focus. There were knots of students dressed in the summer fashion of 1989: white shirttails hanging out of drainpipe trousers; men in khaki shorts worn with socks and moccasins; young women in baggy military pants; pale kids in doctors' coats; white headbands.

At the far corner of the square Brough could make out a delegation of murdered workers. Scruffier and at the same time more genial, they loitered in a tight group, almost clutching each other.

"That's my lot. Beijing Autonomous Workers Federation. Got separated on the day," Big Wu gave a puzzled sigh, drifting back into vision. "Incredibly well-read now! Much more politically astute. Access to everything this side – nothing's banned. It's like friggin' university–Gramsci, Foucault, Saul Alinsky..."

"What will they do?"

"We're not sure – all a bit spontaneous. The students are still demanding to lead the demo. But that's tending to get lost in the arguments between the massacre victims and the rest."

"The rest?"

"Well there's the soldiers. We beat about fifty of them to death on the day itself, you know. Dragged them out of ambulances. But they were victims too, is my argument. And on top of that there's everybody else..."

Across the concrete, hundreds of metres wide, tens of thousands of unquiet spirits had begun to march. There were tortured drug dealers, kidnapped prostitutes dressed in twenty years' worth of cheap fashion; disgraced officials in the fluorescent bibs they'd worn on the morning of their execution. A small army of coalminers, lamps dangling from their necks, faces with that blinking stare of innocence all miners give when they're in the natural light. The dead, scraped up off the floors of unlit factories; the victims of firing squads; workers whose lives had been shortened by cancer and poisoning. A whole delegation of brick-kiln kids, their childhoods stolen by work and physical abuse, skipping along in formation, waving the national flag. Brough watched the coalminers turn their faces skyward and wave, as a bunch of recently killed mates flew in from a mine disaster in Shenyang.

The image of everything living–the trees, the soldiers and the flag–seemed blurred, over-inked, like a smudged gravure plate; the imprint of the ghosts was a shade too light but crisper for it.

The soldiers stood to attention as their officer unfurled the flag. The trumpet fanfare of the national anthem clanged out of a speaker. A male TV reporter stood ready to deliver a hushed commentary through a fluffy microphone.

Suddenly a crowd of ethereal students rushed towards the flagpole, forming a circle. The martyred workers stumbled after them, bowed their heads and raised their fists. The dead soldiers of 1989 held hands and made a semicircle facing the flag, throwing nervous glances at the rest. The endless crowd of victims pressed in behind them, filling Tiananmen Square to its southern gate, clambering over the monuments, cracking jokes and waving to long-lost friends.

"Got to go," said Big Wu.

"Thanks for sorting out that SD card," Brough said.

"That wasn't us, it was him," said Big Wu, gesturing to Grandfather Li, who had just materialised and was hovering in the lotus position next to General Guo.

"Apparently he had some karmic deficit with you: he had to use two decades of accumulated good behaviour to help you out. He's stuck here now, like us. Anyway, see you later…"

Big Wu made a Batman-style dive off the National Museum, swooping over the heads of the crowd to join his delegation.

When the last notes of the national anthem died Brough could hear a quiet chant rolling across the crowd.

"Do not fear tyranny!" Chun-li translated.

It was not an angry chant, more desultory; more like the last words you would shout in some hopeless moment of parting with somebody you would never see again. It unfurled, echoed and died away and the spirit crowd vanished.

In the silence Brough could hear only the flag slapping against the flagpole in the dawn breeze:

Brough pointed a finger at Grandfather Li: "How did you know what my Dad sounds like? And who are you anyway?"

Grandfather Li stared beyond him, contemptuous.

"Have you," a wave of remembered grief surged over him, "met my father?"

Grandfather Li stood silent.

"Can you give him a message?"

"You must be joking!" General Guo intervened, twangy and bright eyed, struggling to break the pall of sadness that had engulfed them: "The unquiet dead are a strictly Chinese phenomenon!"

"China, North Korea and Myanmar." sniggered Grandfather Li.

"How come?" said Brough.

"Nobody knows for certain," said General Guo, "but we think it's probably because of the absence of historical memory. Where history is suppressed, and for generations–suppressed so thoroughly that there are no facts to remember–that's where you get the unquiet dead."

"No facts and then no mental tools to unearth the facts with, or analyse them!" said Grandfather Li: "These maniacs have abolished the past. They've abolished logic. Lies and truth can't challenge each other. They've re-created the iron box."

"The iron box?" Brough's brow furrowed.

"Our intelligentsia compared the dying Qing dynasty to an iron box," said General Guo. "Sealed up, with no means of escape. Inside, people are quietly suffocating. It is cruel to wake them: that was the argument the intelligentsia put to the founders of the Communist Party."

"Communist Party said – better to die in agony trying to escape!" Grandfather Li shook his ethereal fist.

"What everyone forgot," said General Guo, gesturing to the square below, "is that even suffocating people can dream."

"Yes, and when they wake up dead, and find out the truth," Grandfather Li exploded, "they think – excuse me Miss – they think: 'Fuck!' and become very, very angry!"

14

The sunset over the Helan Shan had turned the streets of Tang Lu orange; the green of the mosque walls had turned to shimmering black; the gold leaf on the dragon statues sizzled as if on fire.

The muezzin's call to prayer wandered lazily across the rooftops, competing with the clatter of teapots and taped announcements blaring out of various mobile phone emporia.

At Tang Lu Public Sauna Number One, Chief Superintendent Xiao let the massage girl's fingers walk stiffly across his cranium. On the stage, a monologue artist was playing the rick-racks and reciting a cheeky tongue twister. It was Friday, late June, Xiao's first night back in town.

"Your suntan is orange: probably the effect of radiation," Editor Sheng clucked from the next couch. He was having a lymph-node drainage rub by a pretty girl.

"Yeah, the South China Sea is full of nuclear waste," said Commerce Secretary Zhou, giggling, holding his mobile phone up to Xiao's bare leg. "Hey, Bones, Spock's been fatally exposed!"

"This is jealousy speaking!" Xiao sulked.

Despite the suntan, he was not feeling well. During the whole two weeks at a police veterans' holiday resort in Guangdong he'd been getting nightly visitations from Oktyabr Khünbish: waking up in a slick of sweat, staring into the space one metre above his nose where he had just seen the hoodlum's contorted grimace melt into the air.

"Jealous? What I still…" Sheng began, and then stopped short: "Hey! That's enough. My lymphs are drained!"

He shooed the masseuse away with a hand-flap before leaning furtively to Xiao's ear.

"What I still don't know is how you managed to fix that kid. I mean, he was planning to blow the lid completely off Tang Lu Nickel Metal Hydride. Zheng's people found all kinds of unauthorised searches on his computer; documents gone astray…"

"Wouldn't you like to know?" Xiao growled. "Hey fuwuyuen! Foo-woo-yuen!"–singing the word obsequiously, like Olive Oyl sings the name of Popeye: "Stop massaging my cranium and get the teapot over here! And fast, before I box your ears!"

He hauled his stiff body into a sitting position and his two friends gazed at him with a newfound respect.

"If Superintendent Xiao goes on a mission, it must succeed…" he began, putting on an ancient storytelling voice.

"If Superintendent Xiao signs out a large, ah, *asset* from the inventory of the Public Security Police, it must be accounted for."

"You bribe that kid?" Zhou whispered.

Xiao scowled at Zhou, poker-faced, letting the *Zhongnanhai* droop from his bottom lip.

"Assets have to be signed out. Assets have to be used for the express purpose for which they were signed out. Transactions have to be witnessed."

"But the English journalist refused…" Sheng rasped.

Xiao wagged a sage-like index finger:

"Now it happened that the Kubuqi Desert Propaganda Department also signed out certain large monetary assets for specific use. These also had to be accounted for and witnessed."

"Ho, ho, ho!" Zhou rocked back with glee, slapped his leg, exposing his groin as his robe slipped open.

"What?" says Sheng, "I don't get it!"

"You did a switch? That's genius, Spock!" Zhou hissed.

"Hey, not so loud," said Xiao.

They paused while a waitress poured three bowls of green tea and took their order for Chairman Mao's red-braised pork.

"So the Kubuqi Desert moron signs for your money and you sign for his." Sheng had finally caught up. "Who witnesses the transactions?"

Xiao curled his bottom lip: "A girl."

"That witch from Beijing?"

Xiao shook his head.

"An upstanding citizen of Tang Lu, who just happened to be on hand. Formerly an agricultural worker from Zhejiang Province, later a diligent trainee in the business of manicure and pedicure. Through her assiduous work and saving she has now amassed the capital to start an online portal campaigning for harsh sanctions against Japan over its breach of the International Whaling Treaty."

Zhou whistled. Sheng furrowed his brow.

"How much did she take?"

"Half–of both assets!" Xiao was still capable of being startled every time he thought about it.

"Those Zhejiang mountain folk are wily," Sheng shook his head in disbelief. "And the kid went along with it? What happened to his principles?"

"His penis is now determining his stance on corruption," Xiao sniggered. "They're in Beijing and good riddance! His new job is to coach some students who'll go to a spontaneous town-hall meeting when Obama visits."

"And Chief Superintendent Xiao will soon retire on his life savings?" said Zhou.

"Not likely! My wife's collared the lot: wants to use it for a new apartment!" Xiao shrugged. "What do I care? She's the boss."

The drag act had come onstage and was into his second song by now, wearing a viridian Qing gown and relentlessly taking the piss out of a bald comedian dressed as an imperial eunuch.

Xiao, Sheng and Zhou tugged their towelling robes around their waists, hooked sandals over their toes and padded over to the escalator, Xiao acknowledging waves and tasteless jokes from his buddies in the Tang Lu business fraternity, old and new.

As they stood together on the escalator, each cradling a cigarette and wearing a contented smile, Sheng remembered:

"And the reporter?"

"Gone to Xinjiang!"

"They allowed a Western journalist into Xinjiang?" Sheng looked stunned. "At a time like this?"

Everybody on the Party's rumour network knew there was ethnic tension in Xinjiang following a pogrom against Uighur migrants in Guangdong.

Xiao put on a dirty smile:

"He's gone with a Chinese minder."

"Ho, ho, ho!" said Zhou.

"Female?" said Sheng.

Xiao nodded. The waitresses made a fuss of Xiao as they ushered the men to their usual, chipped formica table. A cast-iron pot of Chairman Mao's Red Braised Pork appeared, steaming; three warm Xingtao beers were delivered in filmy glasses.

Sheng leaned into a halo of smoke and pork-fat breath:

"Maybe that Western reporter will unearth an Al Qaeda plot. Or maybe he will be on hand to witness unspeakable crimes by Uighur separatists. This guy is a specialist in wars caused by Muslims, correct?"

Sheng and Zhou shared a knowing glance.

"Maybe he gets his Chinese scoop after all," said Sheng.

"And his penis sucked by a Chinese lady," sniggered Zhou. "Without paying."

Sheng and Zhou played a game of excited eyebrows with each other.

"What is it?" Xiao shouted.

"Straight out of the textbook–Chapter 20!" said Sheng, and the two sniggered.

But Xiao was despondent.

"What's the matter?" Sheng poked him in the arm. "The reporter's gone. The factory's been cleaned up. Key witnesses are dead. That Li kid's back in Beijing and he's destroyed his secret recording of your bribery attempt–and you are a decorated local hero with three pips!"

"But what if that," Xiao spluttered, "what if that snipe-nosed little foreign bastard goes back to England and turns it all into a novel! Then everybody will laugh at Tang Lu…"

His companions guffawed uncontrollably. Sheng's eyes began to stream with tears and Zhou had to spit a whole lump of pork onto the table to avoid choking. Holding his sides and rocking so hard he nearly fell off his chair Sheng gurgled:

"Nobody will read it! My wife's in a book club. Believe me– she knows: English people will only read novels containing crazy sex or supernatural themes!"

"And anyway," Zhou's eyes had become slits as he struggled for air; "suppose they do laugh at Tang Lu? They'll be laughing at themselves."

CUTTINGS

HEADLINE: VILLAGE TOLD TO CHANGE NAME OR IT WON'T EXIST.
SOURCE: CHINA DAILY, 27 JUNE 2009

STARTS: A village had to change its name because it includes two rarely used Chinese characters that can't be found in a new police computer system.

The characters for "Tang" and "Lu" have been used for decades, but Tang Lu residents who tried to get a marriage certificate had trouble last week since the computers didn't recognise their hometown marked on their ID cards. The system also became a problem for those seeking employment, travellers and those doing real-estate transactions.

Some villagers said changing the village's name is damaging to their culture and customs but a police spokesman said it would be too expensive to change the new computer program.

ENDS

TAGLINE: URGENT: XINJIANG-RIOT – FIRST PIX
SOURCE: EUROVISION NEWS, 5 JULY 2009, 1400 GMT

STARTS: *Warning: footage contains graphic violence, moment-of-death, bodies.* No re-broadcast in People's Republic of China.
DOPESHEET: 0000: Mass demonstration of UIGHUR (pron WEE-GURR) seen progressing through URUMQI (pron

OO-RUM-CHI). 0215: Shop torched by rioters. Bus overturned, on fire. 0322: Burned bodies of women, children believed Han (pron HANN) Chinese. 0400: Riot police clash demonstrators. 0417: Sound of high velocity rifle fire. 0425: Tight shot: u/i rioter, lies dead. Blood. DURATION: 0435. CREDIT: David Brough. NOTE: David Brough (pron BRUFF), freelance, on scene, available phono interviews hourly. Please route all requests via Channel Ninety-Nine bureau chief, Georgina Wyndham, New York City, USA.]

HEADLINE: CHINA, JAPAN DEBATE RESTRICTIONS ON RARE EARTH EXPORTS
SOURCE: PEOPLE'S DAILY, 30 AUGUST 2010.

STARTS: China cut its export quotas for rare earth by 72 percent for the second half of this year, according to data from the Ministry of Commerce released on July 8. Shipments will be capped at around 8,000 metric tons, down from roughly 28,000 tons for the same period a year ago.

Japanese officials told their counterparts that the lower quotas could have a major effect on global industry and demanded early action on easing them. Chinese Commerce Minister Chen Deming said China's restrictions on the rare earth industry will assist in protecting the environment.

ENDS